HOLLY WOULD

By
Phillips Wylly

Large Print Edition

"Holly Would," by Phillips Wylly. ISBN 978-1-951985-49-3(hardcover).

Published 2020 by Virtualbookworm.com Publishing Inc., P.O. Box 9949, College Station, TX 77842, US.

Dedication:

This book is for two people who mean a great deal to me. Their friendship has kept me feeling alive and well. But I have a problem. In this world where everything seems to go “by the numbers,” how do you show two names without implying “first” and “second?” Both friends are FIRST in my mind, So, I will try this:

Thank you, Dona and Charlotte
Thank you, Charlotte and Dona.

Now if you have an iPad, please tell it to reverse the above order every day.

Part 1

The Hole in A Fence

Would you like to go?"

The voice startled her and she looked up quickly from the Hollywood Reporter. She had been reading about the big Star Studded, invitation only party to be held at the Pan Pacific Auditorium following tonight's Opening Night performance of the Ice Capades and telling herself it would be a good place to be "discovered."

She was five foot four, she weighed one hundred ten pounds, she had chestnut brown hair with auburn highlights, her eyes were green, her lips were full and sensual, her measurements were 36C-21-34 and she was beautiful. She knew she was beautiful because she had just won the "Miss Dogwood" Beauty Contest in Passaic, New Jersey and the five hundred dollar prize that allowed her to come to Hollywood to be "discovered." The Ice Capades Opening Night Party would be a perfect place, that was true, only thing, she wasn't invited.

She looked up at the young man who had spoken to her. He was about her age, she judged. Other than a good build, a healthy tan and a shock of wild, blond hair, there was nothing special about him.

"Did you say something to me?"

"Yes. I see you're reading about the big party tonight and I wondered if you would like to go? With me, eh?" he added.

"Do you have an invitation?" She tried to sound more pleasant. You never know, she told herself, a lot of very big stars and producers are supposed to eat lunch here at Nicodels.

"Yes, I've got an invitation," the young man assured her. I'm an H.A.P. in the show so I get to go and bring a date if I want."

"An H.A.P?" She had no idea what an H.A.P. could possibly be. "Why don't you sit down and tell me what on earth is an H.A.P?"

Grinning as he sat down he told her, "Half-ass Principal."

"My name's Todd Wilson. I do one feature number in the show, but I also skate in the line. The feature number earns me a cast invite to the party though, and since I don't know anybody here in Los Angeles and I saw you reading about it, and since you are the prettiest girl I ever saw, I just thought I'd screw up my courage and ask you, eh?"

Located in a row of nondescript, one and two story buildings east of Gower Street on the north side of Melrose Avenue, Nicodels was not at all what Holly had expected to find in glamorous Hollywood but for those in the know it was the unofficial commissary for the RKO Studio, which was located right behind it, as well as Paramount, just up the street to the east.

Under an unimpressive neon sign two small, not very attractive doors that looked like almost anything other than entrances to a restaurant for the glamorous movie world opened into Nicodels.

Behind the doorway on the left a long, softly lit, windowless room, probably intended to be art deco in design, was dominated by a bar stretching the entire length of the room At the near end of the almost always crowded bar an animated neon sign showing a beautiful Coors' Rocky Mountain waterfall provided a warm glow of ever changing light, while at the far end similar light from behind six powerfully built horses towing a Budweiser Beer Wagon did the same..

At Nicodels drinking was by no means limited to the bar room. The second entrance from Melrose Avenue, only a few feet to the right of the first, led into a tiny reception area and the main dining room beyond.

Outside or in, by any standard she could think of, Nicodels did not look like a center for Hollywood's elite, but she knew looks could be deceiving. Two major studios were practically next door. The food was good and the martinis were reported to be the best in town. Maybe that's what made it so popular. She did not know about the martinis, she was too young to buy one, but she did know about the food. Especially Nicodel's famous Caesar Salad, made right at your table with a coddled egg, a real lemon and cheese grated while you watched.

For the past week, ever since she learned about Nicodels three days after she got to town, she had been eating her lunch here. She always waited for a table where she could sit facing the entrance. Facing the people who were arriving. Facing the person who might be the producer or the director who would discover her. The surprising thing about Todd's sudden appearance was the fact that he had approached from behind her.

An ice skating H.A.P. did not sound like someone who was going to "discover" her, but an invitation to the party just might be the passport to stardom she had been looking for, waiting for. She smiled her prettiest smile and extended her hand to him.

"Hi Todd, My name is Holly Sinclair." That was the name she had finally decided on last night before going to sleep. She had been using "Holly Sherman" for a few days, but last night she decided "Sinclair" had more class. "...And I would love to go to the party with you."

"That's great!" He took her hand in a firm grip as he slid into the seat opposite her. "So, what brought you to Hollywood?" .

"I'm an actress," she answered.

"Oh, wow!" Todd's enthusiasm was genuine. "Maybe you can help me. I got here on my skates but I want to find a job in the movies."

"Are you an actor?"

"No. I want to get into production. You know, behind the camera."

"Well," Holly smiled, he was obviously in the same boat she was in. "I can't help you yet, but once somebody discovers me, then maybe I can."

For the next half hour, between bites of his turkey sandwich, Todd told her far more about ice skating than she ever really wanted to know. He spoke of inside edges, outside edges and jumps called "Axles" and "Lutzes" and "Flips". Suddenly, looking at his wrist watch, he told her he had to go. He gave her a show ticket and a party invitation, said he couldn't pick her up because he had to check in an hour before show time but he would meet her at the party, then turned and hurried towards the back of the restaurant.

Strange, Holly thought, why is he going back there? Then she realized he had told her he had to "go." Probably he went to the men's room.

After her lunch with Todd, Holly spent the better part of afternoon in her room at the Paramount Hotel. No connection with Paramount Pictures, but the name and the fact that it was located on Melrose, only a few blocks away from the actual Paramount Studio, plus the fact that the rates were within her budget had persuaded her to take a room there.

Faded green paint clung tenuously to the chipped and cracked plaster walls of the small room. Tired curtains, which might one time had been beige, hung lifelessly in a window looking out at the side of the Western Costume Company building next door. Worn, tan carpeting covered the floor and the bed creaked when she sat on it, but the room was clean and she had a private bath and having never stayed in a hotel room before, she thought it was wonderful.

Her ticket and her invitation to the Ice Capades Opening Night Party had put her mind in a tizzy. What to wear? Her first thought was her lucky dress. The yellow dress she had worn when she won the "Miss Dogwood" beauty contest. She knew she looked good in that yellow dress, but maybe she should wear something less juvenile. Something more exotic. Something more "revealing." Something more mature.

She only had three outfits to choose from. Beauty contest, a rather diaphanous white dress she had purchased in New York City, at Gimbels before she left home. ...Or, the slinky black dress with thin shoulder straps she bought three days ago at The Broadway.

There really wasn't much question about it – Slinky Black!

Getting to the Pan Pacific Auditorium was not difficult. She had only to get on the west bound Melrose Avenue bus right in front of her hotel. She planned to buy an automobile as soon as she could land a part, but until then public transportation, which Los Angeles had surprisingly little of, would just to have to do.

As usual, the evening was foggy and damp so she wore her rain coat over the sexy black dress and, even though she was wearing her very high heel black strap shoes, the coat kept her from looking too out of place on a bus filled mostly with working people heading home.

"Hello, I'm Holly Sinclair," she said to herself as she settled into a seat.

It was only last night that she had finally decided on Holly Sinclair as the name she would use and it was still a little strange on her tongue. "Hello, I'm Holly Sinclair." She repeated over and over in her mind, changing inflections as she did. She wanted to appear warm and sensuous, but slightly reserved. Sophisticated, yet sexy. In a word, mysterious. Someone excitingly unattainable. Well, maybe not too unattainable. “Hello. I’m Holly Sinclair.”

Holly’s seat was not “front row.” In fact it was not even on the main floor of the auditorium. It was eight rows back in the center of the balcony. Not a bad seat really, but one day she wanted to be downstairs, front row center. That is, if she ever went to the Ice Capades again. Not to think about that. The after show party was the thing. Nobody there would know where she had sat for the performance.

She had hoped to make an “entrance”, but with the crowd of people pushing towards the doorway, she just sort of found herself inside the large ballroom. Still, it was exciting. She was inside the velvet ropes with the celebrities, not outside gawking at them. Snatches of conversation she overheard thrilled her:

“…My agent told me there’s a good chance…”

“…He’s not right for the part, I just don’t understand…”

“…They promised to send me a script tomorrow…”

Yes, she really was in Hollywood and she really was surrounded by movie people.

She smiled her best smile, took a deep breath and pulled her shoulders back just a little. Now, if only someone will notice me, she thought. A moment later her "date" came and led her to a table located well back from the dance floor. About the same status location as her seat in the balcony, she told herself. Well, make the best of it.

"Let's dance," she suggested. Surely, there on the dance floor, someone important would see her.

"Great," Todd replied as he jumped to his feet and led her between the tables. She was sure it was her idol, Gene Tierney, seated at a ringside table. And at the next table, she was certain it was Dick Powell.

The dance floor was crowded with lots of people who looked important. The orchestra was wonderful and, to her surprise, Todd was a remarkably good dancer, so they danced and danced and she made every effort to look her best.

When the orchestra "took five," they went to the sumptuous buffet table dominated by an almost life size ice sculpture of a skater. She was certain the man in line just ahead of her was Tab Hunter. As he reached toward the platter of cocktail shrimp she smiled her best smile and told him, "Oh, those look good,"

"Yeah, they sure do," he grinned back at her before taking several of the shrimp and turning away. Well, she thought, at least he smiled at me...

No matter, there are plenty of other actors here and, she guessed, directors and producers too. Surely someone would notice her. Perhaps a lot of people did, but no one asked her name. No one offered her a screen test... Well, she thought, maybe tomorrow.

Todd took her home on the bus. She expected him to want to come up to her room and try for a kiss, but to her surprise he said good night in the lobby and, for just a moment, the thought crossed her mind that maybe she wasn't quite as irresistible as she believed. And just for a moment she felt a tingle of doubt run down her spine.

Whistling happily as he walked the mile or so down Melrose Avenue from the Paramount Hotel to his hotel on Vine Street, Todd's thoughts were not about Holly Sinclair but about Aaron Marks and Anne Bronson. Was it possible there might be a job opportunity with Aaron Marks? Where would it lead? It was these thoughts rather than thoughts of Holly that filled his mind as he climbed into bed that night.

Todd Wilson had grown up in Penticton, BC. He was naturally athletic, but not very big. One hundred forty pounds, five foot nine, well actually five foot eight and a half, but five-nine sounded a little better. Back in his early high school days he weighed only one-twenty. It was his size that spoiled any chance of playing serious ice hockey. Going up against defense men who were six feet tall and maybe one-eighty or better, Todd had no hockey prospects for anything other than serious injuries.

But living in Canada, if you didn't ice skate, what did you do? So, after one near broken arm and one slight concussion, Todd decided to try figure skating. Surprisingly quickly, he became good enough to be offered a contract with Ice Capades just two weeks before he was scheduled to start his second year at Penticton's Junior College.

Todd's mother and father had been opposed to the idea. It wasn't as if he had won a major title and could be a star in the show. they told him. He should stay in Penticton, finish college, then join his father's construction business.

But the construction business held no interest for Todd. Truth be known, neither did ice skating. Ever since his dad had taken him to see his first movie, Errol Flynn in "Dodge City," Todd wanted to be in the movie business. He had never wanted to be an actor. He wanted to be a Writer, or a Director, or a Producer.

There was not a lot he could learn about movie making in Penticton. He worked after school as an usher in the local theater, read everything he could find to read in the public library and never even once thought about the possibility that his ice skating might some day open the door to his dreams. Then, one day, a scout for Ice Capades offered him a job.

Ice Capades might not be the movies but it was show business and Ice Capades was based in Hollywood and played there for four weeks every year. Even more important, a job with Ice

Capades would allow him to get a Green Card to work in the US.

Overcoming his parents' objections, he had joined the company in Atlantic City, New Jersey, on August 10th. Almost ten months later, following a long train ride from Phoenix, the company arrived in Los Angeles for its final, but perhaps most important engagement of the season.

By ten o'clock Monday morning, along with most of the cast, Todd had checked into the Grand Hotel on Vine Street, just across from the Farmer's Market. The only thing "grand" about the hotel was it's name, but the rates were low and the location was convenient. Especially for Todd because it was only a few blocks away from the RKO and Paramount studios.

Todd was very good at "train sleep" so when they got off the train in Los Angels, wearing his brown Florsheim shoes, a clean, white, freshly pressed Arrow shirt, a brown and tan striped tie, one of the two ties he owned, and his only suit, a brown wool suit his folks had bought for him at Eatons before he left home he was ready for action.

Across Vine Street from the hotel, at a food stand in the outdoor Farmer's Market, he ordered a coffee and an English Muffin, "to go," then headed south to Melrose Avenue. As he walked, he decided it wasn't really cold, but a damp fog, something they called a "marine layer," made it seem so and he was glad for the hot coffee.

His steps grew quicker and he forgot the fog as he reached the corner and turned east on Melrose Avenue. The street, and the area was certainly not one in which he would have expected to find something as glamorous as a movie studio, but there, proudly standing high above a three story building at the corner of Melrose and Gower, he could see the shining metal globe and antenna that was the trade mark emblem of RKO RADIO PICTURES.

On Gower Street, a hundred yards north of Melrose, he found the small, unimpressive, RKO Studio Entrance. He adjusted his tie, polished the toes of his shoes against the back of his trouser legs, ran his hand over his hair, then climbed the three cement steps to the frosted glass door he hoped would be the doorway to his future.

A heavy set man, wearing a rumpled uniform, seated at a desk just inside the small lobby looked up from his newspaper.

"What-chu want, kid?" A cigarette dangling from his lips danced up and down as he spoke spilling a few ashes on his jacket.

Todd explained he had written to the studio and hoped he could see someone in the personnel department.

"Naw... they ain't see-en nobody," the guard told him, then went back to reading his paper.

Todd stood there for what seemed a long time, surprised and disappointed at the cold reception. The guard looked up from his paper again. This time he managed a half smile.

"Sorry, kid. Nothin' for you here." The cigarette danced again and more ashes fell on the uniform. "Check with us in a few months."

Okay, he thought, you can't expect to score a goal every time, eh? On to Paramount. He may have said "Thank you," to the guard before he left. He couldn't remember.

A few hundred yards further east on Melrose, he came to Paramount's DeMille Gate – named after the famous director Cecil B. DeMille. Now this was impressive! He had seen a hundred pictures of the curved arch bearing the inscription "Paramount Studio," but actually being in front of it and looking down the road into the studio it spanned caused a little shiver of excitement to run up his spine.

As he approached, a smiling officer stepped out of a small, tile roofed, stucco building standing just outside the gate. The officer's uniform was neatly pressed and looked every bit as smart as the building he had come from.

"Good morning. What can I do for you young man?"

This is certainly a step up from RKO Todd thought as he explained the reason for his visit.

The officer listened politely, then, telling him the personnel department saw people on Wednesdays and Fridays, he invited Todd to fill out an application if he wanted to schedule an interview.

It was while he was filling out the application that Larry Katz came into his life. Actually it wasn't Larry Katz who came into his life, it was the man who stuck his head into the gate house and told the guard, "If Larry Katz shows up, tell him I'm at Nicodels"

"Nicodels" the friendly guard made a note on a sheet of paper, "Yes sir."

On his walk from RKO to Paramount, Todd had noticed a sign for Nicodels 'as passed under it, but were it not for the message left for Larry Katz it would not have entered his mind to go in there. Maybe Nicodel is a place where studio people go, he told himself. Maybe Nicodel is a place where I ought to go... maybe meet somebody, eh?

Nicodel's hostess seated him at a small table towards the back of the dining room. He ordered a chicken sandwich and was quietly eating when one of the three men seated in the booth opposite his table stood up and told his companions in a voice loud enough for Todd to overhear, "No, I got-a go. I've got three reels to sink up before my boss gets back."

The man turned away from his friends and walked through the kitchen door. A few minutes later, as Todd was paying his bill, the two men who had remained in the booth got up and also headed for the kitchen door.

There's got to be some reason for this, Todd thought, and with a look of self assurance he did not really feel followed the two into the kitchen in time to see them disappear out an exit door on the far side of the room. Several busy cooks ignored him as he made his way past them, pushed the door open and stepped out.

And there it was! Only a few feet away. A hole in the fence. A hole large enough for a man to easily step through as the two men he was following had already done. This hole in the fence, he was confident, was going to be his gateway to the film industry.

Chin up, shoulders back, he crossed the few feet of "green belt" that bordered the fence, stepped through the opening and onto the hallowed ground of the RKO Studio.

Walking purposefully up one street and down the next, in his mind he began to map the layout of the studio. On the west side of the studio, where the two men he followed into the lot had headed, two and three story ivy covered, tan stucco office buildings lined a studio street paralleling Gower.

Service buildings housing scenic shops, prop and wardrobe storage, and makeup facilities as well as some dressing rooms lined the street at the north end of the lot. Six Sound Stages, backing on the fence he had entered through, formed the southern border while on the east side, a huge wall, which reminded him of the movie, "King Kong," separated RKO from its neighbor, Paramount. In the world of movies, Todd thought, giant Paramount was very much a King Kong to RKO's small, native village.

As he walked along a studio street he passed other young men, much like himself, hurrying in one direction or another, some on bicycles, some on foot, all carrying something... film cans, note books, stacks of paper. On his next visit, he decided, something to carry would be a good bit of camouflage.

But camouflage, it turned out, was not necessary. Walking back towards the office building along Gower he spotted a man struggling to unload several boxes from the trunk of a Jaguar Convertible, outside one of the office buildings. Only very important people had permits to drive onto the lot, Todd knew, and helping important people was always a good idea.

"Can I help you with those?"

"What?" Surprised, the man looked up.

A nice looking guy, Todd thought. Thirty-five, maybe Forty years old. Thinning black hair, a little on the paunchy side. A cigar smoker, but that was "de riguer" for anybody who was anybody in Hollywood.

"Can I carry those for you?"

"Yeah, sure. That would be great." The man handed the box to Todd then reached for a second. "Can you handle two of them?"

"You bet," Todd assured him.

The boxes were heavy, but one thing Todd was, was strong. Two times each performance he lifted his chorus line skating partner off her feet and up onto his shoulder. Marie weighed one hundred pounds. The boxes didn't weigh more than twenty pounds each.

"Okay. You're the weight lifter here Come-on then." The man closed the trunk lid, gestured "follow me" to Todd and led him into the building which, Todd noticed, had a small brass plaque engraved with the name "TDL Productions" alongside the doorway.

"G-mornin' Mr. Marks." An elderly, uniformed security guard seated at a desk just inside the building entrance nodded a salute. "Looks like yer movin' in fer a long stay."

"You never know, Charlie," Mr. Marks told him. "In this business, you never know."

"I guess you're right about that," the guard called after them as Todd followed Mr. Marks up stairs to the second floor.

Could this be Aaron Marks he was following? Todd wondered. He had read about a writer/director named Aaron Marks.

The narrow second floor hallway, lined on both sides by grim looking, seemingly identical wooden doors boasting frosted glass windows that provided most of the light in the hall, seemed to extend forever.

A few steps down the hallway's bare wood floor Mr. Marks opened a door with the number "22" printed in the lower left hand corner of its opaque glass window. Following him through the door, Todd found himself in a large, apparently freshly painted, almost empty room.

Dark wainscoting met bare, off white plaster walls at the level of the window sills in a row of wind out windows overlooking Gower Street. A desk just inside the doorway and one table accompanied by four green metal "government issue" type chairs, comprised the room's entire complement of furnishings, and only added to a feeling of emptiness.

But the room was not empty. Seated at the desk, a plain looking woman with stringy, brownish hair pulled back into a bun, pushed a pair of heavy, dark rim glasses back up her somewhat predominate nose and greeted Mr. Marks, "Good afternoon Aaron."

So he is Aaron Marks, Todd realized.

A moment later Mr. Marks told him to, "Put that stuff on the table over there. Anne will figure out where everything goes."

"My God, Aaron." The woman behind the desk rolled her eyes. "Did you bring your entire collection of shit?"

"Wait, there's more," he told her. Turning to Todd he tossed his car keys to him. "Lock it when you get the other box. And thanks, kid." He turned to Anne, "See if you can get Crystal on the phone."

With that, Aaron Marks stepped through a door Todd assumed led to an adjoining office and closed it behind him.

When Todd returned with the third box, Anne told him "thanks" and handed him a dollar bill. "Mr. Marks wants you to have this."

"Oh, no thanks," Todd said quickly. "I'm just here to help, eh?"

"Are you?" A slight, somewhat skeptical smile crossed Anne's face. "I don't think I've seen you around here before. What's your name?"

He spotted a small name plate on her desk. "I'm Todd Wilson, Miss Bronson."

"And where do you work, Todd?"

"Ah... well," Todd was stuck. He was usually pretty good at quick answers but Anne's question caught him off balance. Before he could come up with anything to say, the door Mr. Marks had disappeared through opened swiftly.

"Anne, see if you..." then he saw Todd. "Oh, Jesus. Kid you could be a life saver. Can you drive?"

"Yes sir." Todd assured him.

"Great! Look," Marks picked up his car keys from Anne Bronson's desk, tossed them to Todd and handed him a large envelop. "Use my car and take this to Crystal Manning. I need to get this to her as soon as possible."

As he started back into his office another thought came to him. "While you're over that way, stop by my agent and pick up a check will ya?"

With that, as Todd called after him, "Yes sir," the man disappeared back into his office.

Crystal Manning! Todd felt his eyes widening. Crystal Manning was a star! He was going to deliver something to Crystal Manning? Wow!

"All right, Todd." Anne Bronson's skeptical smile turned into something more bemused as she opened a desk drawer and produced a sheet of paper. "Here's directions to Miss Manning's house." She handed the paper to him, "And do you know where Hollywood's Best Agency is?"

"No ma'am"

Anne took back the paper she had handed to him and started to draw a map on it. "...It's in Beverly Hills too, on Canon Drive... When you leave Miss Manning's, you come back down Coldwater, cross Sunset,"

He watched over her shoulder as she drew, "Go to Santa Monica, turn right to Canon, then left for two blocks. It's at the corner on the right. You can't miss it." She handed the paper back to Todd. .

Todd took the paper, "Thank you Miss Bronson."

"You're welcome." She shook her head, smiled again, then told him, "Let's not alert the teamsters to this highly illegal trip you're making."

"No ma'am, Miss Bronson," Todd assured her. He wasn't all together certain what she meant, but he knew enough about "Teamsters" to know they were the people who did the driving and could cause all sorts of trouble.

"We will see you later Todd?" There was something of a question in Anne Bronson's voice that followed him as he headed down the hall.

"Yes ma'am," he called back. "Got to bring Mr. Marks's car back, eh?"

"And don't forget the check!" she shouted after him.

Much to his disappointment, he had not met Crystal Manning, nor Peter Best.

At Miss Manning's house a young Hispanic woman answered the door, told him she was Miss Manning's maid and took the script.

At the agency, the woman at the reception desk handed him an envelope and told him, "Mr. Best said to give this to you."

So much for meeting a movie star and a big time agent, but, what the heck, he had met a famous director and he practically had a job on the RKO Lot. Not bad for only two days in town.

Catering mainly to studio people Nicodels opened early each day and Tuesday morning Todd was one of the first to be seated. He ate a quick breakfast, asked for a coffee “to go” then headed for the kitchen and what he hoped would be his future.

Carrying the coffee Todd again entered the lot through the opening in the fence behind Nicodels then walked confidently to the TDL Building where he told the security guard, “Good morning, Charlie.”

“Good morning, son,” Charlie replied. “Say, what’s your name?”

“Todd, sir. Todd Wilson.”

“Good to know you, Todd,” Charlie called after him as he started up the stairs.

He opened the door to office number 22,

“Good morning Miss Bronson.” Todd carefully placed the coffee on her desk.

“Back again, Todd?” she asked. “Mr. Marks isn’t here. He won’t be in today.”

"That's okay," Todd answered. "I didn't come to see him. I came to see if I can help you." She looked at the young man for a second before reaching into her desk drawer for the ten cents she knew the coffee cost. He was a good looking kid. Well, not really "good looking." His eyes were too wide apart and his nose had the look of one that might have been broken. His hair never wanted to seem like it had ever been near a comb and he wasn't very tall. But he was trim and had muscles a girl could admire. He was sharp and smart and best of all, he was the kind of kid you had a feeling was going to "go somewhere."

"All right, Todd. Let's quit the bull shit. What are you looking for? A job?"

"Yes ma'am. I surely am, eh?" he answered without a second's hesitation.

"Okay. You can be our 'gofer.' Twenty-five a week. God willing, we start production July tenth. Aaron's determined to wrap by August fifteenth so he can go to the Democrat convention in Chicago, You'll get a couple-a weeks wrap which means we'll carry you 'till the end of August. You want the job?"

"Yes ma'am. I do!! Only I won't be able to work this afternoon or Wednesday afternoons or past six o'clock for three more weeks, eh?"

"And why is that?" Anne wanted to know.

"I'm in the Ice Capades," he answered. "We open tonight and we don't close 'till the 29th. I can't quit until then."

"Ice Capades?" Anne's eyes opened wider. "You've got to be kidding."

"No mam. You want some tickets? I can get you a couple of passes. It'll have to be middle of the week though," he added.

"I'd love a couple of tickets," Anne smiled at him. "Next Tuesday or Wednesday would be wonderful. And what is this 'eh' shit?"

"Eh?" Todd looked a bit surprised. "Um, I guess it's just sort of a Canadian thing, eh?"

"Sorry I asked," Anne laughed. "All right, it's still morning, you can start by going up the hall to Number 7 and introducing yourself to our Assistant Director, John Poer. Tell him you are now the official 'gofer' and if he needs anything you are ready, willing and able. Then come back here, put these script pages in order, take them to mimeo and get fifteen copies. Use that desk," she pointed to the new addition on the opposite side of the room.

"Yes ma'am."

It was shortly after one o'clock when Todd got to lunch at Nicodels where Holly Sinclair came into his life.

Before show time Wednesday somebody from publicity put twenty-five or thirty photographs from the opening night party on the company bulletin board. Copies could be purchased for ten cents.

Todd was one of the first to discover the photographs. And there, to his surprise, at the end of the third row was a photo of Holly Sinclair. Well, it wasn't supposed to be a photo of Holly, it was a shot of Gene Tierney, but he and Holly were in the crowd behind her. The thing about it was that Holly stood out just as Gene Tierney did.

My God, Todd told himself, the camera likes her. He remembered an article written by some famous cameraman who wrote that the camera liked some people better than others. The cameraman called them "camera friendly". For some reason, they just stood out in pictures and he considered that the first requisite for motion picture stardom.

Todd put his name on the list for a copy of photo number eighteen and went to find a pay phone. The photo gave him a great reason to call her. He would tell her about the photo and ask her if maybe she would like to go to a movie with him. Best of all, the photo would be a reason for another date when the prints were available.

He telephoned the Paramount Hotel.

There was no Holly Sinclair registered there.

A few minutes after seven that evening, Holly walked into the hotel. "Good evening Miss Sherman," the always eager desk clerk called to her.

"Hi Douglas," she called back. Then, as she was about to enter the elevator, she turned back, "Hey Douglas, I forgot to tell anybody. I'm using the name Holly Sinclair now. If I get..."

"Oh gee, Miss Sherman. There was a call for Miss Sinclair about an hour ago. I didn't know...."

"Damn!" She stamped her foot for emphasis. "I was stupid not to tell anyone. Who was it?"

"Gosh, I don't know. When I told him there was no one registered here by that name he just said thanks and hung up."

Her mind ran through the list of casting agents she had been to see and left her photo with. "Double Damn!" she exclaimed out loud. It did not occur to her that the call might have been from her Ice Capades date.

Missed phone calls and name changes were not on Holly Sinclair's mind Thursday morning. She had a busy day planned.
Without success she had been working her way through the list of Hollywood Talent Agencies and Casting Departments of each of the studios she found listed in a Studio Directory she had purchased at Enterprise Stationers up on Sunset Boulevard. Today she was going to venture across the hill to "the Valley." The San Fernando Valley, just like in Bing Crosby's song.

A number of studios were located in the valley: Universal, Warner Bros., StayCon, Disney, and several smaller ones with a dozen or so talent agencies located nearby.

Like every day since she had arrived in Hollywood the weather was damp and foggy. Someone had told her it wasn't just fog, it was "smog," a combination of fog and smoke. Whatever it was, it had been there every day and it made her think of the lines from another popular song, "Hate California, it's cold and it's damp."

The bus ride up Highland Boulevard, took her past the entrance to the Hollywood Bowl. From the highway she could not see the bowl itself, just lots of palm trees and shrubs and an automobile entrance to a parking lot, but the sign "Hollywood Bowl" was exciting in itself.

Just being here was exciting. Being here and being on her own. Tomorrow she would be eighteen years old. She wondered for a moment where her mother might be and if she would even remember it was her birthday. Probably not. It wasn't likely her mother would be sober enough to know what day it was. She hardly ever knew what any day was.

Sometimes at night she would cry herself to sleep thinking about her mother. Other girl's mothers were different. And other girls had fathers. When she was very little she and her mother were living with a man named Gotlieb and she thought he was her father.

Lots of nights before they moved away from Mr. Gotlieb's place she heard her mother and him arguing with each other. Usually after they had been drinking and had sent her to bed right after super.

She was almost seven when they left Mr. Gotlieb. It wasn't until she and her mother moved into a little apartment over a bowling alley in Passaic that she happened to find her birth certificate and learned her real name was Simon. Mother's name: Felicia Simon. Father: Unknown. Until then she had always thought her name was Gotlieb. When she learned that Mr. Gotlieb wasn't her father, she began to wonder who was. Did he know of her? Would it matter if he did?

It was summer time when they left Mr. Gotlieb and she didn't have to go to school, so while her mother was out doing whatever she did when she was out, she had gone to the movies.

Sitting in the theater, watching two features a short subject, a cartoon and a newsreel, and then watching the whole thing over again, she fantasized herself as every leading lady she saw.

Before school started that fall, they moved into Mr. Oswald's house in Passaic. She had her eighth birthday while they were living at Mr. Oswald's house. Not that anyone cared. Her mother and Mr. Oswald had gone somewhere to a race track and left her home alone.

By the time she was eight she was pretty grown up. She could take care of herself; cook for herself; get herself off to school. She loved school. She loved to read and dream about the women she read about. And dream that one day she would be an actress and be one of those women.

It was while she was in the third grade that she learned of the Play Troop at the Passaic YWCA. A lady named Miss James coached her actors as they red lines from various plays. Then, once every two months, the class would perform one of the plays for everyone at the Y.

"Don't be nervous in front of the audience," Miss James told her. "Just make believe you are the person in the play and behave the way she would behave."

In her first play, in spite of Miss James' counseling, she had been very nervous even though she had only nine words to speak. She remembered the words as if it were yesterday, "Mr. Andrews called to say he will be late."

Six months later, in the fourth play the class presented, she had one of the leading rolls and loved every minute of being on stage.

The bus must have gone over a ridge or a bump in the road as it reached the top of the hill and started it's decent into the San Fernando Valley. Whatever it was, it woke her from her day dream... The sun was beginning to break through "the smog," and with every turn of the wheels the temperature increased. It had been about 50 degrees when she left her hotel. By the time she got off the bus on Ventura Boulevard, the temperature was nearing 80.

The Valley didn't look much like Bing Crosby's song made it sound like and Ventura Boulevard didn't seem much different from most of the side streets in Hollywood. More palm trees and block after block of one and two story buildings that looked like places on the wrong side of town in Passaic.

. MovieCast was the forth agency she visited. A greasy looking man looked at her over his heavy, horn rim glasses. “Lemme see you walk to the end of the room and back,” he gestured with his hand.

She did as he asked.

“No, no. When ya turn aroun’, do it fast. So ya skirt flies up an’ I can see ya legs.”

She repeated her walk, this time with a fast turn.

“Okay. Good legs. That’s important. How come I ain’t seen you before? You new in town?”

She sat down in the chair in front of his desk crossing her legs provocatively. If he likes legs, she told herself, give him something to look at.

“Yes,” she answered. “I’ve only been here a week. This is my first time in the valley.”

“Oh?” The man pushed his glasses back up his nose. “Where you from? Some place back east?”

“Yes. New Jersey. I was Miss Dogwood before I came out here.”

“Hey... all right.” He took the glasses off and began to polish them with the end of his tie. “Miss Dogwood, I’m impressed.” He nodded his head up and down. “So, I suppose you’re all alone out here.”

“Yes. I hardly know anyone.”

“Right... I can understand.” He put the polished glasses back on his nose. “Well listen; I got a full schedule this afternoon, but tell ya what." He reached into a desk draw and drew out several sheets of paper which he handed to Holly. "You study these 'sides,' then come back here about eight... eight-thirty tonight. I live just upstairs, there's a bell right next to the door. You come up an' we'll work on this scene. Maybe I can find somethin' for ya."

Holly took the script pages and, with her prettiest smile, told him "Thank you very much," then hurried out of the tiny MovieCast office.

Back on the street she let out a loud groan. She knew all about "casting couches." She was certain that had she not "submitted" to Judge John Collier, she would not have become Miss Dogwood and she was more or less prepared to participate in that sort of thing again if she had to, but she wasn't going to do it with a sleazy looking grease ball like that. Not even if he could get her a part. "Uggg!"

MovieCast was definitely a depressing experience. She decided some lunch might make her feel better and she had noticed a restaurant named DuPars on the opposite side of Ventura Boulevard before she went into MovieCast.

To her surprise and delight, DuPars seemed to be another Nicodels. A movie industry hang out. People wearing theatrical make up, probably coming from the StayCon Studio only three blocks away on Laurel Canyon, were coming and going, and "Trade Papers" were on sale in coin boxes outside the front entrance. She put a dime into the slot and purchased a copy of the "Hollywood Reporter."

Inside, she decided to wait for a table rather than sit at the counter on the far side of the room with her back to anyone who might "see her." Less than ten minutes later a waitress led her to one of the small tables along the center room divider.

After the woman took her order for ice tea and a California Salad Holly turned her attention to the Reporter. It was always her hope she would find something in "the trades" that would lead her to a part in a movie, but the "Hollywood Reporter" did not report on anything that suggested an opportunity for her. She ate her lunch slowly and decided she better try some of the modeling agencies. She was running out of money, she needed to find a job.

Located in a small stucco building, next to an empty lot near the junction of Highland and Ventura, the third agency she visited, the "Ventura-Highland Agency," proved to be the one she needed.

"Are those boobs real?"

The question came from a hard looking middle age woman seated at the only desk in a room filled with folding chairs and walls covered by framed newspaper and magazine adds featuring models one was to assume were Ventura-Highland clients.

"Yes. Of course they're real." Holly answered, half in surprise at the question and half in anger because of it.

"All right, all right. Don't get your tits in a ringer," the woman told her. "Thirty-six C?"

"Yes," Holly answered.

"This is your lucky day then. The Broadway called not five minutes ago. They last minute decided to do a bra add for the weekend salr and they need a model like right now. Since I ain't got nobody here but you, the job's yours if ya want it. Ten bucks an hour, I take ten percent."

Holly took a deep breath and swallowed hard. She hadn't exactly planned on being a lingerie model, but ten dollars an hour... "Yes. Yes I want it."

"Okay, you got it." The woman picked up a piece of paper and held it out to her, "Sign the contract and go to work."

Fifteen minutes later, clutching a copy of her contract with the Ventura-Highland Agency, Holly was on a bus headed back to Hollywood, twenty minutes after that she walked into the 7th Floor Photo Studio in the Broadway building at Hollywood and Vine.

"Well, it's about time!" A petulant looking young man wearing a red beret and a matching scarf threw his hands into the air by way of welcome. “Go in there,” he indicated a door at the end of the studio. “Ellen is waiting.”

Ellen, turned out to be the “fitter” who, after trying several brassieres on Holly, spent the rest of the afternoon putting her into one snug fitting sweater after another for “Freddie” to photograph, and photograph, and photograph her in. When they finally finished, a few minutes after ten that night, Holly realized it had been seven hours. She had just earned $ 70... Less ten percent, she reminded herself. More than most people she knew made in a week. In two weeks!

In the Ice Capades world Sundays were always a drag. Three hours between matinee and evening was really not enough time to take off make-up, go out, eat, come back and get ready all over again. So, like most of the cast, Todd usually ate in." A pizza and a coke was all he needed.

He sat down on the one, semi-comfortable couch in the men's dressing room. True, he was an H.A.P. with a featured spot, but most of his work was in line and he did not rate a principal's dressing room. He ate his pizza then, having nothing else to do, he picked up a copy of the LA Times someone had left. On page twenty, under a headline reading, "Broadway Bra Sale: Buy One Get One Free!" he found himself looking at a great pair of tits covered by a sweater that might have been painted on, He studied the tits. Then, almost by accident, he looked at the face above them. "Wholly Shit!" He spoke out loud. It was her. Holly.

"What's up, Todd?" George Fredenhoff wanted to know.

"This girl," Todd held up the paper. "I know her."

George got up from his seat at the long makeup table and walked over to see what Todd was talking about. "What girl?"

"This girl." Todd held up the paper and pointed to the picture.

George looked at the ad, then looked at Todd, then back at the ad. "Yeah," he said after a second or two. "She's my sister and I want you to leave her alone."

"No, honest George. She was my date opening night. You don't believe me, go look at our photograph on the bulletin board. Number eighteen."

George rolled his eyes upward. "Dream on kido, dream on."

"No shit, George," Todd insisted. "Go check the photo."

Monday morning Todd arrived at Aaron Marks' office at ten minutes to eight and began setting up chairs for a casting session in the empty room across the hall. Keith Phillips and Crystal Manning, the leads, had been "set" for weeks, now it was time to start picking the actors and actresses who would play the lesser rolls.

Men were scheduled from nine to eleven o'clock, women from eleven until one. Todd was to welcome each actor, check their name on his list and advise Anne Bronson and Doris Rush, the thirty something woman known as "the witch" who was TDL's Casting Director.

Whether it was because of her sharp features and the long black hair that made her resemble the wicked witch in "Wizard of Oz," or her acerbic tongue Todd didn't know, but everybody called Doris Rush "the witch."

A few minutes after one o'clock, as the last actress left, Mr. Marks and "the witch" announced they were going to lunch.

"Bits at two-thirty," Anne reminded them.

"Screw Bits," Aaron grimaced. "Keep 'em on ice 'till Doris gets back." Then turning to Doris he added, "You pick 'em. Todd'll take notes for you."

The following morning things began to really crank up at the production office. Moments after Todd delivered a coffee to John Poer, before John had time to show him what he was doing with the thin, colored cardboard strips he was writing on, Doris Rush charged into John's office looking for him.

"Todd. Take these." Ignoring John Poer, she handed six film cans to him. "Aaron wants to look at these clips but I want you to keep 'em in your hands every second. You take them to the projection room when Aaron is ready to look and you wait right there until he's finished, then you bring them back to me. Understand?"

Todd nodded his head "yes."

"I'm not kidding, Todd. On pain of instant death you don't let these clips out of your hands for even a second. You got to piss, you hold 'em in one hand while you do it. Right?"

"Yeah, sure Miss Rush." Todd couldn't help but laugh. "What if I have to...do something that takes two hands?"

"No one needs two hands to take a shit, Todd." With that Miss Rush turned away and started out of the room.

"And a good morning to you, Doris," John Poer called after her with a look of disbelief on his face. "She is a piece of work, isn't she?"

"I think you could say that," Todd agreed.

Half an hour later Anne Bronson told Todd to take the film clips down to Screening Room Three and Aaron would be along shortly to view them.

Four small, well appointed screening rooms lined the first floor hallway in the Producers Building. Each room had two entrance doors separated by a three step metal stairway leading up to a heavy fire proof door to the projection booth. Although 35mm Safety Film was now in common usage there was still plenty of the old, extremely flammable Nitrate Film around, and rigorous precautions were still taken to see that a film fire did not occur.

Smoking was not permitted in projection booths nor in cutting rooms nor anyplace else where nitrate film was likely to be found. Nitrate Film was not to be fooled with. There were too many first hand stories about fires that had caused serious injuries. Not surprisingly, the smoking ban was generally followed.

Todd carried the six cans of film up to the projection booth for Screening Room #3. “Hi, I’m Todd,” he told the operator. “I’m supposed to stay here and take these back to Miss Rush as soon as Mr. Marks looks at them.”

“Okay by me, Todd.” The man took the cans from him.

“My name’s Augie.”

“Hi, Augie.”

Ten minutes later Mr. Marks’ voice came over the intercom, “Is Todd up there, Augie?”

“Yes sir, he is Mr. Marks.”

“Send him down here to take notes for me, then you can roll.”

Augie could see the flicker of concern on Todd’s face. “Don’t worry, kid. I’ll make sure no body steals ’em. The witch will never know you let ’em out-a your sight.”

Mr. Marks had Todd take a seat next to him at the long, narrow table like desk on a low platform in the center of the screening room. Below the desk two dozen comfortable theater seats were angled towards the screen. The desk itself was equipped with individual reading lights at each of it's six positions, as well as telephones, an intercom and volume controls.

Each of the six rolls of film Todd had delivered to the booth contained scenes of a different actress from several different films. Mr. Marks instructed Todd to list by number each of the actresses they were about to view and write down any comments he might make. Then he pressed the intercom control and told Augie, "Okay. Fire away."

The screening room lights dimmed and the first actress appeared on the large screen...

"Not right..." Mr. Marks said after her second scene. "Next one, Auggie..."

"No, she's too old... Next."

"Ummm. Maybe. What's she, number three? Maybe. We'll look at her again."

When they had seen all six actresses, Mr. Marks asked Augie to run number three again. He watched the screen with his head slightly tilted and a squinting left eye. As the third sequence began to roll he shook his head slowly "no," and reached for the intercom. "Okay Augie, that's enough. Thanks." He released the switch and turned to Todd, "So, what-a-ya think?"

The question surprised him. He wasn't prepared for it. If he had been he might not have been so blunt. "None of them are as pretty as Holly Sinclair. Not as camera friendly either," he answered.

With a look of surprise on his face, Mr. Marks turned to look full on at his young gofer. "And just who the fuck is Holly Sinclair?"

Todd almost said, a girl I know, but realized that might not be the best way to present her. "I've got a couple of pictures of her in the office. As soon as I take the clips back to Miss Rush I'll show them to you."

"Fuck Doris Rush!" Mr. Marks reached for the intercom button again. "Augie, call the witch and tell her to have somebody pick up that shit. I need Todd with me."

"You got it," Augie replied. Todd could almost hear the grin on his face.

Half an hour later, Todd stopped outside the door to the Casting Office, took a deep breath, then with a display of confidence he did not altogether feel, turned the knob, pushed the door open and walked in.

"Yesss?" A "minty" looking young man wearing large, tinted glasses looked up from the stack of photographs on his desk. Todd immediately recognized him for what he was. There were a lot of queer boys in the ice skating world. That never bothered him. It just meant more girls available for him.

"I need to see Miss Rush," Todd told him.

"Is she expecting you?"

"No, but I have something for her from Mr. Marks."

What the young man's answer might have been was lost to the sudden opening of the door to the inner office and the appearance of Doris Rush.

"Well…?"

Before she could add to her petulant question, Todd took the three steps forward necessary to confront her face to face and held out the Broadway Bra add. "Hi Miss Rush. Mr. Marks wants you to find out who this girl is, eh?"

Caught off balance by Todd's demeanor, the woman took the newspaper page Todd was holding out and glanced at the picture. "Big tits'll do it every time," she said half to her self. Todd could not help noticing that in the tit department the witch was sadly lacking. "All right, tell Aaron I'll get back to him in a few minutes." Turning towards her young assistant she told him, "Bobby, get Ellen Green over at The Broadway on the phone." Then, with no further look towards Todd, she went back into her office.

"Well…?" Bobby tilted his head down in order to look at Todd over the top of his glasses for a brief second before picking up his telephone directory.

Since it didn't seem that anyone in the office had anything more to say to him, Todd turned and headed for the doorway to the outside hall. As he pulled the door closed behind him, he couldn't resist the temptation to call back over his shoulder, in his best lisping, lilting voice, "Thank you Bobby."

She was seated in the little lobby area inside the Gower Street entrance. Pointedly ignoring the same bored, chain smoking guard who "welcomed" him on his first visit to RKO, Todd opened his arms to her and said, "Hi Holly."

"“My gosh, Todd." She could not have been more surprised. "What are you doing here?"

"I work for Mr. Marks," he told her. "Our gate keepers here aren't very helpful, so I came down to show you the way to our office. Come on."

He took her arm and led her into the building. "I tried to call you at your hotel but they said you weren't registered."

"Oh Todd, I know. There was a mistake in my name. I should have tried to call you at the Ice Capades but I wasn't sure if I should..."

He wasn't quite certain he believed that, but it was okay. He had found her... well, the witch had found her.

"No matter, you're here. Now listen. There's a part in Mr. Marks' picture for a young, sexy looking girl. I don't know what he will ask you to do, but find a way to loosen your hair a little bit and look seductive."

"Mr. Marks, this is Holly Sinclair."

"Hello Holly." Mr. Marks held the door to his office open as he smiled at her and nodded towards the door, "Come on in and let's talk." As he followed her into the office, he continued, "Tell me about yourself."

Much to his surprise, Holly slowly turned to face him, tilted her head slightly, and with a serious look on her face said, "Mr. Anderson called to say he will be late."

"What???"

She laughed, "That was the first line I ever spoke on stage, Mr. Marks. For some reason I've never forgotten it, and it's about the only thing I can do for an audition."

A short time later Mr. Marks led Holly back out of his office. "Todd, have John Poer set up a screen test and we'll see how this lady looks on film."

Turning to Holly he added, "Thanks for coming in Holly, Todd will call you with a time for the test. Meanwhile you study those sides."

With a look of disbelief on her face, she clutched several pages of script in her hand. "I will, Mr. Marks, I will! And thank you so much for seeing me."

"Thank Todd," he told her. "He's the one who found you."

The part of Carol Reed, in Aaron 's script, "The Professor's Night Out," is indeed small, but Aaron considered it a crucial one.

David and Alice Johnson, played by Keith Phillips and Crystal Manning, are professors at a small college. One day David Johnson accidentally bumps into student Carol Reed as he is walking down a corridor. Although they exchange only a few words, he is mesmerized by her beauty, and her face continually appears and reappears is his dreams and day dreams. Much of the ensuing story hinges on his fascination for her and his wife's reaction to it.

Aaron believes the interaction between Carol and David is so important he asks Keith Phillips to come in and do the screen test with Holly. His meeting with Holly had convinced him she would be good for the part, but unless he were to see the kind of chemistry between Phillips and her that he knows his picture needs, he will continue looking for a girl to play Carol Reed.

Happily, and not really unexpectedly, further looking is not required. There was no mistaking Keith's reaction to Holly

When they finished shooting the test, Keith asked her if she would like to have a drink with him at the Bel Aire Hotel. To everyone's surprise, she said she couldn't. Later, she told Todd she thought he wanted to go to bed with her and she didn't want to seem that easy.

The following morning, Todd was invited to view Holly's test with Mr. Marks and the witch.

Half way through the screening, a very different witch than Todd had seen before turned to Marks and told him "Jesus, Aaron, she's damn good! And my God, she photographs like a million dollars."

"Todd calls it 'camera friendly'," Aaron chuckled. "He found her."

"Oh for Christ sake." Turning to look at Todd she added, "Kiddo, you better come see me when you finish working for the genius here. Bobby's leaving at the end of the month and I have to find someone to replace him."

When Ice Capades closed at the end of June Todd expected his days would be a little shorter even though everyone at the studio had told him they would get really busy when production began. Being a somewhat relative term, at the time "really busy," had little meaning to Todd. Working for Aaron Marks all day while skating ten shows a week for Ice Capades, seemed, to him, "really busy." But following the 4th of July holiday, he began to learn the true meaning of the phrase.

One of its meanings had to do with the requirement that he move into the guest cottage at Mr. Marks' house and become his personal driver, so that Mr. Marks could get a little extra sleep on the way to and from the set. "Other wise," Anne Bronson had assured him, "Aaron might fall asleep at the wheel, run off the road and production would be held up for several hours while the studio found another director!"

God knows, Todd was beginning to understand, once begun, nothing should ever be allowed to stop production!

Mr. Marks and John Poer always got to the set 45 minutes before the 7AM crew call and the company did not normally "wrap" until 7:30PM, but that wasn't the end of the day for Mr. Marks. From the set, he went directly to the screening room each night to view "dailies," then he sometimes sat in the office making script changes for another hour or so. And where Aaron Marks went, Todd also went. It was assumed he was young enough, he didn't need sleep.

Probably the most important thing about finding himself livening in Mr. Marks' guest cottage for four weeks was the fact that during the week before Ice Capades closed, Todd had found an inexpensive, furnished apartment, on Windsor Street, just a block and a half from the studio. It wasn't until after he paid the first month's rent that he learned about his new assignment. What made it important was what he decided to do about it. He invited Holly Sinclair to use the apartment. "It's all paid for and I have to stay at Mr. Marks' so use it and save some money."

Holly was not scheduled to work until the second week of production and Todd did not have much hope of seeing her before that, but late Saturday afternoon, after he had driven Mr. Marks to check, for the third time, the location where the company would be shooting on Monday, Mr. Marks told him he wouldn't need him again until Monday morning. If he wanted to go out on the town he could use the Jag, or if he just wanted to sleep in he could do that. "Just don't bother me or make a sound until 5AM Monday morning."

The prospect of using the Jaguar and the remote possibility that Holly might not have a date was more than enough incentive for his adrenaline flow to kick in full blast and make him forget the fact that he'd had less than four hours sleep any night in the last five. In fact, the adrenaline rush was so strong, he wasn't really surprised when she answered his phone call and told him, yes, she would love to have dinner with him, and insisted they would split the cost.

One morning as they had been driving down LaCienega Boulevard, Mr. Marks had pointed to a restaurant named "Tail of the Cock" and told him it was a great place to eat and not too expensive. "Too expensive" being another relative term, Todd was leery about suggesting it, but decided it was time they celebrate their good fortunes and, if she agreed, they would take a chance.

Holly thought it was a wonderful idea and, indeed, it turned out to be a happy choice.

Built in the style of a French country cottage, the "Tail of the Cock," was a charming, multi-room room restaurant, decorated in the same country French style its exterior predicted. They ate a sumptuous meal, listened to the first set played by Shelly Mann and his Men and Todd fell asleep.

Holly smiled, then nudged him. "Come on, let's pay our bill and get out of here."

Somehow Todd managed to stay awake for the short drive from LaCienega to the apartment on Windsor but when he pulled up in front of the building, Holly put her hand on his arm and told him, "You are too tired to drive all the way to Beverly Hills. Stay here tonight."

Sunday morning Todd awoke slowly, luxuriating in the fabulous dream he'd had. Then something next to him in the bed moved. He opened his eyes. For a moment he wasn't certain where he was. Then he realized he was lying on his side, looking at the little bedroom window in his Windsor Avenue apartment.

"Are you awake?" It was her voice. He was sure of it.

"Jesus, Holly? Is that really you?"

"You don't even remember I'm here?" Her voice was soft as she whispered in his ear. "That doesn't make a girl feel very special."

He could feel her breath on the back of his neck, then her tongue began to trace his ear lobe. He counted slowly to himself, one, two, three, then turned and took her in his arms.

"You will never know how very special you are to me." He wrapped his arms around her and felt her warm, bare breasts against his naked chest...

"My God, I have nothing on and neither do you."

"I suppose we could get dressed," She pushed her pelvis against his, "If you really want to."

He found her lips and whispered, "No, I think this is just fine," before he kissed her.

Todd's hope for a repeat engagement the following weekend was doomed from the beginning. First, the company was scheduled to shoot that Saturday in order to wrap on the 15th. The Wednesday wrap date was a "must" for Aaron because he had a reservation on TWA's Thursday morning, 7AM flight to Chicago. Aaron was going to the Democratic Convention to cheer for Adlai Stevenson and he was determined nothing would prevent him from getting there..

Working on Saturday would not have prevented Todd from seeing Holly on Sunday except Mr. Marks had other plans for him. "Todd, I've got a job for you tomorrow," he told him as they pulled away from the from the down town office building which had been the location for the day's shooting.

"When we get home there will be a car in the driveway just like the one Keith was using today. We need some shots of that car traveling around the city, in and out of the garage at the building we've been shooting, stuff like that. There's a cameraman named Dennis Stern who has an office on Ventura Boulevard. You're going to pick him up tomorrow and bring him down here. You put on this jacket," Mr. Marks held up a jacket that was identical to the one Keith Phillips had worn, "Have Dennis shoot some MOS shots of the car as you drive around. Make sure he gets angles that won't show your face. Okay?

"Wow! Sure. You bet Mr. Marks." Todd's excitement was obvious. Eight weeks in the business and already he was directing! "...But, what's an MOS shot?"

Mr. Marks laughed... "Good question. MOS is from what an old German director used to say, 'Mit out sound'."

"Okay," Todd joined in the laugh. "I can do that."

"Good enough," Marks paused for a moment, then continued, "Two things more. Making these shots is strictly illegal. The unions will kill us if they find out. Dennis will process the film then we will buy some 'library' footage from him. Comprehendo?"

"Yeah, sure."

"Second thing, as of now you are officially promoted from 'gofer' to 'schlep,' and you can call me 'Aaron' like everyone else does. Comprehendo dos?"

"Si, Mr. Aaron." Hearing his own voice speak Mr. Marks' first name sounded strange to him but he was sure he could get the hang of it in time.

Five weeks later at 1:28 in the morning John Poer announced they were on "the martini."

Throughout the film world the last set up of the day is known as the martini shot. The next to last shot of the day was getting to be known as the "Abby." The reason for this being another very busy, and much admired assistant director named Abby Singer and his frequently heard end of the day pronouncement, "This and one more."

"Cut! Print!"

Aaron Marks finally completed the martini at ten minutes to two and John Poer shouted, "That's a wrap everybody!" There was a sprinkling of applause but everyone was too tired to celebrate very much.

Aaron told everyone "Thanks" and promised he would see them all at the "Wrap Party" when he got back. Then he told Todd to drive him directly to the airport. He would catch a nap in the VIP lounge rather than risk going home to bed and not waking up. "I'll get plenty of sleep on the plane."

Todd's hope that the end of production would mean more time with Holly was quickly squelched when she announced she and Keith Phillips were leaving for his place in Palm Springs.

"Keith is starting a new picture in a few weeks," she told him. "He thinks there is a part in it that's just right for me. He wants to show me the script and work on a couple of scenes."

"Welcome to Hollywood," Todd muttered to himself.

Aaron's hero, Adlai Stevenson, won the nomination and enthusiastic excitement filled the film world.

Having been constantly at Aaron's side during the long days of shooting Todd had become more and more aware of how many people on the lot were wearing Adlai Stevenson buttons. Actors, directors, even "the suits." If everybody is so interested in politics, he decided, maybe he should be too.

He didn't really care much about American politics, Canadian either for that matter, but he remembered his father telling him, "Sometimes it ain't what you know, it's who you know," and the possibility that Stevenson Headquarters might be a place to meet more people definitely seemed worth looking into.

Post Production days were slow and Todd's job with Aaron was ending. He was sure Aaron would approve if he were to volunteer some of his free time to "the cause." So, after work one evening, he decided to visit the "Stevenson For

President" office, located on the ground floor of the RCA building at Hollywood and Vine, and ask if he could volunteer his services.

Boy! Could he ever!

A chubby young woman, who introduced herself as Gail, welcomed him as he entered and could not have been more enthusiastic.

"We can always use more help! Come on over here." She led him to an unoccupied desk, handed him a telephone, a list of phone numbers and a type written "pitch."

"Make as many calls as you can. Change the wording any way you like. Just try to get people to vote and send money!"'

It turned out Todd was very good at phone soliciting. As the amount of pledges he received grew regular staffers at the office took more and more notice of him with the result that a week later he was asked if he would like to "help out" at a one hundred dollar a plate fund raising dinner to be held at the Ambassador Hotel.

Few rooms are as lavishly beautiful as the Ambassador's main ballroom and few affairs more eagerly attended by Hollywood's aristocracy than a Democratic Party dinner. Wearing an "All The Way with Adlai!" button pinned on the lapel of his brown suit he welcomed guests: "Hi, I'm Todd. May I show you to your table?"

Arriving early, on the arm of studio tycoon Howard Fabric, a stunning Crystal Manning gave Todd an affectionate hug as she introduced him to her escort. “Howard, this is the wonderful young man I told you about.”

Crystal Manning had to be getting close to forty, Todd thought, yet she still looked every bit as glamorous as any of the newer stars. For some reason she had never quite made it to the top rung of stardom and the chances are she never would now. None the less, she was a genuine movie queen and ever since he first met her on the set of Aaron’s picture, she had always treated him as if he were someone special. And to him, that was very special indeed.

Moments later Aaron himself arrived with his guests. Peter Best, and an attractive looking woman Todd learned was Peter’s wife Beverly. When Aaron sent Holly to see him he had told Todd Peter Best was perhaps the most respected and most powerful agent in Hollywood. So now Holly was a client, and she had a feature roll in a movie. Good for her, he thought, but he couldn’t help wondering how he could become one of Peter’s clients too.

“Hi Todd.” Aaron put an arm affectionately around his shoulders. “What are you doing here?”

Trying to save America for democracy, eh?” Todd answered.

The day after Todd began working as an assistant to Doris Rush he received a phone call from Holly. She had just returned from Palm Springs and wanted to pick up the few things she had left at his place... unless he wanted to have a room mate for a while.

Wow, Todd thought to himself. She's been away, presumably screwing Keith Phillips and now she wants to come back and play house with me? Well, what the hell! It isn't like we're married or anything. And she is certainly fun to play house with!

You still got a key?"

"Yes," she answered.

"My place is your place then. I'll see ya tonight, eh?" He made certain his inflection conveyed the question he was asking.

"I'll see what I can find for dinner," she told him. "What time will you be home?"

"Probably about seven," he answered.

Later that same day, David Dill, an Associate Producer on Keith Phillips' next picture, walked into the Casting Office and asked if Doris was in.

David Dill might be an Associate Producer but he did not look much like other producers and associate producers Todd had seen on the lot. David Dill looked more like a "suit." He was wearing a dark blue pin stripe suit with a "Stevenson for President" button on the lapel, highly polished black shoes, a white shirt and a tie. He was slender, had brown hair that was cut very short, and a voice and demeanor Todd thought was somewhat affected.

David had come to tell Doris that Keith Phillips wanted them to consider an actress named Holly Sinclair who had worked with him in Aaron Marks' new picture, and was it possible Doris could arrange for them to see a couple of clips from the picture even though they knew Aaron was still editing.

"Gee David, that's a tough one," the witch answered, then turned to Todd. "Todd here worked on the picture and is very close with Aaron... What-a you think, Todd?"

Remembering Doris' rule number one: "Never let them know how easy it is," Todd tried to look doubtful as he answered, "Gee, he really doesn't like to have people looking at things before he's finished editing, but I can certainly talk to him."

"That will be very much appreciated... Todd? Right?"

"Right," Todd nodded agreement.

"Good." David Dill clapped him on the back. "We hate to book an actress we haven't seen."

"I'll do what I can, David."

After he left, Doris smiled at Todd and said, "You do know his father is the 'D' in TDL, eh?"

For a moment he didn't understand what she was telling him. Then he realized, David Dill is the son of one of the company's owners. That translated into: David Dill can do you a lot of good!

"This is truly a wonderful town," Aaron smiled and shook his head from side to side as Todd told him of David Dill's request. "From bra add, to bit part, to a staring roll in less than two months."

"I don't know if it's exactly a starring roll," Todd replied, "But I guess it could be really good for her if she gets it... So, what-a you think?"

"Hell, yes." Aaron slapped his hand down on his desk for emphasis. "Go over to the cutting room and tell Harold to pull a couple of her best takes and give them to young Mr. Dill with my compliments. Tell him to call me if he wants any more information."

"Thanks... Aaron." Calling him "Aaron" was still not altogether comfortable for Todd, but he was getting better at it. “This could mean a lot to her, eh?”

“I hope it’s doing you some good too... eh?” The smile on Aaron’s face made his meaning perfectly clear.

As Todd headed for the cutting room, he heard Aaron call to Anne Bronson, “See if you can get Peter Best on the phone. Maybe we can get an agent for the young lady.”

Aaron’s film editor, Harold Bowman listened to Todd’s request then asked his Assistant Film Editor, Albert, to pull good takes of the girl from scenes 42, 92 and 137. Moments later Albert handed several rolls of film to a young woman about Todd’s age and said, “Meg will splice these up for you.”

As the girl took the rolls from Albert and started towards the Bell and Howell hot splicer in the corner of the cutting room, she turned to Todd, “Apprentice Editor Megan Schmidt at your service, Mr. Wilson.”

“Well thank you Miss Schmidt.” He followed her. “It could make things easier if you call me Todd and I call you Meg.”

“Okay. That works for me, Todd.”

She sat down at the machine and began splicing the rolls of picture together and winding them onto a reel. Then she began the same process with three rolls of what appeared to be clear celluloid.

"I know this is a dumb question, but what are those rolls?"

"These?" The girl held up one of the rolls of seemingly clear film. "Sound tracks." She held the roll out towards him and showed him the quarter inch wide metallic strip running just inside the sprocket holes along one side of the film.

"While we're editing, the sound is on one roll, the picture's on another. We call it 'double system'. This way, if Mr. Bowman wants to, he can cut away from the picture of the girl talking to a picture of someone else listening while her voice continues. It isn't until the editing is complete that the sound and the picture are put together on one piece of film called a 'composite print'."

"Wow!" Todd blinked. "There's a lot about film I don't know."

"You want lessons," the girl finished splicing the takes together, "Give me a call."

The morning after Todd delivered the clips of Holly Sinclair to David Dill's office, he answered his telephone to hear: "Hello Todd. David Dill here." Todd thought his telephone voice was even more affected than it was in person. "Say, we really like this Holly Sinclair. Is she under contract?"

"Good morning, David. No, I don't believe she is. She was just a day player on "Professor."

"Humm. That's too bad. Tell you what, see if you and Doris can get her signed up, will you? We want to have our director meet her, but I think it will be best if she is under contract before we do. Don't you agree?"

"By all means, David. Doris and I will get right on it. I think she just signed with Peter Best." Todd added.

He was aware of a groan from David at his mention of Peter Best, but he chose to ignore it. Peter Best was considered by most people in Hollywood to be "the best" agent in town. His clients were "the best" and he always negotiated "the best" contracts for them. Todd wasn't certain Holly actually was his client, but he did know that Aaron had arranged a meeting with him for her, and he hadn't said she *was* a client... he just said he *thought* she was.

It was only a short walk from the Windsor Avenue apartment she was sharing with Todd to the bus stop at Santa Monica and Gower, but it was a long ride from Gower to Canon Drive in Beverly Hills. A long ride that gave Holly time to do a great deal of thinking, which was something she did not particularly like to do much of. . Thinking always seemed to turn into remembering, and too much of what she remembered was unpleasant.

Growing up, she and her mother lived with a different man every few years. None of them had ever been like a father. None of them ever offered her the kind of advice other girls talked about getting from their fathers. The only useful advice she could remember ever getting was from her mother, something to the effect that "men only want one thing so make sure you get what you want in return."

She had begun to put that advice to work when she was a junior in High School. By then, she knew she wanted to be a movie star and she believed the more movies she could see, the more she could learn about acting. But movies were expensive and she needed all the money she could earn working after school behind the soda fountain at "Joe's" next door to the Beacon Theater. She had been working there about a month when Art Griffy, the theater's assistant manager, came in for a soda one day and realized he had forgotten his money.

"That's okay," she told him while Joe was in the back room. "You let me in for free sometime and the soda's on the house."

Two weeks later Holly lost her virginity on the coach in Art Griffy's office and never paid to go to the movies again.

Well momma, she told herself, it still seems to be working. She thought of her week with Keith Phillips in Palm Springs. According to Todd, Keith had kept his promise. They were considering her for a part in his next picture. And Todd! Funny that she should think of him just as the bus was passing the Pan Pacific Auditorium. What an amazing bit of luck had brought him into her life. She thought about last night. "Doing it" with Todd was wonderful. More than that, when she was in his arms she had a feeling of well being. She felt safe. If there is such a thing as love she thought, she was in love with him. But he was too young. And he didn't have any more money than she did. No future there. Nonetheless, if there was to be a future for her, Todd was certainly the one who got her started. Todd and Aaron Marks.

What is it with Aaron Marks, she wondered. He isn't married but he doesn't seem to be one of those men who like other men, still, he hadn't given her any indication he liked girls. From the day she had first met him Aaron had been kind and thoughtful and helpful to her. He had gone out of his way to help her with her scenes. He had made a special effort to send clips of her to David Dill and he had told Todd to make certain she did not sign anything until she had an agent. Then he had arranged for her to meet Peter Best.

Holly was awe struck just being in Beverly Hills, but it wasn't until she arrived in front of the six story building on Canon Drive, with the small brass plate along side the entrance reading "Hollywood's Best Agency," that she began to feel uncomfortably out of place. A feeling which became suddenly overwhelming when she stepped through the entrance doors into the building's magnificent lobby.

Magnificent, and intimidating!

Holly hesitated. Did she really belong here? She was on the verge of turning around and leaving when the icy looking blond woman at the reception desk called to her.

"May I help you, Miss?"

"...Ah," For a moment Holly was at a loss for words. "Ah, I'm Holly Sinclair. I think I have an appointment with Mr. Best."

Before the words were out of her mouth, the icy looking receptionist had gotten to her feet. "Ice" turned to warm syrup as she hurried to Holly's side. "Oh, Miss Sinclair. We've been expecting you. Mr. Best is waiting for you in the conference room, let me take you to him."

"Hi Holly." A tall, well built, good looking older man with salt and pepper hair jumped to his feet as the completely thawed icy blond held the door open for her. Hurrying towards her with his hand extended, he continued, "I'm Peter Best. It's great to meet you."

She took his hand, "How do you do Mr. Best..."

"Please call me Peter. Mr. Best is my father."

In actual fact, "Best" was not the name of Peter's father. It was Tucci.

Shortly after the end of World War I, Franco Tucci had met Hugh Alan Crawford, an enterprising young British Navy veteran who had come to Staten Island. They became friends and partners as Hugh developed highly successful boot-legging, loan sharking, book making and gambling businesses.

In 1926, during a liquor delivery gone wrong, Franco Tucci had been gunned down and Hugh Crawford assumed the roll of family protector and father figure, helping Franco's widow, Rosa, raise his two sons, Franco, Jr. and Pietro, almost as older brothers to his daughter, Kathleen.

Over the years, since the end of prohibition, most of Hugh's activity had turned to legal businesses, but back in the mid thirties, when Kathleen first ventured out from out from under his protective shield to sing with Chuck Stacey's Orchestra, in order to hide her identity from his enemies, she did so under the name Cathy Connors. In 1937 when she left the Stacey band to pursue a film career, believing she should have someone out there in Hollywood to look after her interests, Hugh sent twenty-three year old Pietro to California. Since the Tucci name was closely associated with Staten Island's notorious Hugh Alan Crawford, Pietro had done so under the name Peter Best.

"Okay, Peter it is then." Holly held out her hand to shake his. "I'm afraid I don't know what I'm supposed to say or do, Peter. Aaron just told me to come see you and that possibly you might consider representing me, but there's something you should probably know," Holly reached into her handbag as she spoke, "A couple of weeks ago I signed a contract with a modeling agency. I didn't read it very carefully... I needed a job and they had one."

She handed the contract to Peter. “I think it sort of says they represent me for everything…”

Peter took the one page document and scanned it quickly. He had seen many like it before, it was a standard, all encompassing agreement designed to take advantage of the countless hopefuls who would do almost anything to find a job. People who used this kind of contract were not exactly unscrupulous, they just figured that one out of a hundred… maybe one out of a thousand, might get a crack at the movies and then they would have a cash-cow in hand.

“Ummm… I’m glad you told me about this.” Peter looked up from the paper, “It won’t be a problem.”

“It won’t?” The relief in her voice was obvious. “And you might consider representing me?”

“Holly, Aaron Marks is one of the best directors in the business, even if he hadn’t shown me clips of your work, even if I hadn’t met you, his recommendation alone would have made me want you as a client. But I have seen clips and I have met you and if Aaron hadn’t said a word, I would want you to sign with us.”

Holly opened her mouth to say something, but before she could speak, Peter smiled and continued, “Then, too, the fact that Keith Phillips has asked TDL to put you in his next picture doesn’t hurt…”

"Oh... He did?"

"Yeah." Peter cocked his head and looked at her. "Is there anything I should know about you and Keith?"

She knew Peter Best was considered to be just that; the best! And she desperately wanted to be his client, but just how much about her private life did he need to know? Maybe not everything, she decided, but maybe some things...

"After we finished Aaron's picture," she spoke slowly, but without embarrassment, Keith told me there might be a part for me in his next picture and he wanted to work on some scenes with me. I spent a few days with him at his place in Palm Springs."

"Okay. Is this a relationship you plan to continue?"

"Is that something you really need to know, Mr. Best?"

"Yes. It is. If I'm going to represent you properly I need to know what you're looking for and where you want to go. ...And remember, I'm Peter."

"Okay Peter." She smiled and glanced away briefly. Then, turning back, she focused her eyes on his. "I want to be a star. It seemed to me Keith Phillips could help me get started. Beyond that, I have no interest in him."

"Then I suggest from now on you keep your relationship with him on a strictly professional level."

"I can do that; but I'm not sure he can."

"I'm sure he can." Peter nodded his head up and down. "I'll have a word with him."

A few minutes after Holly left his office, Peter used his private phone to call Hy Abrams. "Hello, Hy. I need a favor."

"Peter, of course, anything. How are you anyway? I haven't seen you in ages."

I'm great. Busy, but feeling fine," Peter answered. "We need to get together for diner some time soon."

"Yeah. That would be good. Meanwhile, what do you need?"

"Hy, there's a modeling agency over in the valley..."

Peter looked down at the contract Holly had signed... "The Ventura-Highland Agency. A few weeks ago they signed a girl named Holly Sinclair. I need to get rid of that agreement."

"I'll take care of it right away, Pete. Now what about that diner? Can we make it next week? Maybe Wednesday?"

Peter looked at his desk calendar. Wednesday looked clear. "Seven o'clock, Musso and Frank?"

"Wonderful!" Hy's enthusiasm was contagious.

"Okay," Peter grinned. "See you there."

There were several young women seated in the Ventura-Highland office, waiting for... hoping for assignments when she entered. Although she was not unattractive, it was obvious from her walk... her stride, that she was not a model. She walked quickly past the hopefuls and held out her Police ID as she spoke to the woman seated at the desk.

"You got someplace we can talk?"

The woman looked at the badge. "Yes..." she got to her feet, "In the back office."

The police woman followed the agent into the small office behind the main waiting room. "What's the trouble?" she asked as she closed the door.

"You signed a girl named Holly Sinclair a couple-a weeks ago. She's underage. You can gimme the contract, or I can close you down. What'll it be?"

"I'm not sure..." The agent started to protest.

"I got two men in the car outside." There was no quarter in the police woman's voice. "Gimme the contract or I close the place and take you in."

"Well shit!" The agent was angry, but what could she do? Things like this happened now and then. All you could do was go along with it. Police trouble, no matter how unfair or unreasonable it was, was not something you wanted.

"All right... all right. I'll give you the contract."

"Mountains! Real Goddamn Mountains! That's what I'm talking about!"

Director Zack Seguine stood in the middle of Sedona's main street holding his arms outstretched to encompass the rugged, thousand foot high cliffs that surround the village. "Fucking spectacular is what they are! And September is the perfect time. This is 'Out West' country!"

"Out West" was to be the Western to End All Westerns. Holly knew it's star, Keith Phillips believed that. And it's producer, Ira Shuman believed it. The writer, Morrie Sparks, believed it and, most important of all, Zack Seguine believed it. So, if the Director, and the Star, and the Producer, and the Writer all believed it, she believed it too.

And so did the very eager Associate Producer David Dill.

To her surprise, as Peter had assured her would be the case, since arriving in Sedona, Keith Phillips had been cordial, friendly, charming, but had made no attempt at renewing their Palm Springs relationship. On the other hand, although somewhat timidly, Associate Producer David Dill was apparently becoming interested, and she was very aware of the fact that his father owned the company.

All this, combined with the excitement of being on location with a movie company, was almost too good to be true. In fact, Holly had just one problem: she had never been on a horse in her life! Aside from horses she remembered seeing pulling milk wagons when she was a tiny girl, and horses she had seen policemen riding in Jersey City, she had practically never even looked at a real live horse. Especially not up close. Now she was expected to ride one of the damn things. Maybe she shouldn't have told David Dill she could ride. But if she had, she might not have gotten the part.

Thinking of David made her smile. He didn't know how to ride either. The thing was, he didn't have to ride. She did! Fortunately, although she was practically the only woman in the picture, her part was not that big and she had a few days during which she was able to take some riding lessons from head wrangler "Tom Mix" before her first horseback scene.

Everybody knew the wrangler's name was not really "Tom Mix," but his Indian name was virtually unpronounceable, so he was "Tom Mix" to cast and crew.

The best thing about her riding lessons was the fact that David Dill decided he should also learn to ride, so they frequently took lessons together. They rode what Tom Mix called "rocking horses" and made short trips into some of the deep canyons slicing between the spectacular mountains and red rock cliffs that made Sedona one of the wonder spots of the world. There were no mountains in Passaic. In Hollywood she had been in awe of the Hollywood Hills, but they couldn't compare to the cliffs surrounding Sedona. Thousand foot high walls in shades of rust red and pink with horizontal striations of light tan cutting across. Looking in one direction, she could see huge, protruding shoulders that seemed to enfold towering columns and slender fingers of red rock which, from a distance, looked almost like the New York City skyline as seen from the Jersey side of the Hudson River. In another direction the outcroppings and shadows looked like animals and human faces. No wonder Indians believed spirits lived in these mountains along Oak Creek.

It was on one of their evening rides together that David made his first, gentle, pass at her: Mesmerized by the deepening colors and ever changing shadows the setting sun was creating on the cliffs around them, they had stopped their horses along side the creek when he said. "I guess you and Keith are pretty good friends." It was more of a question than a statement.

"Oh, yes," she said with enthusiasm she didn't really feel. "Keith is such a wonderful man. He's like a father and a brother to me all in one." She hoped referring to Keith Phillips as a "father" and "brother" figure would cancel out questions that might arise regarding the time she had spent with him in Palm Springs. "Why if it weren't for Keith," she continued, "I wouldn't have this part in your picture."

"Well, I'm not certain of that, Holly. We heard about your work in 'Professor.' Keith did speak to us about you, but I think we might have found you without his help."

"Really?" Holly's normally large eyes grew even wider.

"As soon as I saw... I mean as soon as we all saw the clips Aaron let us look at..."

"Oh, David," she broke in. "I didn't know it was you."

Holly was a young lady who knew very well how to play her cards. The way she said "you" would have caused any man under the age of 80 to feel a tingle.

"Oh, gee Holly," David protested, "I can't claim anything like that. I did ask a fellow in casting if he could get some clips of you from

Aaron, but really all of us looked at them and decided you were right for the part."

David," she lowered her voice. "You are very modest and very sweet and I thank you for giving me this chance."

At which point Holly's "rocking horse" gave a start and turned away from the creek. If the horse's sudden movement was caused by a kick from Holly, David Dill was not aware of it, but the moment was broken and when Holly said, "I guess we should be getting back," he quickly turned his horse and followed her up the trail towards the little motel in which the entire company was staying.

Next morning, for her first day of shooting, Holly arrived in the make up trailer at 5:30AM.

Today. as seems to be mandatory in the film business, Zack Seguine planes to begin her work with the final sequence of his movie. Holly's character, Naomie, a beautiful half-breed girl, struggles to climb Bell Rock to reach the dying man she loves. And Zack intends to have realism! He intends that by the time Naomie reaches Tim Dalton, her dress will be torn, her fingers bloody and she will be tired beyond belief.

It is at the foot of Bell Rock that Holly's day begins as an assistant director and the stunt coordinator help her up to the first area Seguine has selected. After several rehearsals,

Seguine's camera finally rolls for it's first "take" a few minutes after eight o'clock.

Almost three hours, with four "prints" in the can, Seguine says it is time to move to location number two.

Eight hours later, as the sun is nearing the horizon, there are tears of real exhaustion on Naomie's face when she finally kisses Tim Dalton "goodbye" and Zack Seguine says they are through for the day.

That evening, her body "all aching and racked with pain," Holly Sinclair asked Leonard, the company medic, if he could give her something to make the aches go away and help her get to sleep.

"You bet, Holly. I got just the thing for that."

She took a hot bath, two of the blue pills Leonard had given her and switched on the TV set. She had been surprised to find they actually had TV in Sedona and her room had a TV set complete with its own "rabbit ears." She climbed into bed, lay back against the pillows and fell asleep before the screen came to life.

The day after "Out West" wrapped, Holly telephoned Todd to tell him she would not be returning to Windsor Street. She thought it was time she had a place of her own. The call was not a major surprise, he knew she was becoming a Movie Star, and sharing an apartment with an assistant in the Casting Department was probably not very good for her image. None the less, he felt a twinge of sadness mixed with an equal amount of envy. They had met a couple of days after they each arrived in Hollywood looking for fame and fortune. It seemed she was very much on her way. He, on the other hand, as an assistant in the Casting Department, certainly was not. But, Hey! This is Hollywood. You take things as they come. He wished her good luck. He knew he would miss her. A lot.

Election night found Todd back on duty at the Ambassador Hotel. Balloons were suspended in overhead nettings, awaiting a signal for release. The popping of dozens of champagne corks sounded like small arms fire while the musical strains of "Happy Days Are Here Again," played time after time by the eighteen piece orchestra set up on the festively decorated stage at the far end of the room tried to drown out the ever growing buzz of excited conversation. Excitement that began to diminish as the evening wore on and it became more and more obvious the General was going to be re-elected.

As the crowd began to melt away, those who remained watched the TV screens in disappointed silence and listened sadly as their man Adlai told his supporters, "I'm too old to cry, but it hurts too much to laugh."

"Cheer up son, It ain't the end of the world. We did pretty good here in California."

Todd looked up to see who's hand was on his shoulder and who's warm voice was consoling him. It was silver haired, straight as a ram rod, ruggedly handsome, Jordan Lustig, a City Councilman he had met once or twice at the campaign office.

Now in the middle of his sixth, four year term, and in spite of his distinctive, distinguished white hair, Jordan Lustig was not yet fifty, and indirectly owed his political success to Chicago's own, Al Capone.

In 1925, with the new film industry coining money at a rate no one could believe, Hollywood was becoming a place where you could make a lot of money providing entertainment for the new rich of the movie world. Every night, gambling ships anchored outside the three mile limit were filled to capacity. Ladies of the evening were some of the best looking and most expensive to be found anywhere in the world, and, particularly at private parties, the demand for liquor was insatiable.

Big Al had decided he wanted some of this action and picked jovial, outgoing, salesman type Hy Abrams to go to Hollywood and set up shop. Something Hy did with great success and had continued to do long after prohibition ended and Big Al went off to prison.

Shortly after the market crash in 1920, a young college student needing money to stay in school, came to Hy's agency looking for a job. Something about the young man struck a chord with Abrams. He hired him, and never regretted his decision to do so. The young man was Jordan Lustig.

In 1933, following the demise of Prohibition, with his auto business and call girl service and other interests all doing remarkably well, it occurred to Hy that some influence in the local body politic might be a great asset. To this end, he suggested his young protégé consider a run for City Council. With a campaign that was well financed by Hy and others with similar interests, Lustig had easily been elected by a large majority.

"Oh. Hello, Councilman Lustig." Todd managed a smile, "Yeah. Yes, I guess we did good in California at that."

"Politics is like the ocean tide, my boy..." The councilman liked to speak in centurion tones. "Ebb and flow, ebb and flow."

"I suppose so. But this was my first election. I don't guess I can even call it that, I can't vote, I'm a Canadian."

"Don't worry about that, son. You can get your citizenship in no time and you'll have plenty of years for voting. I like to see young people like yourself getting involved in politics. I've heard a lot of good things about you. You keep up your interest and come visit me down at City Hall sometime. A sharp young man could do himself a lot of good in politics."

Weather patterns in Southern California are so predictable there doesn't seem to be any good reason for TV Stations to hire people to "forecast" the weather, but they do, and the forecast for Christmas week 1956 was about the same as it had been for 1955 and for 1954, the year before that, and the year before that: "Rain, heavy at times." Surprise, surprise.

It was also common knowledge in Southern California that on New Year's Eve the weather would clear and by Rose Bowl time next day the sun would be shinning, the temperature would be 73 degrees and some more people in Denver and Chicago and Pittsburgh and almost anyplace else where there was snow on the ground and temperatures in the teens, would begin thinking about moving to Southern California.

All this Aaron Marks knew, so why didn't the studio? Why had they decided to preview his picture on December 27th?

The 27th, was exactly like Aaron expected it to be, except maybe the rain was a little heavier than "heavy at times." At least it was heavier in Carona Del Mar, the small, charming, seaside village some fifty miles south of Los Angeles where the Del Mar Theater's marquee proudly boasted: "Studio Preview Tonight."

.

"Rain is for shit!" according to Aaron Marks. "Rain like this, nobody goes out. They sit in front of their TV sets and keep warm and dry. But what do those shmucks at the studio know from TV? They got their fucking heads up their ass!"

Be that as it may, for better or worse, the studio had arranged the preview of "Professor's Night Out," and there was nothing Aaron could do about that other than hope anyone who braved the rain to see his picture would be happy with what they saw.

The problem, according to Aaron, is that laughter's contagious. If you are in a crowd and someone starts to laugh, others quickly join in. But, with only a few people in a theater that has six hundred seats, laughs can die a horrible death.

All this Todd was told as he drove his old boss through the pouring rain, down the Pacific Coast Highway, past the refinery lights of Long Beach and into the wilds of Orange

County. Orange County, according to Aaron, was California's version of Schenectady, New York. Most people have heard of it but not too many know exactly where it is.

The thing about Orange County was the fact that there, according to studio mavens who were supposed to know, only a few miles from LA, you could find simple people, "real people," people not influenced by the world of movie making. There, you could get a valid indication as to what the rest of the country would think about a picture.

Aaron might be depressed at the evening's prospects, for Todd, however, it was an exciting time. His first "preview." The preview of a picture he had actually worked on. Maybe best of all, that was four months ago and his old boss had remembered him and asked him to be his driver once again. He was sorry for the problems the rain might cause, but it was hard for him to feel too badly about the evening.

Of the one hundred twenty-seven people who attended the preview, seventy-three turned in mostly favorable Comment Cards. What was considered surprisingly important by the studio's assistant publicity director, was the fact that seventeen respondents asked "Who's the girl who played the student?" Or, "Like to see more of the student girl." One said, "Wow! I want to go to school with HER!"

"Aaron, this is phenomenal!" The assistant publicity director was obviously excited, "Almost twenty-five percent of these cards single out a girl who doesn't even get screen credit! I'm going to recommend we shoot some additional scenes with her and we should put her name up in lights." He raised his arms with his hands framing the marquee he could see in his mind, "Introducing...." he paused then turned to Aaron. "What's her name?"

The preview audience reaction to Holly Sinclair in Aaron's picture was pleasing to Thoman, Dill and Levy, but the suggestion that scenes of her be added to Aaron's picture, "Professor's Night Out," was not.

"Aaron's picture is finished." David Dill proclaimed. "Better we "introduce" her in "Out West," which was still in post production and which just happened to be the film Mr. Dill's son David, Jr. was involved with.

While they were shooting "Out West" David Dill, Jr. had spent a lot of time with Holly learning to ride. And Holly knew his father was the "D" in TDL. She thought David was "hot for her body," and believed she knew exactly how to keep him that way. Whenever David tried to get closer to her, she reminded him they were working together and said "no," with a tone of voice that said "maybe."

The day after “Out West” wrapped Holly rented a room at the Studio Club for women and waited for David’s next move. It was not long in coming.

“Have you heard about the preview of Aaron’s picture last night?” David’s voice was low, controlled.

“No, I haven’t. Did they cut me out?”

“Oh, not exactly...“ His voice began to break, he couldn’t keep up the pretense. “Holly, they had more comment cards about you than they could count and the studio wants us to shoot some added scenes of you for our picture and put your name up in lights!”

For a moment she could not speak. Tears filled her eyes as she began to cry. “Oh, David.” She sobbed, “I... I... Can I call you back...?”

“You don’t have to. I’ll call you as soon as we set a date for shooting.”

The more Holly asked herself why she was crying, the more she cried. It took several minutes for her to stop. Then, suddenly, she realized she wanted to tell her mother. She didn’t know why, she hadn’t talked with her mother in more than six months. She doubted her mother would be the slightest bit interested, but she wanted to tell her anyway. She wanted her to know her daughter was actually in a movie.

The only place she knew of where she might contact her mother was where they had been living when she left. The Hudson Apartment Hotel in Passaic, a run down three story ware house building next to the Pennsylvania Railroad tracks that had eight, one room "efficiency" apartments on the top floor. There were no telephones in the apartments, at least not in the room she and her mother shared.

Probably her mother had moved in with another man by this time, but the Hudson office was the only place she could think of where she might find out how to reach her.

The telephone in her room at the Studio Club was for local calls only. To make a long distance call she had to go through the club operator and pre pay just like using a pay phone in a phone booth.

She gave the number to club operator, paid four dollars and fifty cents for three minutes, then waited for her call to go through.

"Yeah, Hudson, Apartments. What-cha want?" The voice that answered had a slight slur to it.

"I'd like to get a message to Mrs. Simon in Apartment five, please."

"Who...? Mrs. Simon? Wait a minute."

She could hear muffled voice, then the man with the slurred voice came back on the line.

"She ain't here no more."

"Do you know where I can reach her? I'm her daughter."

"Wait a minute..."

Again muffled voices, then another man spoke to her. "You Felicia's daughter?"

"Yes. I'm Myra."

"Yeah? Well Myra, your ol' lady died about two months ago. How come you don't know dat?"

She did not realize the telephone had slipped from her hand. Nor did she hear the voice coming from the receiver asking her to pay twenty-three dollars "the ol' lady still owes us."

Tears filled her eyes for the second time in a matter of minutes and she began to cry softly... uncontrollably. "Oh momma... momma... momma."

Word of the comment cards and TDL's decision regarding Holly reached Producer Ira Shuman when he arrived at his office Monday morning.

"Studio's all excited about Holly Sinclair," his secretary told him. "They want us to add a couple-a scenes of her."

"Really?" Ira's eyebrows elevated along with the corners of his mouth. "That's a nice Monday morning surprise. . Better give Morrie a call and tell him we need a couple of new scenes. Tell him to come up with something we can shoot here in the studio, "I'm not going to piss away money on a location just to get a few more close-ups of her good looking tits!"

The Tuesday morning surprise was even better:

"God damn Morrie" Ira Shuman's expression was a mirror of his happiness. "These scenes are great. How the hell did you come up with 'em this quick?"

"Ira," Morrie took a deep breath then continued, "The scenes were in my original draft. You cut 'em out. Remember?"

"Oh." Ira slapped his hand against his head. "That's right. But who knew the chick was going to be this hot?"

"I did," Morrie smiled.

"Fuck-off." Ira laughed as he flipped on his intercom.

"Gloria, tell David to set up a couple of days shooting. Soon as possible." He switched off before Gloria could reply.

Zack Seguine knew perfectly well he could shoot the three added scenes of Holly and Keith Phillips in one day but if Ira was willing to go for two why should he push the crew. Besides, with extra time, he could fool around with a few more angles on her boobs. And that was always fun. Even so, stretching things as much as he could, they finished a little after five on the second day.

"Holly..." David Dill caught up to with her as she headed for her dressing room trailer. "It's still pretty early. How 'bout a celebration drink over at Sportsman's?"

"Oh, gee David, that would be wonderful."

The drink at Sportsman's Lodge lead to several dates to see movies, and three evenings at the Macombo and Palm Garden before David told her he wanted her to meet his parents and would she like to have lunch with them on Sunday, at their home in Bel Aire..

Sunday was a perfect January kind of day in Los Angeles. The cloudless sky was azure blue, the humidity free temperature was 71 degrees and the crystal clear air made it seem as if the snow covered mountains, framed by the stately palm trees along Wilshire Boulevard, were just at the end of the street, not fifty .miles away..

As David turned into their circular driveway his parents came out onto the front terrace of their imposing three story mansion, then walked to the car, where David's father opened the door for Holly while his mother went round to great her son with a warm hug and kiss.

Introductions completed, Mrs. Dill suggested they take a short stroll through her gardens before lunch.

"That would be wonderful," Holly exclaimed. "David has told me so much about your beautiful roses, I'm dying to see them."

After ten minutes of strolling across immaculate Dicondra grass, past perfectly manicured privet hedges and through exquisite rose gardens, they arrived at an awning covered patio overlooking a swimming pool which, Holly was reasonably certain, was somewhat smaller than the Atlantic Ocean, but not much.

Next to the two flag stone steps leading from the pool decking up to the patio, a uniformed houseman stood waiting to serve champagne and canapés.

"I thought we should celebrate your picture, Holly." Mr. Dill told her as he signaled to the man to begin serving.

"Oh, Mr. Dill," Holly's shy giggle was not lost on Mrs. Dill. "It's not my picture. It's Mr. Seguine's and Mr. Shuman's and, maybe most of all, David's."

"David's?" His father's pride was obvious. "Why do you say that? He was just an associate producer."

"Mr. Dill," Holly's voice took on a slight edge. "Maybe you don't know it, but without David I don't think our picture would have ever been finished. David was everywhere, watching over everything."

"I'm glad to hear that, Holly. None the less, I saw a rough cut yesterday and it certainly is your picture too."

Before she could respond, the houseman presented her with a tray carrying filed champagne glasses. She reacted with a quick, slightly alarmed glance towards David before reaching for a glass.

"Dad, Holly doesn't drink. Maybe Harry can bring her a coke or some orange juice." David put his hand on her shoulder. "What would you like?"

"Oh, no David," she looked quickly from David to his father, then back to him.

"Celebrating your picture, I think I should have champagne."

"Okay." David laughed and turned to his mother. "You may have to put her to bed Mom..."

"Oh David." Holly's blush was also not lost on Mrs. Dill.

After luncheon on the patio, as Harry was clearing away the desert dishes, David's father suggested he and his son have a game of pool "while the ladies finish their tea."

"Well, Holly," Mrs. Dill began the grilling she had anticipated and prepared for. "David tells me you are from back east. New Jersey, I think he said."

"Yes. Passaic." Holly smiled a lovely smile. "It's a tiny little town you probably never heard of. Not far from New York City."

"Umm, no. I don't know New Jersey too well," Mrs. Dill admitted. "Are your parents still living there?"

Holly blinked and Mrs. Dill could see a quick look of sadness flash across her face. "No. I'm an orphan, Mrs. Dill."

"Oh, my dear. I am so sorry. I didn't mean to pry."

No, of course you didn't, Holly thought. But her face did not reveal her thoughts. "Oh, no. That's all right. I don't mind."

"But your mother and your father, they're both... gone?"

"I never knew my dad," Holly began slowly. "He was a... a country doctor. You know, the kind who used to make house calls." She took a deep breath. "He was coming home from one of those calls when a car ran a red light and...he was killed."

Mrs. Dill could detect definite dampness in the corners of Holly's eyes. "I was only two, so I never really knew my father."

"Oh, what a tragedy, Holly. I'm so sorry." Mrs. Dill reached over to put her hand on Holly's arm. "And your mother? You lost her too?"

Now there were real tears in Holly's eyes. "Last year. She caught pneumonia..."

Holly could not go on. Grabbing up a napkin, she turned her head away and tried to dry her eyes. "I'm sorry, Mrs. Dill. I shouldn't cry. It's been nearly a year. But I miss her so... She was so... wonderful."

While the ladies were "finishing their tea" on the patio outside, inside David sank the eight ball on the first break and, as his father began to re-wrack, he jumped in with the subject he could no longer contain, "Dad, I read a book that I think will make a great movie."

"Oh...?"

"Yeah. It's about a beautiful spy. World War Two, most of it takes place in Venice."

"Venice, Italy?" his father asked as he sorted the pool balls then pushed the wrack into position.

"Yes. Dad, with TV sucking away our audiences I think we have got to get out of the studio and show people things they can't see on TV." David's enthusiasm was genuine and contagious. "UA, MGM and Universal all have pictures going overseas and we need to do that too."

David knew his father well enough not to push. Instead he carefully placed the cue ball four inches to the right of the spot and with a smooth, strong stroke, drove it into the rack. The four ball found it's way into the side pocket.

"Guess I'm solids," he told his father as he moved down the side of the table looking for his next shot.

"I suppose..." His father looked up from the tip of his pool cue he was chalking, "You want to produce this picture"

"You bet!"

"And can I guess who you plan to have play the lady spy?"

"Gee dad, I don't know... Can you?"

For Todd Wilson the year did not have the same auspicious beginning it had for Holly. On his first day in the office following the preview of Aaron's picture in Corona Del Mar Doris Rush called him into her office and told him he no longer had a job.

"Aaron is going to take a couple of months off. Ira says he isn't going to do anything for at least six months and David Dill is going to make a picture in Europe this summer," she explained. "With almost no production going on here at the studio, they won't approve an assistant in the department any longer."

Todd remembered a story he once heard about a man who had been fired from MGM after fifteen years. "Well," he was supposed to have said, "They told me it was only temporary when they hired me." Temporary or not, for Todd the news was, if not devastating, certainly very unhappy,

"I got you a week's severance," Doris added. "And you're welcome to come in and use the office if you want."

Twice since election day Todd had visited Councilman Jordan Lustig at his office in LA's mammoth City Hall. Each time he walked into the vast, tile floored marble rotunda, he felt as if he were entering the world's largest mausoleum. But, if LA's City Hall was not warm and wonderful, Councilman Lustig's welcome always was. On both occasions he had expressed his delight at seeing Todd again and made noises about the possibility of a job there if Todd ever got tired of the movie business. He certainly was not tired of the movie business, but on the sixty dollar a week salary he had been making as Doris' assistant, he did not have a bank account that would allow him to be out of work for very long. Working for Councilman Lustig was a possibility he needed to investigate.

"I'm really glad you came to see me, Todd," the councilman told him after he explained the reason for his sudden and unexpected need to find a job. "I need a Studio Liaison. I'm up for re-election next year and it's time I start buttering up a few people. There's a lot of movie studios in my district and a lot of people living there work in the studios. I can pay you three hundred dollars a month, plus expenses and the use of an automobile." The councilman smiled at Todd. "I know your heart's in the movie business and this can be an opportunity for you to meet a lot of important people. So, what-a-ya say?"

"Wow! That's great! When do I start, and what do I do, eh?"

Lustig explained Todd's duties would not be complicated. He would contact Studio Executives, Union Reps and prominent industry people. He would ask them for suggestions regarding regulations and legislation dealing with the business. He would impress upon them how much the councilman respected their input and how sincerely he appreciated their advice. He would remind them of the many ways in which the councilman had supported the industry in the past and point out that he had always been, and continued to be "Strongly opposed to the legalization of gambling here in our wonderful city, or in our state, or any place else in this country!" Jordan Lustig believed gambling worked economic hardships on the poor and took people away from movie theaters. "Movies," the councilman insisted, "Are what makes this city... this state and this country great!"

As he continued, Todd could hear his father's voice echoing over and over again in his ears: "Not always what you know, but who you know!" This job would be a direct pipeline to anybody and everybody in the industry. He could imagine the telephone calls he would make: "Hello, this is Todd Wilson calling from Councilman Lustig's office. The councilman wants your advice on what he can do to help keep the industry moving forward." Bingo! There wasn't a person in the business who would not respond to a call like that.

"We also want to remind people..." Todd realized Lustig was still outlining his duties, "...That we are up for re-election next year and we need their votes and their support if we are to continue working in their behalf."

The councilman held out his hand a rubbed his fingers together when he said "support," confirming Todd's suspicion that "support" meant money.

Working a "day job" seemed strange to Todd. What to do at night? Thoughts of Holly Sinclair were always in his mind. "But shit!," he told himself. "That's over. So what now?"

Well, he had a job with the councilman and politics might be a good future but making movies was what he really wanted to do. Did he know enough about how movies are made? He was pretty familiar with how actors are picked. His job with Aaron had taught him just about everything about production, but post production. What really happens to the film when it comes out of the camera? Probably something he should learn more about...

Megan! One evening her name suddenly popped up in his mind. The Apprentice Editor in Harold Bowman's cutting room. He didn't remember her last name, in fact he wasn't sure he ever knew it... but she had told him if he wanted to know more about film editing he should call her. At the time he and Holly had been together and some other girl was the last thing in his mind. But Holly was gone and... well, Megan wasn't. Meg's offer just might be an opportunity he shouldn't overlook. And besides, he remembered, she was a pretty good looking lady.

"Hi, this is Todd Wilson, eh? Is that offer to teach me about film editing still good."

"Jesus Todd, it's only been what, six months?"

"Maybe more than that, which just proves how good my memory is and how much I value a chance to go to your school. Could we have dinner tonight?"

"No way. I'm moonlighting on a project for a friend of mine and I'll be working tonight and every night."

Before he could think of a retort, she continued, "...But if maybe you wanna come over to the cutting room and help me out, I'll make sure you learn everything there is to know about cutting film."

"That sounds good to me. What time?"

"Any time you want... after six that is. Harold and Albert go home at six then the cutting room is all mine."

"Want I should bring a pizza?"

"Pizza's good," she laughed. I like mine with sausage."

"Get it while it's hot..." Todd used his elbow then his rear end to open the cutting room door while he held the pizza box and two bottles of beer in his hands.

"Don't put it down in here," Meg almost screamed. "Take it in the office." She pointed to a door at the far end of the cutting room then turned her attention back to her Moviola.

"I'll be right there," she added before stepping on the foot pedal, starting the machine again.

Todd watched her for a moment, then followed her instructions to carry the food into the small office adjoining the cutting room. Before he had the caps off the beer bottles he heard the Moviola stop and almost immediately she joined him.

"God, that smells wonderful! I didn't realize how hungry I am."

Todd held up a bottle, "Is there a glass somewhere?"

"Never mind glasses, the bottle will do fine."

She had pushed her frameless eye glasses back up on top of her head, where they did something to her hair, and the combination of no glasses and changed hair made her look surprisingly pretty.

Todd bit off half a slice of pizza, chewed for a moment then said, “Sooo.. tell me about film,”

“Didn’t your mother ever teach you not to talk with your mouthful?” Meg grinned as she attempted to swallow her own first bite.

“Okay.” Todd nodded his head and pushed the rest of the slice into his mouth.

“What’s to tell?” She took a swig of beer. “There’s negative and positive. Color and black and white. Sixteen frames to a foot, projection speed is twenty-four frames a second, ninety feet a minute.” She took another bite. “Ummm. Love Italian sausage.”

“That’s all?” Todd asked. “Negative and positive and ninety feet a minute?”

“That’s all you need to know about film. It’s what you do with it that’s tricky.”

They finished their suppers and she led him back into the cutting room to the Moviola where she was working.

“I’m cutting a documentary for a friend who has absolutely no money. We couldn’t afford to make a work print, so I’m cutting the original negative.”

“That doesn’t sound like a good idea. What if you fuck it up?”

"Then it's fucked up. That's why I have to be careful, not only with the cuts I make but how I handle the film so I don't scratch it or get it dirty."

Pulling on a pair of white cotton gloves she reached for one of several strips of film hanging from a rack over a barrel lined with a soft cotton bag. Holding the strip up for Todd to see, she continued.

"When raw stock comes from Kodak it ain't nothin' until a cameraman exposes it, the lab develops it and a director and an editor look at it, That's when the creative part begins."

She threaded the film strip carefully into the Mviola. "Each of these strips is a different 'take' of basically the same scene. A cutter's job... Pardon me, I mean a Film Editor's job, is deciding which take to use, how much of it to use and how it should be juxtaposed with the other takes."

"Juxtaposed!" Todd couldn't help the laugh. "Where did you get a word like that?"

"Film school. Now shut-up and watch."

She ran the strip of film back and forth several times deciding where it should begin and end. "On most pictures the director and the editor make a lot of these decisions together. On a documentary like this, there aren't that many takes nor that many ways to put them together. Besides, our director is too busy trying to finish shooting before his money runs out."

"I thought you said he has no money."

"Yes, well he practically doesn't."

She picked up a pair of scissors. "There are four sprocket holes to each frame," she continued and held the film strip up for him to see. "When you cut it, you cut right in the middle, between hole number two and hole number three." She made the cut. "Then you overlay the half frame I have here with the half frame left on the previous take..."

As she spoke she put the new scene in what she told him was a sync machine, ran it through and wound it onto a reel which held the sequence she was building. "When you splice all this together, the half frames get cut off.

"How come if you are an editor, you're working here as an Apprentice?" Todd wanted to know.

Meg turned away from the Moviola to look straight at him. "That's a dumb question. You got any idea how hard it is to get a job in this business? I went to film school with about ten million other kids. The only reason I have this job is because my sister is married to Harold's sister's brother-in-law."

"Nepotism, eh?"

"Call it anything you want. All I know is ever since I started film school I wanted to be an editor and a chance to get into the business and work for a man like Harold Bowman is about as big a break as anyone can have.

"Besides, I can do okay with a documentary, but I've got a lot to learn about the subtleties of feature editing. And this is a great place to learn because Harold is the best there is."

For the next hour and a half Todd sat close behind her watching the negative images in the small Moviola screen and marveling as she selected part of this one and part of that one, then put them together, to build a sequence.

"Okay. That's it for tonight." She turned the Moviola switch to "off" and swung around to face him. "The stuff I've been working on is all MOS...that's..."

"Mit out sound," Todd jumped in. "I ain't totally stupid."

"Good boy!" Meg laughed. "You get a star on your chart. Tomorrow I've got to get started on a couple of dialogue sequences so I'll be working with a sound track too. If you bring another pizza you're welcome to come watch."

"Thanks, Meg." For a minute he thought about asking her to have a drink with him, but so far their relationship hadn't been anything but teacher/pupil and he decided against it. "You are a fantastic teacher. I'll be here unless my boss needs me."

Todd was sitting in the office thinking about Meg's "film school" when the telephone began to ring. He suddenly realized Councilman Lustig's secretary, Tanya, had gone to the Ladies Room and he needed to answer the phone.:

"Councilman Lustig's office..."

"Hello. This is Hy Abrams calling," a slightly accented voice told him. "Is he in?"

"One minute please, Mr. Abrams." The name was unfamiliar to Todd. "He may have gone down the hall to a meeting..." Putting the call on "hold", he switched on the intercom. "There's a Hy Abrams on the line, boss. You wanna..."

Before he could finish asking, Lustig told him, "You bet," and picked up the blinking line.

Ten minutes later Councilman Lustig called him into his office and asked him to have dinner with him at what he considered the "finest restaurant in all of Los Angeles": Musso and Frank.

"You bet, boss. That will be great."

Todd was confident his enthusiastic tone of voice covered the slight disappointment he felt. He had spent several recent evenings in the cutting room with Meg, and had finally made a date with her for dinner that evening.

"Meg, I'm sorry about this. My boss just sprung it on me, he wants me to have dinner with him tonight..."

"Don't worry about it." Her voice didn't sound as if she were angry. "That's show-biz. Things like that happen all the time. Besides, I have plenty to do here. I really shouldn't be going anywhere."

"Can we try for tomorrow?"

"If you're free and I'm free. Why don't you call me in the afternoon and we'll see where we stand."

"Thanks, Meg. I really am sorry about tonight. I'll call tomorrow."

Located a few blocks west of the NBC Studios, close to Grauman's Chinese, The Egyptian, The RKO Palace and Colossal Cinema, the biggest and best theaters in town, Mussso and Frank was a collection point for Hollywood's famous and infamous. The formal entrance on Hollywood Boulevard was not used nearly as much as the small, rear doorway that led in from the parking lot behind.

Divided into two rooms, the main room featured small booths, made both cozy and private by wood and glass dividers between each one. The second room, where reservations were usually required, featured large, semi circular booths with comfortable, well upholstered red leather benches embracing heavy tables of warm, polished, well worn wood. Solid looking, carved mahogany bars in each of the dining rooms completed the decor which was often described as looking a bit like a German Hoff Braun. Todd and the councilman were escorted to Lustig's regular booth in the second room.

"Todd," the councilman turned to him after they were seated and he had ordered a beer for Todd and a Burbon Old Fashion for himself. "Todd, there's a couple of matters I want to talk to you about..." The councilman paused, pursed his lips once or twice, then continued. "...Matters of ahh, shall we say 'some delicacy'?"

Their waiter arrived with their drinks. "You gentlemen ready to order?"

"Not yet," Lustig said. "Give us a few minutes." He picked up his drink, took a sip and waited until the waiter was out of ear-shot. "There's something I would like to have you handle for me, but it must be kept very confidential..."

"Boss, my favorite word is 'discretion'," Todd assured him. "What's up?"

"I'd like it if you could set up a meeting with a man named Herman Zeigler some time soon," the councilman said slowly. "He has a company named Zeigler Developments. I have a confidential proposal for him but I can't talk with him directly and I don't want anyone to think my office is involved with him in any way."

Three days later, Todd and Herman Zeigler met for lunch at the Original Brown Derby just across Wilshire Boulevard from the beautiful Ambassador Hotel. Built in the shape of a derby hat, the restaurant had once been a place for Hollywood's royalty to see and be seen, but in recent years, with the opening of the Hollywood Derby on Vine Street, more and more the original had become a tourist hang out where little but framed pictures of the famous who once dined there remained of the glory days. None the less, it was located only a few blocks from Zeigler's office and, judging by the reception he received from the hostess, it was apparently a favorite of his.

After the hostess seated them and took their orders for ice tea, Zeigler turned to Todd, "Okay young man. This is your party. What are we here for?"

Councilman Lustig had carefully prepared Todd for this meeting. He had explained that Zeigler was basically a small time crook who had grown wealthy in the post war building boom by means of shady dealings and skull duggery.. A combination not uncommon in Hollywood.

Lustig had gone on to tell Todd that he didn't know much about Zeigler's personal habits, but, as Todd would soon discover, when many of the men he would deal with learned he was involved with the movie world, he would frequently be asked questions about "getting fixed up with one of those starlets." Lustig had then given Todd a business card for Westland House. "You run into something like that you tell them to call this number and ask for Miss Dunn.

A woman will take the call and tell them Miss Dunn isn't in, can she take a message. They tell her they're a friend of Miss Dunn's brother, just in town for the evening, and wanted to ask her out for a drink. The gal will offer to take Miss Dunn's place. The price is two hundred. If you're dealing with somebody we really need to take care of, don't give out the number, just tell them you'll see if maybe you can arrange something, let me know and I'll take it from there." Lustig had looked at Todd and asked, "Understand?"

Todd had understood, but, so far at least, Zeigler had not expressed any interest in "starlets." He seemed much more interested in whatever proposal he expected Todd to make.

"I want to talk about the StayCon back lot over in the valley." Todd said easily.

StayCon Lot #2 was located in an area of the Valley Zeigler considered ripe for development, but he was not willing to pay StayCon's price and had, therefore, begun negotiations for another property further west, in Woodland Hills. Peter Best had then asked Hy Abrams to see if Council Lustig might have an idea for making the property more attractive. It did not take the councilman long to come up with an idea it was now Todd's job to sell Zeigler on.

Lowering his voice, he began. "What I want to talk to you about is very confidential. If word gets out, you can forget everything I tell you..."

"I'm in a business where keeping secrets is a requirement," Zeigler assured him.

"Okay, good." Todd hesitated just enough to indicate he was somewhat uncomfortable about giving out confidential information. "Well, in the past two years the lot has been used a total of twenty-three days and, frankly, the cost of maintaining it is hurting. They want to sell, but they really need the three million five.

"Yeah, so?" Obviously intrigued, Zeigler cocked his head and took a sip of his ice tea. "Am I supposed to feel sorry for them?"

"No, not at all. But here's the deal, Todd twisted slightly in his seat in order to look directly at his guest. "Mr. Zeigler, if that studio goes into bankruptcy, it will mean a lot of people in my boss' district will lose their jobs and with an election coming up next year, that isn't something we want to see happen, because jobs mean votes."

"I can understand that," Zeigler agreed.

Todd leaned closer and dropped his voice another notch. "We know you made an offer on that property, but it was just too low to get the studio off the hook. Now the councilman is convinced that if you did develop that property, it would only be a matter of a few years before the area would significantly add to the city's tax base. Because of that, if you were to come up with the money StayCon needs, Councilman Lustig is in a position to see to it that the new freeway they're building will have on and off ramps at the entrance to the lot and the entry road will be extended in both directions, south to Ventura Boulevard and north to Victory Boulevard. He thinks if you factor in the advantages that kind of access will give to your project it should be possible for you to reconsider your offer."

"Can I get that in writing?" Zeigler asked.

"Yeah. You bet!" Todd laughed loudly. "Just as soon as you sprout wings and fly out of here. If word about this gets out, StayCon will deny there is any truth to the story about their financial problems; the councilman will deny having ever heard of such a scheme," Todd's voice took on a slight edge, "And the freeway will probably never have an off ramp anywhere near any place where you decide to build."

"Okay, I get the picture..." Zeigler's voice told Todd he definitely did get the picture. "But what kind of assurance do I have about all this?"

"Just my honest face," Todd told him. "But in your business I'm sure you take a chance now and then. What's having direct freeway access and a major Valley cross street mean to a project like yours?" Todd couldn't help a quick wink before adding, "Maybe they'll even name the cross street after you. And just think what a beautiful piece of property that is, and how nice it will be to have building inspectors who are happy about what you are doing there.

"Todd, you did a hell of a job!" The councilman was practically skipping into Todd's little corner of the outer office. "I just got word Zeigler upped his offer this morning and the deal's set."

"Wow!" Todd put down the phone he was talking on. "That's great boss." He paused for a brief second, then added, "Does that mean I can get tonight off and take my girl out for dinner?"

"Hell yes!" The councilman slapped his hand down on Todd's shoulder. "I'll even pickup the tab."

Todd picked up the phone. "Meg, did you hear that? My boss says I can have the night off and he'll pay for our dinner. Are we still a go?"

Located on Vine Street just south of Melrose, The Auberge was housed in what had once been a private home. It was set back just far enough from the road, and surrounded with just enough shrubs and trees to make it a place you could easily miss if you didn't know where you were going.

"The Auberge," Meg read from the menu cover. "That sounds very French to me."

Ah. mon Cherie," Todd used his French-Canadian accent. "You are so very perceptive..."

"I must have passed this place a thousand times and never knew it was here," Meg smiled as she looked around the small dining room. "How did you find it?"

"Ahh-haa. Zat is a very, very long story."

"That's okay," she assured him. "I'm not planning on going anyplace until we eat."

"Ahh yes, zee food." Todd signaled the waiter. "With your permission, I shall order for us both."

Using his best French, Todd ordered entrecote with pommes frites, green salads and a bottle of Cotes du Rhone.

"Cotes du Rhone? Is that a Canadian wine," Meg asked.

"God, no!" Todd rolled his eyes upward and winked at their waiter. "There is no wine in Canada. Cotes du Rhone comes from the Rhone River Valley in France." As he spoke the words "Rhone River Valley in France," Todd straightened in his chair and saluted as their waiter broke into song with the first notes of "The Marseilles".

"Jesus, Okay. I get the picture

The waiter joined in their laughter, then hurried off to get their wine.

"So, you were going to tell me the long story about how you know of this place..."

"Okay. I'll give you the short version anyway. When I came to Hollywood I was skating in the Ice Capades. There was a French/Canadian girl named Gertie DesJardines in the show, we dated a few times, when we got to L.A., she knew the people who own the place and we came here for dinner a couple of times."

"...And...?

"No 'ands'. That's it."

"You call that a long story? And what's that about the Ice Capades? You were a skater?"

"There, you see, that's what makes it a long story, eh? Yes, I was a skater in Capades. That's how I got here and if it hadn't been for that hole in the fence between the lot and Nicodel's, I'd probably still be skating in the show."

"Todd. What are you talking bout now? What hole in what fence?"

Ansers to her questions would have to wait as their waiter arrived with the wine and their steaks.

"Oh... my... God."

"What...?"

"It's steak with French fries and beans."

"You were expecting...?"

"I don't know." Meg laughed. "What happened to our salads?"

"I told you, this is very French. Salad after the main course, not before."

"I knew that."

The steak was so tender she could cut it with her fork.

"This is wonderful."

"Would I take you to a bad place? Especially when the boss is paying!""

"I guess not." She tried the potatoes and the beans and took a sip of wine before adding, "so, what's all that about the fence?"

Todd told her how he had discovered the hole and how he had met Aaron Marks. He did not mention Holly Sinclair.

More than an hour later, when they had finished their wine and eaten their salads – a practice Meg thought she could easily get used to – Todd told her, "I live just down the street, on Windsor. If you don't want to drive all the way out to Reseda tonight, you can bunk in at my place."

She looked at him for a moment, then, in a voice laden with sarcasm, told him, "That may be the most romantic thing anyone has ever said to me..."

"I didn't mean it like that. I'm not trying to put the make on you. You said you have to be in early in the morning and I have a couch that makes up into a second bed. You can have it if you want. No strings attached."

"Jesus Todd. That's even more romantic."

They had walked to the restaurant from where their cars were parked at the RKO Studio. During the walk back, both were strangely silent until Meg finally stopped and turned to him.

"Todd, I don't think this is a good idea..."

"Staying at my place?"

"Yes. You're a nice guy. Maybe I'm a nice girl but I don't think we're exactly passionate about each other and if I go to your place one thing could lead to another... and I just don't think that's a good idea."

"You don't..."

"No, I don't. What I see is one of these days I'm going to want to be the editor on one of your pictures, and I think it would be better if we were just friends."

"Wow! One of my pictures, eh." Todd laughed as he slapped himself on the forehead. "I'm working for a city councilman and you have me making pictures?"

She started to continue their walk to the parking lot. "You will. And I don't think it will be very long either. I just hope I'm ready to cut it for you when you do."

At that moment Todd had more respect and a higher regard for Megan Schmidt than almost anybody he could think of. He had to admit to himself that the idea of making love to her had certainly been in the back of his mind, but she was right. He knew she was going to be a top notch film editor one day, and if the day ever came when he actually did make a picture, she would be his first choice for the editing job. Being friends was going to be far better than ex-lovers.

"If I ever make a picture, you'll have the job, Meg. That's a promise."

It was just a few minutes after ten in the morning when Peter's secretary buzzed him to let him know, "Holly Sinclair is on the phone."

"Holly. Good morning. How good to hear from you. What's up?"

"Good morning Peter," she hesitated for a brief second, "Peter, I have a problem. I was wondering if you can help me with something..."

"Well I can certainly try. What is it?"

"Umm... It's sort of personal. Could I come in and see you?"

"Sure. Better yet, why don't I take you to lunch?"

"That's very sweet of you, but I'd rather just come to your office if you don't mind."

"Whatever works for you..." He glanced down at his appointment schedule. "You want to try for this afternoon... about two, two-thirty?"

"Two o'clock would be fine."

"Good. See you then."

She blew him a kiss, hung up the phone and looked down at her engagement ring.

She did not wear it in public because she and David wanted to keep their engagement more or less a secret but it was time Peter knew about it, and about David's plans for the picture in Europe.

At two o'clock on the dot, Peter's secretary signaled with two short beeps on the intercom that his guest had arrived and seconds later she held the door open for Holly to enter his office.

Peter met her half way to the door, embraced her, then, while holding both her hands, stepped back and looked at her. It seemed every time he saw her, she was more beautiful. "My God, you look sensational. Next picture we've got to double your rate."

Raising her left hand up to where the ring should almost blind him, she smiled. "That's part of what I want to talk to you about."

"Pictures, or that rock on your finger?" Peter grinned as he shook his head from side to side, then led her to one of the comfortable easy chairs by the window.

"The two are sort of tied together. David Dill has asked me to marry him and then I'm going to be the star of his new film."

"Oh? " He sat down opposite her. "Some agent I am. Congratulations on your engagement and what new film?"

Holly quickly filled him in on the details of the upcoming wedding plans and David's movie. "So, my problem is this. I need to get a passport."

It took her less than two minutes to tell him that her real name was Myra Simon. That she thought she had been born in Bergen County, New Jersey. That her mother was unmarried, her father unknown. To get a pass port, she was going to need a birth certificate and she didn't know how to get one.

"Getting a copy of your birth certificate shouldn't be a problem. Just contact the Hall of Records in Bergen County."

"Yes, but part of my problem is that I told David's mother my father was a doctor and she thinks my real name is Sinclair..."

"And you think a copy of your real birth certificate might... make problems?"

"I definitely do!"

Peter thought for a moment, then took a sheet of paper out of his desk drawer and pushed it towards her. He handed her a pen and told her, "Write down exactly what you told Mrs. Dill and I'll see if maybe we can come up with what you need."

Ten minutes after Holly left his office, Peter was on the phone with Hugh Crawford and his brother Frank. "We need to get a fake birth certificate for Holly."

"And why is that?" Hugh asked.

"Well, she made up quite a story to impress the Dills and now that David wants her to do his picture she needs to get a pass port..."

"...All right. Bergen County?"

"Yes, At least she thinks so. I don't think she really knows. But that's a place to start anyway."

"Okay. Give us the details."

Hugh listened carefully while Franco made notes. When Peter finished they said goodbye, Franco hug up and looked at Hugh.

"What-a ya think boss, Sean Phinney?"

Ever since his father's death when he was just a little boy, Hugh Crawford had been very much a father to him and his brother but he had never been able to call him "dad" as Peter did.

Hugh nodded his head, ."Yes, I think so,"

A native Staten Islander, Sean Phinney had started his professional life as a Richmond County Building Inspector. Sean was very good at a number of things but picking horses was not one of them. Early on, in one of those "good news...bad news" situations, he got himself seriously in debt to his bookmaker, Hugh Crawford, and found himself presented with three options: Pay up. Work off his debts by being helpful. Or find himself in the middle of New York Harbor, in no condition to swim.

Since he could not pay up, and since he hated the water, he had elected to be helpful.

Now, more than twenty years later, a wealthy Sean Phinney ran the detective agency Hugh Crawford financed and had handled any number of "sensitive" matters for Hugh and his organization.

"So, can we do something over there in Jersey?" .

"Yeah, sure Frank. In Jersey you can do almost anything you want."

Sean began writing down the information Franco was giving him... "What's her father's first name supposed to be?"

"I don't know. Let's pick one...Umm, what goes well with Sinclair?"

"I don't know. Let me think..." Sean looked down at the racing form on his desk. The owner of the first trotter in the first race at Roosevelt Raceway that evening was listed as George Wentworth. "How 'bout George? That goes good with Sinclair."

"All right, Doctor George Sinclair...better give him a middle name too... Let's name him after Peter..."

"George Peter Sinclair..." Sean wrote the name down. "That works. How about the mother. Felicia doesn't really make it, and we ought to keep away from anything that could tie her to her real old lady."

"Sure, Let's make it Beverly.," Frank chuckled. " We got Peter, we might as well keep it in the family and have his wife's name too. Besides, Beverly Sinclair sounds very prestigious. Ought to impress Mrs. Dill no end."

"Okay. Got it, Doctor George P. and Beverly Sinclair. Call you in a couple-a days."

Two days later Sean Phinney climbed the solid wooden outdoor stair way up to the office above Original Angelo's, knocked on the door and waited for the buzz that told him the lock was opened. Inside Frank Tucci welcomed him with a warm handshake.

"Here ya are Frank. Phinney handed him a large envelope. "Signed, sealed and part of the permanent Bergen County records."

"Thanks, Sean. What do we owe you?"

"You don't owe me nothin' . Any time I can do somethin' fer you and Mister Crawford it makes me feel good."

"That's very nice, Sean, but lousy business. What did you spend?"

Sean shook his head. He knew it was useless to argue. . . "About a grand."

"Okay., Have a cup pf coffee while I write you a check."

After much thought, Mrs. Dill and Holly decided to ask Aaron Marks if he would give her away as it was he who first put her in a picture and therefore was responsible for her and David meeting each other. Aaron had been flattered by the request and replied he would be "a bit jealous," of David, but none the less proud to give away so lovely a bride.

Thus, on Aaron's arm Holly made her way across the manicured south lawn of the Dill's Bel Aire estate to where her husband to be awaited her. And there, under an arbor of roses from the Dill garden intertwined with exotic Hawaiian orchids, flown in for the occasion, Holly and David exchanged their vows.

According to the Los Angeles Times: "The bride wore a magnificent, full length gown and cathedral train of Italian satin all over embellished with Florentine lace, the bodice accented with pearls and embroidery."

The report also noted, "The groom wore a navy blue jacket and white trousers."

The wedding was everything Mrs. Dill hoped it would be, a simple, afternoon affair with "just a few good friends" in attendance.

Following the ceremony, the "few good friends," which included Crystal Manning, Keith Phillips, Mr. & Mrs. Zack Seguine, Mr. & Mrs. Peter Best, Councilman and Mrs. Jordan Lustig, Todd Wilson and an august list of more than one hundred industry notables were wined and dined at pool side and on the awning covered patio while a fifteen piece orchestra played for their dancing pleasure. As they began "You Came To Me From Out of Nowhere," Todd asked for his turn to dance with the bride.

"That seems an appropriate song for us to dance to, doesn't it?" Holly asked him. "I'll never forget our first lunch at Nicodels, eh?"

"No, I wont either." Todd chuckled at her "eh?"

"You've come a long way since then."

"Yes, thanks to you..." She hugged him and thought, I wouldn't have made it without you. You discovered me. You gave me a place to live and a feeling of security when I needed it most. More than that, you gave me love. But, she realized, that road might never have led any further than to the apartment on Windsor Avenue, rather than this estate in Bel Aire.

"I've been lucky," she added. "You'll get there too. It's easier for girls at first."

Before Todd could reply, husband David cut in claiming that no one had a right to more than half a dance with his new wife.

As the memorable afternoon slowly turned into evening, David and his beautiful bride smiled their way through a blizzard of confetti and rice and hurried to a waiting Rolls Royce sedan that whisked them away to the Beverly Hills Hotel where, in the private cottage David had reserved, Holly acted the part of the perfect, breathlessly beautiful, virginally demure young bride.

Following what David would always refer to as, "two wonderful nights" in the Beverly Hills cottage, the couple arrived on a non stop TWA flight to New York's Idlewild Airport. A waiting Cadillac Limousine whisked them across Queens, the Tri-boro Bridge and Manhattan Island to the Hudson River pier where the Ile de France awaited them.

Almost 800 feet in length, the Ile de France had been launched in 1926 as the pride of the French Merchant Marine. During World War II, she had served as a troop ship then, at war's end, in an attempt to regain French pre-eminence in the world of ocean going luxury liners, she underwent extensive refurbishing before returning to passenger service.

In the summer of 1956, she had enjoyed a moment of fame when she rescued some 750 passengers from the sinking Andrea Doria. Other than for that moment in the limelight, she had served her country and her passengers in quiet elegance.

The only time Holly had previously been on a boat was when she was very young, maybe four or five. Her mother and a man she could not remember, took her across the Hudson River to New York City on a Hoboken Ferry boat.

The Ile de France is bigger, she told herself.

Having Insisted on carrying her across the threshold of the exquisite, Art Deco suite he had reserved, David sat her down on a delicate, blue, Le Corbusier settee and directed a waiter to pour champagne.

Next morning, prior to their noon sailing, Holly found a few moments to address a post card to "Mother and Father Dill."

"We are so happy." she wrote. "Thank you for our lovely wedding. Thank you for your unbelievable gift and, most of all, thank you for my wonderful, wonderful husband."

To herself she whispered, "He's not much in bed but he is rich! And the Malibu beach house they gave us is marvelous!"

What David may have lacked "in bed," he made up for in other ways. "The Venice Connection" was the first film on which he was to be the soul producer, an assignment he would not likely have enjoyed were it not for his father. But an assignment he was very ready for.

Not surprisingly, his father's partners had been... nervous. The preliminary budget David submitted was well over fifteen million dollars and that was more than either "T" or "L" were comfortable with.

But shortly before the wedding the concerns they had were dispelled when they learned David had cajoled Manny Levine into writing an excellent script which had attracted one of Great Britain's finest directors, Malcolm Printer.

Malcolm Printer had a reputation as a "woman's director." Many of his films had introduced actresses who went on to become major stars. It was this reputation that caused David to seek him out.

In spite of Levine's script, however, and the attractive offer David made to him, Printer insisted on seeing film of "this Holly Sinclair girl," before he would accept the assignment.

Six hours after the plane carrying clips from Holly's previous pictures landed in London, David received Printer's enthusiastic acceptance via trans-Atlantic telephone.

And "T" and "L" were very happy.

After seven days at sea, Holly and David traveled by train from Le Harve to Paris and the Georges V Hotel where David planned to spend a week with Malcolm Printer working on casting and a production schedule before going to Venice. It was at lunch, their second day in Paris, that Holly first met Printer.

The Toure d' Argent matre de' and several waiters hovered discretely in the background as Printer welcomed Holly and David to the window table he had reserved. He kissed her hand then, while still holding it, stepped back to look at her framed against the back drop of the Seine and Notre Dame Cathedral that seemed to be almost an extension of the restaurant itself. Shaking his head in wonderment, he told her, "Few women can make me look at them rather than that scene. You, my dear, make me forget all the beauty that is Paris."

Often described as "looking very British," Printer was quite tall, perhaps an inch over six feet, slender, yet muscular as a tennis player might be. At thirty-eight his wavy brown hair was beginning to show a few strands of silver at his temples and in his small mustache. His face featured wide spread, bright blue eyes above a slender, slightly curved nose. Most women considered him rather handsome, most men thought he looked "a bit prissy."

As with many of filmdom's better directors, Printer had certain peculiarities that members of his cast and crew chuckled about, yet admired. First of all, in a world where almost everyone was known by their first name, no one was to ever call him "Malcolm!" He was "Mister Printer," or in some cases simply "Printer," but never Malcolm. And Printer never said "cut" at the end of a take. Instead, he would say, "All right…" which would then be followed by the words, "let's try that again, shall we?" or, to everyone's delight, "That's a 'Printer'."

Three weeks after their meeting in Paris, three weeks of wonderful, luxurious travel through France, and Italy, the newly weds arrived in Venice where Printer was waiting for them. Holly could feel a sense of excitement in the air as they stepped down off the Venice Express where Printer greeted her with a smothering hug, shook David's hand, then asked for their luggage claim checks which he handed to two swarthy young men who saluted and quickly hurried away towards the terminal building. “Now then, we can take our time,” Printer told them. “They’ll have everything loaded by the time we get there.”

For Holly, once they entered the station building it was like a fairy tale come true. Passengers from the train were rushing past her and out the glass doors that led to a series of wide steps... and a canal. A real Venetian canal, just like the ones she had seen pictures of. A canal complete with gondolas, and launches and small boats of every description. Gondolas and launches and boats that everyone seemed to be trying to get aboard. She was sure there were many more people than boats to carry them.

“No rush,” Printer assured them. “Our launch is just over there,” he nodded towards something Holly could not see as he led them down the steps, through the crowd and finally to a handsome blue launch flying the flag of the Hotel Gritti Palace.

In spite of the choppy water in the canal Holly insisted on standing along side the cabin so she could see everything there was to see. Beautiful old buildings in lovely, soft pastel colors of pink and peach. Buildings that stood right in the water. Gondolas everywhere, with slender, muscular men standing in the stern and somehow moving them with only one long paddle.

Filming in Venice turned out to be much more of a problem than David had thought it could be. When Printer insisted on twenty days to shoot eighteen pages of script, he had wondered if perhaps he'd made a mistake in asking him to direct the picture. Now, after sixteen days, he was beginning to wonder if twenty days would be enough. The problems in moving the company from location to location were enormous. Many of the moves had to be made by boat where loading and unloading equipment seemed to take forever. When moves could be made overland, the narrow little bridges that crossed canal after canal, and the tiny, crooked, always crowded with tourists alleys that passed for streets made it a nightmare. During any given twelve to fourteen hour production day they were lucky to be on camera more than four hours.

For the cast, the long delays were boring and artistically draining. For the crew the moves were physically exhausting. For David, the entire process was mentally and financially stressful. Only Printer seemed to be comfortable, unruffled and completely at ease. After each move, when the camera was finally ready to shoot, he called his cast together, reinvigorated them with the power of his artistic dedication and carried on with a spirit that inspired them all.

Having finally reached their third and hopefully final Sunday in Venice, not surprisingly, Holly and David slept in until almost ten o'clock. Finally awake, after pulling a robe over her nightgown, Holly opened the blinds covering their bedroom window and stepped out on to the balcony which overlooked a small canal three floors below.

"Oh David, it's such a beautiful morning, come look." From the balcony she could see not only the narrow canal below, but some of the Grand Canal it joined in front of the hotel.

Easily swinging his legs out of their bed, David stretched, yawned, then slowly crossed the room to join her on the balcony.

"There is such a lovely, soft light here in Venice." She slipped her around his waist as she leaned forward to watch a black and gold gondola passing below them. "I've heard Printer talking about it. He says it makes everything on film look even more beautiful. Look how the colors reflect in the ripples."

"Yes. It is beautiful, isn't it."

"Let's go over to that island," she said after a moment. "...What's it called? You know, where they make all the glass."

"Murano, I think that's the name of it."

"Yes. Yes that's it. Can we go?"

"Gee Holly, I can't this morning. I promised Printer I would go over some production notes with him. Why don't you call Peggy and see if she'd like to go with you. I know you'll have more fun shopping with her than with me anyway."

"Oh... I'll miss you," she told him, although actually she wasn't particularly disappointed he didn't want to go. He wasn't that much fun to shop with. "You're sure you wont mind?"

"No. Not at all. It will give us time to work and I wont have to worry about you."

"Okay," Holly walked back into the room and picked up the telephone. "I'll call Peggy and see if she'd like to go."

Forty-five minutes later, dressed in white slacks, a gondolier's striped shirt and a sky blue jacket toped by a matching sailor's cap, Holly gave David a quick "good-bye" kiss and headed for the elevator where she met Printer getting off as she was getting on.

"Good morning, love." He waved at her with the script he was carrying.

"Morning Printer. Don't you two work all day. Go out and take a walk. A little exercise will be good for both of you."

"We may do that," he smiled. "Have fun shopping."

A native of Rome, Peggy Zea had gone to college in New York where she earned a degree in Accounting before returning to Italy. Once back home she found her way into the Italian film industry and now, with the advantage of nearly perfect English, she was a tremendous asset to any English or American company wanting to work in Italy. In the few weeks she and Holly had known each other the two had become good friends and both were delighted at the prospect of a day of shopping together.

The captain and a seaman from the elegant hotel launch assigned to them were waiting at the hotel dock. With sweeping bows, they were escorted on board and made comfortable in the pair of cushioned, leather upholstered swivel chairs near the stern of the boat. Almost immediately, a third member of the crew appeared to offer them coffee or champagne and a selection of Italian pastries.

Once certain his guests were comfortable, the captain ordered his men to cast off and pointed his low, narrow craft down the Grand Canal towards the bay beyond.

Half way to Murano Island, merrily bouncing over the choppy waves which a light breeze had churned up all over the bay, they had nearly finished the bottle of champagne when Holly realized she did not have her passport with her.

"Shit!" She muttered to Peggy. "Without my passport they'll never let me use my Traveler's Checks."

"Not a major crises," Peggy laughed. "We'll go back and get it." She signaled to the Captain, "Capitano, dobbiamo ritornare indietro. Abbiomo dinesticato qualcoso."

The Captain nodded, slowed the engines and spunn his wheel. An hour after she had left, Holly arrived back at the door to their suite. Not wanting to disturb her husband and Printer, she opened the door very softly and tip toed towards the bedroom.

"Jesus Christ!" Printer and her husband were in bed together. Naked, in each other's arms. Stunned, she started to say more then caught herself and looked away. She realized her discovery was going to have some serious ramifications which she needed to consider carefully before saying or doing anything more. Without again looking at the two men, she quickly picked up her passport and left the room.

She knew she had reached a momentous turning point in her life. There seemed to be a feeling in the company that they were making a very good film. A film her husband was producing. A film that might very well catapult her into real stardom. And she had just discovered her husband is queer.

What should she do now? She was in a foreign country, surrounded by people who worked for her husband and Printer. Think carefully about it before you do anything, she told herself. Put it aside for now, have some fun with Peggy, then come back to it. Just don't be hasty. Don't do anything for a while.

That afternoon Holly gave one of her best performances as a happy bride shopping for her new home. At the Murano Glass Factory, she and Peggy watched an unbelievable demonstration of glass sculpturing, marveling at how the artist could create a delicate little deer from a light bulb size glob of bright orange melted glass clinging somehow to the end of a metal rod. Then, exploring the numerous show rooms, they delightedly spent an exorbitant amount of David's money buying vases and bowls and figurines that Holly insisted would be perfect for their beach front house in Malibu. The shipping charges back to California alone totaled nearly eight hundred dollars.

Arriving back at the hotel dock late in the day Holly suggested she and Peggy wind up their adventure with cocktails at Harry's Bar.

Before the wedding, Peter Best had given her what he called a "non-wedding gift": A book about Venice. Among the many sights to see and things to do in Venice, the book went to great lengths describing Harry's Bar which was supposed to be a favorite hang out for Ernest Hemmingway. It sounded to her like a place that would be fun. The kind of place where rich and rakish men tended to hang out. Since she was obviously not ever going to get in bed with David again, even though they were scheduled to leave Venice in four more days, it still might be interesting to meet someone. When you think about it, four days can be rather a long time, she told herself, and there's always a possibility they could be delayed.

There were one or two men at Harry's who looked interesting. Holly smiled at each of them, but did not extend an invitation for them to join her and Peggy. Instead the two made "girl talk" as one martini led to another, and finally dinner. It was well after dark when they made their somewhat unstable way back along the canal to the Gritti Palace.

When Holly reached the door to their suite, she paused for a moment wondering if perhaps she should knock. No, she decided. If they're still at it... well they'll just have to get dressed and get the hell out. She did, however, make rather a lot of noise putting her key into the lock.

"Hello Myra."

David was sitting in the dark, on the large sofa looking out the glass doors towards the lights along the canal.

"What?" His greeting surprised her. How did he know that name?

"I said 'Hello Myra.' That's your real name isn't it? Myra Simon? At least your mother's name was Simon. I don't suppose anyone really knows what your father's name is."

Three, or was it four, martinis had slowed her reaction time so it took almost five seconds for her to respond: "Fuck you, you goddamn queer! Half the people in Hollywood changed their names. Fucking your own sex is a little different!" She turned and headed for the door.

"Then stop and think about the career you are about to blow off." David's voice had an edge to it she had not heard before. "So you know my secret. It isn't something I'm proud of. You're so beautiful, when I saw you for the first time I thought maybe I could change. But I can't. I am what I am. If you can keep quiet about it, in a year or so we'll get a divorce. By that time everybody will believe I'm a real macho stud and you'll be a bigger star than Ava Gardner."

Holly stopped and waited with her back to him. "Go on."

"This picture is going to get you a lot of notice. When it's finished, Malcolm's going to do a major epic for Production Associates. You can have the lead if you play your cards right."

This sounded like something she should think about with very carefully and with a very clear head tomorrow.

She closed her eyes for a moment, but that wasn't a good idea. With her eyes closed she had the sensation that the room was somehow moving... she opened them and the room began to steady. Changing her direction to head for the bedroom door, without looking back she told him, "We'll talk in the morning. You sleep right there on the sofa. I get the bedroom."

"That's okay by me," he answered. "I don't really like sleeping with you anyway."

The glairing sunlight hurt her eyes. She had taken two of her little blue pills before going to bed and forgotten to close the blinds. Not only did the light hurt her eyes, it made her head ache. "Fucking sunshine" she muttered as she put her hand to her brow to shade her eyes.

And the pounding in her head. No... it wasn't a pounding in her head, it was someone knocking on the door that had awakened her. She closed her eyes to a squint and look around the room. Before she was fully awake, the door opened and someone pushing a food service cart entered the room. Oh shit! It was David.

"Good morning. I thought some black coffee and one of your 'feel good' pills might help." He pushed the cart to the edge of the bed and handed her a cup full of coffee.

Her eyes were becoming used to the sunlight and without the knocking sound, the ache in her head seemed to have lessened. She reached out and, with a slightly shaking hand, took the cup.

Her first sip brought a whole new pain into being. It was scalding hot. But it did seem to help.

"I thought we should talk a little if you feel up to it."

"What's to talk about?"

"A lot of things," he answered. "First off, you don't have to sweat this morning. Printer's going to shoot around you until noon."

"Oh, Christ!" She looked at the clock and groaned. It was twenty after seven and she had been due in make-up at six AM.

"Second," he continued, "We need to talk about us."

"What's to talk about, faggot?"

"Look, Holly." David's voice took on an edge. "You wanna be bitchy, we can wrap it up right now. You go home, get a divorce, we'll find somebody else to play the part and re-shoot all your scenes."

Back off, Holly told herself. Let's not jump out of the frying pan, into a fire. "All right, David. Let's talk."

"That's better." His voice returned to the warm, cordial tone it had been when he offered her coffee. "I'm sorry you had to find Printer and me. I'm sorry you had to learn about me that way... I'm sorry you had to learn about me at all."

He paused and picked up one of her pink pills. “You want this?” She took it and swallowed it with a gulp of coffee. “As I told you last night, I really thought I could change when we got married. It didn’t work out that way.”

Whether the coffee was clearing her mind or the pill was already starting to work, she didn’t know, but what David was saying was beginning to reach her.

“I love you, Holly. I really do. I’m sorry I can’t be the husband you expected, but I can take care of you. And I will if you let me.”

“What is it you want from me, David?”

“I want you to finish our picture. I want you to play the part of a happy wife for a year or so. You know, Hollywood marriages never last much longer than that. I want you to do Printer’s next picture and become a major star, then we’ll get a divorce and no one will ever have to know the truth about us… about me.”

She thought about it for a minute. The pluses obviously far outweighed the negatives. “All right David. You got a deal.”

Todd's job with Councilman Lustig was mostly nine to five. With Holly gone forever and Meg wanting to be his film editor rather than his girl friend he had nothing to do at night. His type writer seemed to be calling to him and he was free to stay in the office as late as he wanted to so he stared to write a story that had been growing in his mind. The more he wrote the more he enjoyed writing and it was not long before it seemed as if he were reading the story rather than writing it.

Without realizing it Todd was about to begin a new page in the book of life:

"What the hell do you do here half the night?" the Councilman asked him one day.

"Oh, I've been trying to write a story," Todd told him.

"No kidding? Let me see it."

The councilman had read his script and made an appointment for him with Peter Best without ever telling him. Now here he was, in the HBA building at nine o'clock in the morning, riding in an elevator with an attractive blond receptionist, up to the third floor and Peter's office.

Todd had met Peter Best on several occasions. The first time was at the fund raising dinner for Adeli Stevenson when he arrived with Aaron Marks. After that, in his capacity as Councilman Lustig's Industry Rep, he had run into the agent at various social functions, but he never thought to contact him about the movie idea he was working on.

"Hi, Todd." Peter got up and came from behind his desk to shake Todd's hand. "It's good to see you again."

"Thanks Peter." For just an instant he wasn't sure he should have used his first name, but it was too late to worry about it now and if being on a first name basis was not to Peter's liking he gave no evidence of it as he led Todd to a comfortable chair by a coffee table in a grouping of furniture in front of one of the large picture windows overlooking Canon Drive.

"Coffee?"

"I would love some."

He looked around Peter's spacious office while his host poured from a black and silver thermos into dark blue cups with gold embossed HBA emblems on them.

Rich green deep pile wall to wall carpeting covered the floor of the room that was probably twice the size of the studio apartment he was living in. On one side, Peter's desk... carved wood, probably cherry, he thought, not dark enough for mahogany and much warmer tones.

A matching table was placed in front of the desk so as to make a "T", with six chairs, three to a side, providing comfortable seating for a working session with the boss. Picture windows made up one entire wall of the office, the other three walls were floor to ceiling book cases, interspersed with light green sections of wall on which a few sea seascapes were carefully hung.

Leaning against a book case behind the big desk, Todd spotted a putter and an indoor golf hole. "I bet it's a bitch trying to put on this carpet, eh."

Peter couldn't help the laugh that almost caused him to drop the creamer he had just picked up to offer Todd.

"Jesus, you are so right." He laughed again as he held the cream out for Todd to take. "All right. I've had my laugh for the day," he continued. "Now what is in that ominous looking binder you're holding?"

"My script for the greatest movie ever made," Todd answered easily. His crack about the carpet had broken the ice as far as he was concerned and now he felt comfortable talking to him.

"Good gracious! I better see that quickly."

Todd handed the binder to him. Peter flipped it open and read the title page, "Homeroom"?

"Right," Todd assured him.

"Tell you what," Peter pointed, "See that door over there?"

Todd looked towards a door directly opposite Peter's desk. Not the door he had entered through. "Yeah..."

"There's a pool table in there, and a bar if you want something. Go fool around for a while and give me time to read this."

"Okay if I take my coffee with me?"

"Yes, but be damn sure you don't spill it on the carpet."

Peter could hear the click, click of pool balls hitting each other as he read Todd's script. When he finished, he poured himself a fresh cup of coffee and slowly read it again.

It really was no better or no worse than dozens of other scripts he had read and passed on. Fact is, the young man's personality impressed him far more than his script which in no way would make a feature film. But maybe that isn't where it should go, he thought.

Todd had done a good job on the Zeigler matter and helping him would also be appreciated by their friendly councilman and their friendly councilman was going to be a lot of help to them when the plans for expanding the StayCon Studio were ready for city approval. So, he thought, we'll see what we can do. He stood and walked to the door to the game room. "Todd, come back. Let's talk."

"Your talent as a script writer is limited but I think you have a good idea here," Peter began when Todd had re-joined him, "However it isn't a movie."

He watched the expression on Todd's face change from eager anticipation to disappointment.

"What I think you've got here is an idea for a half-hour TV sit-com."

The look of disappointment deepened.

"Something about that bother you?"

"No, no. It's just... well, I've always wanted to be in the movie business... not television."

"Todd, listen to me carefully. TV is just beginning to get cranked up and it wont be too long before television is running this town. Believe me, there is no better place for you to get your feet wet and maybe make some money.

Now OGB is looking for a family show for Palmer Foods and, with the right ingredients, this could be it. So, don't give me any grief about TV being beneath you."

"I'm sorry Peter. I didn't mean what I said to come out that way. You can't imagine what it means to me to have you like my idea. And if television is the right place for it, then I'm going to become the best TV Producer in the world!"

"Well you are going to have to, because this idea of yours is only going to succeed if it has a great star and some wonderful writing." Peter leaned forward in his chair. "Got any ideas about that?"

"Yesss..." Todd answered slowly. "I've been thinking Crystal Manning is the perfect Miss Ridley."

"Now that is a hell of an idea," Peter cocked his head to one side. "Do you have any reason to think she might be interested?"

Todd knew what he said next might have very lasting effects on his future. The idea of Crystal Manning obviously intrigued Peter Best, so he better keep Peter on the train with him.

"I worked with her on Aaron's picture when I first got to Hollywood." Todd mentally crossed his fingers as he added, "We've kept in touch since then..." it wasn't really a lie, he had sent her a Christmas card each year, and she had sent him one in return... "And yes, I'm sure she'll be interested."

"You go get her to give us a commitment based on script approval," Peter was suddenly all business. "And I'll find you a writer."

So all I have to do is get Crystal Manning to agree to do my show, Todd told himself as he walked down the curved stairway from Peter's third floor office to the ornate lobby below. He had never liked elevators and avoided them whenever possible.

Just get Crystal Manning. That shouldn't be so hard. After all, I know her... sort of. And she knows me... two years ago she knew me.

As he left the building, he was oblivious to the lobby that had impressed him so much when he arrived.

Shit! A movie star who had been nice to him two years ago didn't exactly qualify as a good friend. So, okay, if it were easy they would only hire relatives.

He walked up Canon Drive towards the coffee shop at the corner of Little Santa Monica. Coffee would help him think.

The coffee was hot. He found a seat in front of a window overlooking the street and sat the cup down to let it cool. It was hard to believe there could be so much traffic in Beverly Hills at eleven o'clock in the morning. And it was hard to believe his mind could be such a complete blank at eleven o'clock in the morning. He watched the cars creeping bye and wondered why Beverly Hills had a Santa Monica Boulevard and a parallel street, only a hundred yards away, named Little Santa Monica Boulevard. Couldn't they think of another name? Maybe not... sometimes thinking could be very difficult. Like now. For him.

He took another sip of steaming coffee then opened his mouth and tried to fan his burning tongue.

Suddenly it came to him... Roses! Crystal Manning loved roses. He remembered Aaron had him deliver a rose to her every day of shooting. He remembered the flower shop they came from because it had such a crazy name, "Toyo Griffith Park Florist." It was owned by a Japanese family but it wasn't located anywhere near Griffith Park. It was located in the middle of Hollywood and a lot of movie people had accounts there. The councilman had an account there. He looked at his wrist watch, it was only eleven-thirty, if he called right away they could probably make a delivery within the next hour or so.

At noon he checked with the florist. A woman with a strong Japanese accent assured him, "Yes, all deliver. Fifteen minute ago. All deliver to Miss Manning, please."

"And my note? Did she get my note?"

"Note, yes. Son write note, very good English. She have it."

"Thank you, very much."

"You welcome, please. Tell Councilman 'hello' for me."

He hung up, then dialed Crystal's number:

"Hello, Miss Manning, this is Todd Wilson."

"Todd. What a delightful surprise to hear from you. Thank you so much for the lovely roses. Now, tell me, what's on your young mind?"

Crystal Manning had such a warm, happy voice, it made him feel good just to hear it. "I have an idea I hope might interest you Miss Manning, and I was wondering if I could tell you about it."

"I would like that, Todd. Do you want to come over here?"

"Yes, if that would be okay."

"That would be fine. Where are you now?"

"Canon Drive in Beverly Hills."

"Oh, that isn't far. Come on over. If you haven't had lunch, I'm sure Inez can put something together for us.

;Wow! That's great, Miss Manning. I can be there in fifteen minutes. Is that okay?"

"Yes, of course. You remember where I live?"

"Sure do. I'll see you in a few minutes."

As she put the phone back in its cradle she told Inez to expect company for lunch, then went to check her makeup at the dressing table in her bedroom. She studied herself in the three panel mirror.

"Mirror, mirror on the wall..." she whispered. "I look pretty damn good for thirty-eight, don't I?"

Deep, deep in her sub-conscious the little voice she always tried to ignore reminded her she was actually forty-three. Thirty-eight was the age she admitted to. Thirty-eight was the age everyone thought her to be. Everyone except the little voice.

She began to brush her hair. Brushing her hair always made her feel warm and sensuous.

And she needed to feel warm and sensuous as she thought about the two parts she had missed out on in the last month. Parts she thought were perfect for her that had gone to actresses who were in their twenties. Her agent had assured her age had nothing to do with it and that she still looked as youthful and beautiful and lovely as ever, but something in his voice… something in the way he looked at her, told her he wasn't being totally honest. And she knew very well that for actresses there always came a time when scripts were no longer offered; when agents seemed to forget to call; when careers came to an end so quietly one never actually realized it was over…

She put down the brush and picked up her lipstick then looked at the roses Todd had sent as she touched up her lips. Finishing with the lipstick, she picked up the note he had sent with the flowers. She again read the words: *"…a project that might interest you…"* and wondered.

Todd drove north on Canon to Sunset, east past the Beverly Hills Hotel then north again on Coldwater. Thanks to the councilman, he still had use of a city automobile and that made life ever so much easier.

What's the best way to persuade her to consider my show, he wondered. The idea of television probably won't be particularly pleasing to her. So the first thing I have to do is convince her TV is good.

Peter Best said TV is soon going to run Hollywood. Tell her that.

Peter said OGB might be looking for a series like "Homeroom," for their client, Palmer Foods, and Crystal would be the perfect star. Tell her OGB *is* looking for a series like "Homeroom," and it wouldn't be much of a stretch to tell her *they* want her.

She's getting too old to play juveniles, but, he thought, what little I know about women tells me this is a dangerous area. Being a teacher instead of one of the students might not exactly sit too well. So how do I tell her she's perfect for the teacher roll, eh?

Well gee Todd! He mentally clapped a hand against his forehead. You don't tell her anything yet. You just get her intrigued with the idea of doing television. What her roll is going to be, she can find out when she reads the script Peter is going to find someone to help me write.

Crystal opened the giant front door herself and wrapped her arms around him as though he were a long lost son.

"Todd. How wonderful to see you again."

"I can't tell you how good it is to see you, Crystal." He had decided that if he could call Peter Best by his first name, he could, and should do the same with the actress he was hoping to hire.

She led him to the "family room." A bright, warm, friendly room filled with comfortable furniture that induced a feeling of tranquility and relaxation. In Canada, rooms like this were called "dens", he thought, but in California, probably in an effort to make up for the fact that there is so little family life, they are called family rooms.

Before they were seated, a slender, young, Hispanic woman brought in a gold tray carrying glasses and bottles of red and white wine.

"Todd, this is Inez."

He smiled at her as she nodded and murmured, “Mr. Wilson...”

“So, what would you like?” Crystal pointed at the bottles. “Red...? white...? Or something stronger?”

“Oh gee, no. Nothing stronger.” He had not expected lunch to include wine. “A glass of red will do fine.”

“Good.” She turned to the girl, “I’ll have red as well, please Inez.”

Inez poured, then left the tray on a table. “Lunch is ready when you want Miss Manning,” she told Crystal.

“Thanks Inez. We’ll let you know.”

Crystal held her glass up to Todd, “I’m overcome with curiosity, Todd. What sort of project is on your mind?”

He did not reply immediately but tipped his glass toward her before taking a sip. Then, avoiding a direct answer, and hoping he was not about to build a trap for himself, he asked her a question. “Do you know what I saw on TV last night?” Without waiting for an answer, he continued, “‘North of the Rio Grande’.”

“Oh my heavens. When was it on?”

“I’m not sure. Sometime late...”

In actual fact, he had not seen the movie last night. He had seen it almost two years ago when he was working in Casting for Doris Rush. But old movies were common late night programming and he didn’t think she would know if the picture had been on last night. “I woke up and couldn't sleep," he continued. "So I switched on the TV and there you were riding like the wind, getting away from a band of outlaws."

"Goodness. I wish I'd known. It would have been fun to see it again. I think that was my first picture."

It always surprised him how Hollywood people referred to any movie they had even a small part in making as "their" picture. Yes, a major star or top director or producer might properly call a movie "theirs", but it seemed to be stretching it a bit when the assistant prop man spoke of "his picture." Then again, maybe it was just an indication of the intense sense of belonging and contributing felt by everyone working on a picture. Certainly it was a team effort, and members of a movie company always became "family" if only for a little while.

He took a sip of wine then asked her, "Do you watch much television?"

"No, not a lot. I try to watch the news... I love Chet Huntley, and every now and then I'll catch one of the variety shows, specially Jimmy Durante. He's always fun in spite of the commercials."

"You know," Todd said thoughtfully, "Something like twenty million people watch TV every night."

"I've heard that," she nodded her head up and down. "Isn't it amazing?"

"Yeah, it really is. Peter... my agent, Peter Best, he says TV is going to run this town in a few years. He wants me to get in on the ground floor, eh...? "

Peter Best is his agent? Good grief, she thought, that's pretty impressive. She remembered once hearing about how Todd had something to do with discovering Holly Sinclair. That probably has something to do with his representing Todd, Holly was becoming one of Peter's most important clients. The bitch...

Why do you think of her like that? Her subconscious voice asked. You've never even met the girl. Is it because she's young and beautiful and obviously very talented. All the things you once were, or tried to be? Is it because you're jealous?

So what if it is? She shut the voice off and returned to Todd's thoughts about television. "Peter is a very savvy man," she nodded her head in agreement. "He's probably right about television."

"I think so." Todd took a second sip of wine. He's talking with one of the ad agencies about a series I have in mind."

"Really. Why Todd, that's wonderful. I wish you all sorts of good luck."

Now's the time, he told himself.

"All of the good luck I need is sitting about four feet away from me..." He locked eyes with her and saw a flicker of excitement in hers.

"That's why I'm here. Would you consider doing television?"

Her eyes suddenly lost their sparkle as acting skills quickly controlled emotions. "Oh, Todd. That's so sweet of you. But, no, I don't think television is what I should be doing."

"I told them that, but the agency guy said if you knew that on TV, in one night more people would see you in their living rooms than were likely to see you in ten movies, you might give some serious thought to the idea. And Peter said since you can make more money in a year of TV than two years of movie making maybe... just maybe, you would consider it..."

He had shot his load. Now all he could do was wait for her...

"This is all very flattering, but I don't know..."

She is such an actress, Todd thought. There is no way to guess what she is really thinking.

"Is there a script I can read?" she said after a moment. "You'll have to talk to my agent of course, but I don't suppose it could hurt to look at a script."

"There is a script," Todd was amazed at how easily one little fib could lead to another. "But I'm not going to show it to you until we finish making a couple of changes."

"All right, I wont make any final decision until I read it, but Todd dear, I don't want you to be too upset if I say no. I don't really think I want to do TV."

"Upset?" Todd threw both his hands into the air. "If you say no I'll probably kill myself."

"Oh Todd." Her laugh was more of a girlish giggle. "Come on, let's have lunch."

Gardeners were hosing down a driveway near Crystal's house and water had collected in the street. He wasn't driving fast, none the less, as he ran through the puddle, his tires splashed a considerable amount of water onto the sidewalk. He was glad no one had been walking there.

Wow! He blinked as the idea popped into his mind. The puddle of water he had just driven through... sure, what a great opening... The series begins with Miss Ridley walking on her way to the first day of school. A couple of kids, who will wind up in her Homeroom, come whizzing past her in their hot rod and splatter mud all over her new dress.

Welcome to Summerville High!

He needed a telephone and the closest place he could think of to find one was the Beverly Hills Hotel. There were lots of advantages to driving a City of Los Angeles car. For one thing, people like doormen at ritzy places like the Beverly

Hills Hotel never questioned him when he pulled up and told them not to put his car too far away because he would need it soon.

He walked into the magnificent lobby, asked a bell boy where he could find a house phone and called Peter.

"She wants to do it!"

"She does? You've already talked to her?" Peter's surprise was obvious.

"Yeah. I had lunch with her."

"Jesus Todd, you work pretty fast."

"I'm doing the best I can Peter." He took a deep breath, looked out over the hotel lobby, then continued. "I told her she can see a script by the end of the week."

"Told her what?"

"That shouldn't be so hard. If you have a good writer we can start to work tonight."

"Son of a bitch!" Peter couldn't help laughing. "All right wise guy, I can match you. I've got not one, but two. A husband and wife team. Lucienne and Ron Rubin. She used to teach high school French until they got married and started writing together."

"Can they meet me tonight?"

"Yeah, probably. You wanna use an office here?"

"No. That's no place to talk about kids and school." Todd thought for a moment... "You know the drive-in on Sunset near Highland?"

"Yes..."

"Have them meet me there, about six-thirty."

"What if..." too late, the son-of-a-bitch hung up! What kind of a whirlwind have I invited into my comfortable world, Peter asked himself.

The drive-in manager was far more impressed by the city car than Todd's promise to spend at least twenty dollars in return for the exclusive use of a table next to a window overlooking the car hop service area.

"Yeah, sure..." he took another quick look at the business card Todd had handed him... "Mr. Wilson. You can have that table if you want." It wasn't the twenty bucks that persuaded him to keep the table open for Todd, the table would bring in twenty bucks anyhow, but you had to be careful of people who drove city cars. Health inspectors were all over the place and when you ran a restaurant you had to watch out for them. Especially if you ran a drive-in. Not only health inspectors, you had to watch out for guys looking at your traffic flow. There were always people who wanted to close down drive-ins.

"Great!" Todd gave him a friendly slap on the shoulder. "I'll see you about six o'clock."

He hadn't thought to ask Peter what Lucienne and Ron looked like, but he didn't think he would have too much trouble spotting them in a crowd that was primarily high school and college kids. And he didn't.

They arrived in an almost new, Buick convertible and drove to a parking spot at the far end of the lot.

"Lucienne? Ron?" He called as he dodged between roller skating car hops and walked towards the Buick.

They did the prescriptive hand-shakes and nice to meet yous, then Todd took Lucienne's arm and led them both toward the restaurant building and the table by the window.

"Welcome to Summerland High." He pulled out a chair for Lucienne. "In just a minute I'm going to introduce you to your new your homeroom teacher, Miss Ridley."

As they sat down, almost as if on cue, two kids in an open hot rod wheeled in the driveway and screeched to a stop just outside their window.

A cute, young, teen age car hop, wearing a short, blue skirt, white top and red pill box hat, skated towards the two boys in the car.

"See those two kids in the car?" Todd pointed to them.

"In our opening episode two kids just like that have a good laugh when they splash mud all over Miss Ridley on the way to her first day of school. After the commercial break they are going to find out she is their new homeroom teacher."

"Oh, wow…" Ron exclaimed.

"This is gonna be fun," his wife finished the thought.

The only thing wrong with the movie world, Peter Best often thought, was the fact that it was such an early morning business. On Monday mornings, production companies started shooting almost as soon as the sun came up and a good agent needed to be available for upset clients soon after that. Yes, he now had a number of very capable assistants who could handle almost any problem that might arise, but having got into the habit years ago, he still made it a point to be in the office by 7:30... 8:00 at the latest, on Monday mornings.

On this Monday morning, he had hardly taken his hat off before Caroline buzzed him on the intercom. "Malcolm Printer is calling from London."

"My God." Peter was surprised. "Put him on."

'Printer Hello What a pleasant surprise."

"Hello, Peter..." The connection was very clear. "It may not be all that pleasant when you here what I have to tell you."

"What's the problem?"

"Partly me, partly Holly Sinclair, partly Donald Lowman,,.." Printer paused, then added, "Mostly Movie Associates."

"So what's the trouble? And what has Donald Lowman got to do with it?"

"Lowman is putting up the money. He wants me and I want Holly but Movie Associates is insisting we put one of their stars in the picture. You know David Dill and I promised the part to Holly and I certainly do not want to disappoint her, but if things go on like they are, I may find myself sitting this one out too. I'm wondering if you have some magic that can sort this thing out?"

"I don't know..." Peter thought for a moment. "Let me think about it. I'll see if I can come up with something."

"I know you will, Peter. That's why I called you."

"Well, we'll see, Printer. I'll let you know."

Donald Lowman got up from his desk and walked to the corner window over looking the cloud covered East River and told him self "No More Fucking Movies!"

In the years following World War II Don Lowman had made a lot of money building houses for veterans covered by the G.I. Bill.

Hundreds of houses in tracts on Long Island and in New Jersey. Houses that brought him millions of dollars. But successful as he had been, and continued to be, deep in his heart, he always wanted to make movies. The history of Anne Boleyn had always intrigued him and a movie about her is what he wanted to make.

Well, by golly, it seemed if a fellow with millions of dollars to spend wanted to make a movie, Movie Associates would be glad to help him spend it.

"No Problem" MA assured him and quickly put screen writer Dean Rudas to work.

Rudas wrote a script. Then he re-wrote the script. Then he re-wrote the re-write. Finally, after almost $350,000, the script was acceptable to MA and to himself..

Next, at their urging, he hired Malcolm Printer to direct the picture.. Printer's fee of $500,000 had come as a shock, but Printer he had heard of, and he had not been displeased when MA suggested him.

But now. Good God, the casting. Who was to play Anne Boleyn? MA wanted Elizabeth Taylor or Lana Turner. Printer was insisting on relatively unknown Holly Sinclair. Neither Printer nor MA seemed willing to budge an inch. What was he going to do?

MA had insisted he make the deal with Printer, and now with a signed "pay or play" contract in force, a contract that gave Printer cast approval, the only way he could accept

MA's casting was to pay him off and, rich as he was, he still wasn't ready to kiss $500,000 goodbye. Plus which, he respected Printer and honestly believed he was the right director for his picture. So here he was, battling with MA who were telling him that without Taylor or Turner, they wouldn't handle the picture.

"No more fucking movies!" He said again as he watched a pair of tug boats that seemed to be racing one and other down the East River.

A moment later his secretary's voice came over the intercom. "Telephone call from Peter Best, Mr. Lowman..."

"Who?" He turned back towards his desk and his secretary's voice.

"Peter Best," she told him. "He's a big Hollywood agent and he represents Holly Sinclair."

"Oh shit!" He put his hands to his forehead. "Who needs this?"

"Shall I tell him you're tied up?"

"No, no. Put him on."

Five minutes later, Don Lowman realized the clouds covering the river had cleared as Peter Best told him if he went with Holly Sinclair, he could make a deal with StayCon to handle his picture and he could kiss MA goodbye.

"Hello David, this is Peter Best, is your beautiful bride around?"

Hi Peter. Yes, she out on the beach getting a little sun tan. Shall I call her?"

"Please, I've got some good news for her."

A moment later Holly came on the line. "Hello Peter. David says you have some news...?"

"And how! I just set the deal for you to play Anne Boleyn. You are now very definitely in the top echelon, my love."

"My God, Peter." She turned and sat down on one of the little Italian chairs she'd had sent home from Venice, "That's fabulous, Peter. When do I start?"

"It's going to be at least two months before Printer's ready to shoot, but he wants you to spend some time with an acting coach here in LA named Trevor Courtney. I've met him a few times. He's very British and I understand he's very good. Printer doesn't want to turn you into an Englishman, but he thinks Trevor can help you with a few mannerisms, things like that."

The drive along Pacific Coast Highway from the house in Malibu to the steep ramp leading up to Santa Monica's Main Street took Holly less than thirty minutes.

Running parallel to PCH, 200 feet below, Main Street is bordered by a lovely park like green belt which is complete with palm trees, walkways for strolling, comfortable benches perfect for sitting and enjoying the view out over the Pacific Ocean.

Trevor Courtney's studio was located on Main Street, just half a block south of Wilshire.

"It is delightful to meet you, Miss Sinclair." His voice was deep and wonderfully British. "Malcolm has told me so much about you."

"Malcolm," Holly said to herself. Very few people call him that. The fact that Courtney did served to reinforce her suspicion that he was another one of "the boys."

"It's good to meet you too, Trevor, I'm so looking forward to working with you. I know you're going to help me a great deal. Where do we begin?"

"What we are going to do first of all..." he took her hand and led her towards a door at the end of the studio, "Is dress you for the ccasion..."

"Dress...?"

"Yes indeed." He opened the door that led into a comfortable looking library room where she saw a metal clothes rack holding several medieval looking dresses.

"A friend of mine at Western Costumes loaned these to us. They're very much the sort of things you'll be wearing in the film. I want you to put one on."

She walked to the rack and held out the skirt of one of the gowns. "Oh they look beautiful..."

"All right. You pick one and put it on. I'll be in the studio when you're ready."

Fifteen minutes later Anne Boleyn made her entrance... well, tried to make her entrance. The voluminous gown she was wearing somehow got caught in the doorway causing her to step on the hem of the skirt and loose her balance. Grabbing hold of a chair just along side the doorway was all that saved her from a fall.

"Wow! This is going to take a little getting used to Trevor..."

"Yes, exactly." He smiled and nodded his head in agreement. "What we call 'body language' is a major part of acting. One of the most important things I hope we can do is make you comfortable with those sort of garments."

Two sessions later, Holly arrived to find a long wooden table set with brocaded cloths, heavy plates, goblets and silverware standing in the middle of the studio,

"Good afternoon your highness," Trevor told her as he bowed her into the room. "Please dress quickly for dinner."

It wasn't until she turned away from the table, which looked for all the world like a picture from a history book that she noticed the two uniformed "servants" standing next to the wall.

"Elmer and Victor. Students of mine..." Trevor said by way of introduction.

His lovers, Holly told herself as the two young men bowed in unison and said, "Your highness..."

Eating and drinking with unfamiliar utensils and glasses was even more difficult than learning to move comfortably in the costumes.

"Remember," Trevor cautioned her, "The secret of lasting through a day of shooting a scene like this is not to really eat or drink anything."

Holly took his admonition seriously with respect to the food. However the wines Elmer and Victor stood ready to pour were very good and she had been thirsty so perhaps she was not quite so careful where the wines were concerned.

After an hour or more of being served, drinking, and make believe eating, Trevor, who was not in costume, said, “Enough of this,” and told his two students to “clear away the mess,” while he and “her majesty” went into the library to run some lines.

“Don’t bother us when you’re finished. Just lock the door behind you when you leave and I’ll see you both tomorrow.”

“Love scenes in a period piece can sometimes be quite challenging,” Trevor said as he closed the library door. “Particularly for women,” he continued. “Back in the dark ages women were so totally inhibited that even the slightest hint of passion could terrorize them.” Taking her hand in his he drew her closer. “And dresses like the one you’re wearing were designed to excite men while protecting women from their advances.” He put his arms around her. “Now, as I try to kiss you, lean away. Be very lady like but try to avoid my lips...”

Holly did.

“Now, at some point, even fifteenth century women eventually gave in,” Trevor continued,

"But even so, their clothing made everything difficult." He leaned closer, "Now kiss me."

Wow! Holly blinked as his tongue slipped between her lips. Perhaps it was all the wine, perhaps it was just her surprise, but she found herself enjoying and responding to him as his hand somehow found a way to slip the dress off her shoulder, then locate her breast.

Maybe he isn't queer after all, she thought as he lifted her off her feet and carried her to the large sofa at the far end of the room.

“Acaaa...” It certainly wasn’t a word, just sort of a guttural sound that might have come from something being strangled. Todd blinked. He didn’t think he was so nervous he couldn’t speak. He didn’t feel overly tired, or excited, or anything else, but the word just hadn’t come out.

When Michael told him he should kick off the first shot, he had definitely been surprised, happy, and, yes, excited, but still... He looked at Michael, “I guess I should try that again, eh?”

There was some general laughter until Michael said, “Let’s have it quiet on the set.” Then he looked towards Todd. “Hey, boss, camera’s rolling. It’s your film we’re burning up. You can do what you like.”

“Great.” Todd grinned at him. “Okay, ready everybody...?” this time his voice was strong. “And ACTION!”

The empty classroom door opened and a slightly disheveled Crystal Manning, wearing a Janitor’s smock stepped into the room, snapped on the lights by the switch just inside the doorway, then walked to the teacher's desk where she put her purse and briefcase down. She looked over the empty room for a moment, then turned to the blackboard, picked up a piece of chalk and wrote, "Miss Ridley," in large, clear letters.

"...And CUT!" Michael stepped out from alongside the camera. "That was great, Crystal. Now if we can just get the electrical department to turn on the lights at the same time you snap the switch, we may even get to do some other scenes today."

Peter Best joined in the laughter. Along with Maureen and Jordan Lustig Peter and his wife Beverly were among several special guests Todd had invited to this first day of shooting. Peter didn't know the director, Michael Lange. He had suggested Todd ask Aaron Marks to direct the pilot, but Todd had not wanted Aaron involved. He had worked for Aaron and thought of him as a combination teacher, father, older brother and super mentor. If Aaron were to direct the pilot, Todd felt it would become Aaron's project, and he wanted it to be his own.

Todd's film editor, Megan Schmidt, had worked on a show Michael Lange had directed; she had recommended him to Todd, and Todd had total confidence in Meg Schmidt. So Michael Lange it was. And, Peter had to admit, Lange was certainly getting things off to a very happy start. A happy company usually made for a happy show, Peter thought, and that would be good.

Thinking of Todd's position regarding his director, reminded Peter of his insistence about Dennis Stern. Of all the cameramen in all of Hollywood, Todd wanted Dennis Stern and Dennis Stern was not a member of the union. Fortunately that was not a serious problem. Peter had Todd establish his own company, when the company signed with the IA, people who worked for the company, were required to join the IA in order to keep their jobs. So, once the company was formed, Dennis was hired, the guild agreements were signed and he was "forced" to join IA Local 600.

"Cut!" Lange's voice brought Peter's attention back to the set.

While he was thinking about Todd's determination to do things his way, the company had rehearsed the scene again and although Michael seemed pleased, he had joined Crystal on the set and was conferring with her. A moment later he called for the makeup man to join them.

Story wise, Peter knew, this scene would immediately follow the opening sequence in which Miss Ridley is soaked by a student's hot rod as it flashes past her. However, between that sequence and the scene they were now shooting, there would be a commercial break and apparently Michael felt the need for something stronger than the janitor's smock to tie the two scenes together. He was suggesting Crystal's hair could still be wet and perhaps fall down in front of her face once or twice...

"So, what-a-ya think of my director now?" Todd's voice startled him. Seated in a director's chair on the floor of the almost dark stage while looking at the brightly lit set, he had not noticed Todd approach.

"I have to say I think he's a damn good choice, Todd."

"Peter, I think I have a problem."

"What's up?" he wanted to know.

"I think I'm pregnant."

"Holly. I think that's great. I'm sure David is delighted."

"It isn't David's." Her voice was low, icy cold. "That's another story I'll tell you someday. Today we need to figure out what to do about this one."

Peter switched the telephone to his other hand, leaned back in his desk chair and looked out the window at the blue sky above the Wrather Building across the street. It took him a few seconds to adjust to Holly's news.

"...What is it you want to do about it?"

"I need to be sure, and if I am... I have to get rid of it, Peter."

"Ummph." He felt as if the air had been knocked out of his chest. Things like this happened, he knew. Still, the idea of aborting a baby did not sit well. He thought of his wife, Beverly, and their two children, and how much happiness they brought into their lives. Why did things like this have to happen? Why are so many girls like Holly, with so much talent, such tramps?

"I'm supposed to be in London in just a few weeks," she continued. "So I need to do something quickly and quietly. Very quietly," she stressed.

Peter's mind turned slowly to the real world and practical solutions to problems. His first thought was Hy Abrams. Westland House girls sometimes found themselves "in trouble," and Peter knew Hy had a place to take care of those things. On second thought, he realized Holly was getting to be known here in LA and there was always a chance someone might recognize her. Better send her to Vegas.

"Yes, all right Holly. I'll see if I can arrange something."

Olympia Gonzales knocked on Holly's s bedroom door. "Mr. Best is here."

"Thank you. Tell him I'll be right down."

She had sent Olympia to the May Company store in Santa Monica the previous afternoon to buy her a simple, one size too large house dress, a mousy, gray cloth coat, and a pair of "sensible" shoes. Weaaring this outfit she doubted people would recognize her and, fortunately, David was in Europe looking for locations for his next picture, so there was no need for him to know anything. Not that he would care anyway.

"All set?" Peter's voice was a bit too cheerful, she thought.

"Yes. All ready." Then, turning to her houskeeper, " Olympia, if anyone calls tell them I'm away for a few days and I don't want to be disturbed." It was the third time Holly had given these instructions to Olympia. "If there are any problems, call Mr. Best at his office. Okay?"

"Si. I understand, Miss Holly."

As she slid into Peter's car Olympia handed him the small overnight case she had packed with a few necessities she thought Holly might need: fresh underwear, a blouse, a skirt and a dozen pills..

Shortly after her marriage to David, Holly had hired Olympia Gonzales and her husband Ernesto to be live in custodians and care takers of their Malibu house. For Olympia and Ernesto the job was a God-send. They were what President Eisenhower had termed, "wetbacks". They had crossed the border illegally and, until finding a home with Holly, had lived in constant fear of being apprehended and sent back to Mexico. Their gratitude for the home and the protection it afforded them was manifested in their total, complete, and unquestioning loyalty to her.

Peter drove south along Pacific Coast Highway into Santa Monica, then east on Wilshire Boulevard to the VA Hospital adjacent to the San Diego Freeway. He pulled into the parking lot where a two or three year old Lincoln was waiting to take her to Las Vegas.

You have the money?" Peter asked her.

"Yes, three thousand..."

"Good. Don't give it to anyone other than Noreen Pierce. She'll be waiting for you."

Holly gave him a quick kiss on the cheek, whispered,
"Thank you Peter," picked up her hand bag and slid out of Peter's car.

The driver of the Lincoln did not get out to welcome her. Instead he reached back, behind himself, and opened the rear door for her.

"Ready?"

"Yes." she told him.

Holly did not know exactly how long she slept but when she awoke the sun's angle told her it had been several hours. "Where are we?"

"Almost there, Miss," the driver answered. "Just a few more miles. "Off there," he nodded his head to the right, "You can see Las Vegas."

She looked. In the day time there was not much to see. At night, she knew, there were millions of lights that could be seen for miles, but in the daytime, the low buildings did not look very impressive. At least not from this distance.

She realized they were climbing slightly and circling the city. Moments later they turned off the highway onto a two lane road. A sign told her the road was headed towards someplace named "Parrump."

The entrance to the "Desert Sanitarium," could easily be missed by anyone not familiar with its location, and the gravel road leading to it was not designed to attract curious visitors. Three hundred yards up the gravel road, a heavy gate attended by two uniformed guards made certain that only those who were expected could go further.

The Sanitarium itself looked charming. Pink stucco, Spanish style buildings, with wide verandahs and red bougainvillea vines climbing the columns which supported the second floor balconies, made the place look like the home of some wealthy Spanish Don.

As they pulled up in front of the main building, a pleasant looking, heavy set middle aged woman, wearing a wide smile, came out to welcome her. "Hello, I'm Noreen Pierce."

The woman opened the car door and held it for her, then took her arm and led her into the building, down a wide, well lit hallway to a comfortable bedroom with a large window overlooking a sparkling fountain in a small garden.

"This will be your room," the woman told her with unnecessary enthusiasm. "Isn't it lovely? Doctor will be in to see you in a few minutes. He probably won't want you to eat too much this evening, but if he says it's okay," she picked up a small control box from the bedside table, "Just press this button. Room service is available twenty-four hours."

"Thank you," Holly told the woman and took an envelope from her purse. "Am I to pay you now?"

"Oh, that would be lovely," the woman gushed.

It was less than five minutes since Holly had met her, but she was already sick of her overdone effervescence.

"Three thousand, right?" She handed the envelope to the woman.

"That's just perfect." The woman took the envelope and headed towards the door. "Now you make yourself comfortable dear, doctor will be along any minute."

She left, gently closing the door behind her but somehow, to Holly, it sounded very loud and ominous and suddenly she felt very alone. She sat down in a comfortable chair facing the window looking out at the fountain. How could she have gotten herself into this predicament? How could she have been so careless... so foolish?

She wasn't sure how long she sat there watching the clear water bubble from the top of the fountain, then fall in sparkling streams to the little pond in which it stood. Perhaps five minutes, perhaps twenty-five. Her mind seemed devoid of thought.

A knock on the door brought her back to awareness. She turned as a gray haired man of medium height entered. His white lab coat and the stethoscope around his neck served as introduction enough.

"As I understand it," he began with no "hello" or introduction, "You asked for a test to confirm your condition."

"...Yes. I think I'm pregnant, but it's too early to be sure."

"We can do a blood test, but it takes a bit of time to get the results and they aren't always accurate."

The doctor walked across the room to her and took her wrist. Although "matter of fact," his demeanor was not unpleasant. "Your pulse is good." He let go of her wrist. "A little fast, but that's just nerves. Quite understandable. The best thing is to do a D&C," he said slowly. "That's certain, and it will remove any foreign matter or infection."

"I'm not sure what a D&C is," Holly told him. "But if you think it's best..."

He pulled a chair away from the writing desk and placed it where he could sit and face her. "D&C. Dilation and Curettage. It's a procedure by which we clean out your womb. Before bedtime tonight the nurse will give you a pill to help you relax and slightly dilate your cervix. In the morning, we'll take you into surgery, give you a general anesthesia to put you to sleep so you won't feel anything, and do the procedure. It won't take more then fifteen or twenty minutes. Before you know it you'll wake up back here in your bed."

"You make it sound very simple."

"Actually it is." He stood and returned the chair to its position in front of the desk. "Very simple. Very safe. You'll spend tomorrow relaxing and taking it easy, then Thursday you can go home."

Not surprisingly, perhaps, coincidence is sometimes responsible for the collapse of the most carefully made plans. In the case of Holly's visit to the sanitarium in Las Vegas, "coincidence" came in the form of an attractive young nurse named Coco who was not only a movie buff, but from time to time actually worked as an extra when film companies came to the Vegas area. With or without makeup, old clothes or new, made no difference to Coco, she immediately recognized Holly Sinclair that evening when she delivered her bedtime pill. Having been most carefully instructed that sanitarium patients were always incognito, and warned that never, ever, under any circumstances, were patients to be recognized, nor their identities revealed to anyone, Coco carefully hid her surprise and said nothing to Holly. In fact, she said nothing to anyone until later that evening when she and her boy friend left the hospital. Then together, they began hatching a plot they felt certain would bring them the money they needed to realize their dream of setting up a smaller version of the sanitarium near the city of Reno, Nevada.

The same driver who had picked her up Tuesday drove her back to LA on Thursday, and Peter was waiting when they pulled into the VA parking lot that afternoon. Once again the driver reached behind himself and opened the door for her without getting out of the car. As on the trip to Las Vegas, she and the driver had scarcely looked at each other and exchanged very few words during the nearly six hour drive. She told him "Thank you," as Peter took her overnight case and walked with her to his waiting car. Neither she nor Peter noticed the brown, Ford sedan that followed them out of the parking lot. Even if they had, it's unlikely Holly would have realized the dark haired woman driving it was Coco, the nurse who had tended her at the sanitarium.

Holly felt all right on Friday morning, but somewhat listless and she asked Olympia io serve her breakfast in bed. After she had eaten, she pulled on a sweat shirt and a pair of comfortable old slacks then took her script out on the second floor deck adjoining her bed room. With the warm sun and the soft sound of waves washing on the beach below lulling her, she dozed off before she had read more than half a dozen pages.

"Miss Holly..."

It wasn't like Olympia to awaken her when she was napping.

"What is it, Olympia?"

"I sorry to bother, but there is this man who say he was-shur driver and he muss talk wit-chu."

"My driver...?" For some reason Olympia's announcement caused a wave of fear to make her tremble.

"Where is he?"

"He downstairs at de door. I don't let him come in de house."

Holly took a deep breath and got up from her deck chair. "All right, let's see what he wants."

If it were the man who had driven her to Vegas and back, something was wrong. That man should not know her name nor have any idea where she lived. If he were the driver, it could mean a problem. Well, she told herself as she headed for the stairway, I can handle problems.

"Hello Miss Sinclair. Can I talk ta-ya privately fer a minute?"

It was him; the man who had driven her to and from Las Vegas.

"What is it you want?"

"Better we should talk private," he said looking at Olympia.

"All right." Holly turned to Olympia, "Excuse us for a minute please."

Somewhat reluctantly, Olympia started back into the house. "I be chuss inside if you need me."

Holly looked back at the man, "Now, what is it?"

"Well the thing is, Holly, I need some money."

"Some money," Holly repeated. "And you want me to give you some money?"

"Yeah. That's sort-a the idea."

"I see." The fear she had felt earlier was gone, replaced by a growing anger at the man's presumptuous use of her first name together with a feeling of self assurance that she could deal with whatever problems he might have brought to her doorstep. "And just how much money are we talking about?"

"It's gonna take ten thou, Holly."

"Ten thou...? Are we talking about ten thousand dollars?"

"Yep. I know that ain't a lot to you, but it is ta me, an' it's what I need."

"And why in the world do you think I'd give you ten thousand dollars?"

"Well, see, I need some dough, an' I know this reporter guy who would probably pay me pretty good fer some information 'bout that little package you dumped off in Vegas..."

"What package is that?"

"Come on, lady. Don't play dumb, You know what I'm talkin' about."

"No, I don't. I don't think you do either. And I don't think anyone would be dumb enough to believe whatever story it is your trying to invent."

"Yeah, well, the pictures will help."

"Pictures?" Holly could not imagine what pictures he was talking about.

"Yeah. My girl friend took a few while you were sleepin'."

This was going on too long, Holly realized. This man could become dangerous and she needed to send him away. Once he was gone, she could call Peter. He had been able to arrange the Vegas situation, so he probably would have some idea how to take care of this. Meanwhile, she had better convince the man that she was frightened and would find some way to pay him.

"Why are you doing this to me?" It didn't tax her acting talent to project a degree of helplessness and fear. "I haven't done anything to you."

"No, no." The man put his hands up in a gesture of futility. "Hey Holly. Nothin' personal here. You-n-me got along fine. It's just I need money, see?"

"I don't... I don't have that kind of money..."

"Aw, come on Holly... How can you stand here in front of this mansion an' tell me you ain't got money. Besides, I'm sure your studio'll pay plenty to keep things quiet. Right?"

Holly let him see a spark of hope in her eyes. "Yes, yes they might. I could talk to somebody..."

"Right. You could talk ta somebody." The man grinned at her. "So, you do-dat. Tonight I'll call ya an' we'll figure out where you can deliver the money. Okay?"

Holly nodded her head skowly up and down. "Yes... I guess. I don't know..."

The man looked at his wrist watch. He was due to make a pick up in Beverly Hills at one o'clock. "Holly." His voice suddenly became strident, demanding. "Enough-a this shit! You talk ta who ya need to and get the dough. Now gim-me ya phone number an' I'll call ya tonight."

To say Peter was surprised by Holly's phone call would be like saying the ocean is big. Both statements are true, but neither quite captures the full depth of the situation. He was shocked... stunned! Holly's report of the driver's visit was unbelievable, inconceivable! Confidentiality was the key to the sanitarium's success. People who worked there were very carefully selected, and very carefully instructed in their duties. Not only were they supposed to be trustworthy, they were supposed to be smart. Nobody intent on blackmail… nobody who had any brains, that is, could be dumb enough to personally confront their intended victim. Could they? Obviously this guy could.

Well, this was a situation needing immediate attention. He told Holly he would get back to her, then telephoned Jeffery Flanagan.

Jeffery Flanagan was the General Manager of the Fabulous Sirocco Hotel in Las Vegas. Not too many people knew the Sirocco was part of Hugh Crawford's empire.

"Jesus! That's very bad," Jeffery told him. "We don't own the place, but like everybody, we use it and this sort-a thing can make problems fer everybody."

"Yeah!" Peter agreed. "You're damn right Jeff. Especially for my client. So what should I tell her to do?"

Jeffery thought for a moment… "You tell her to say she gona pay him. If he wants her to deliver the money someplace, she should tell him she's afraid to go alone, she'll send a messenger. Then, right away, she should call you and you call me. We have people to take care a things like this."

"Okay Jeff. Keep me posted, and I'll let you know what happens at this end.

Noreen Price was nervous. Very nervous. Dexter Poole was her boss. He had found Dr. Weinstein, and he had built the Sanitarium, but he almost never came out for a visit... unless there was a problem; a big problem! She was certain his unexpected arrival this afternoon could only mean trouble of some kind.

Moments after he arrived she began to realize just how much trouble there was.

"Who picked up the woman in Los Angeles last Tuesday?" Dexter asked her.

"Sal," she answered. "Salvatore Indence."

"Where is he now?"

"Right now," Noreen looked at the clock on her desk. It was ten after three, "He had a noon time pickup in LA. That means he ought to be somewhere this side of Barstow. I expect him back here by five o'clock." She wanted to ask why he wanted to know, but knew better. Dexter was not a man you asked question of.

"How did you find him? When did he start?"

"He started about a month ago. He's Coco's boy friend." She realized Dexter did not know Coco and added, "Coco is one of our nurses. Someone Doctor knows recommended her."

Dexter closed his eyes and thought for a moment, then opened them and stared at her again. "We got a serious breach-a security here, Noreen. Gimme their pictures."

Dexter's eyes were hard, cold, and he had not taken them off her since asking about the driver. She felt a chill run up her spine as she took hold of the gold chain necklace she wore and pulled the small key ring attached to it from between her breasts. She selected a key and used it to open the file draw in her desk. A moment later she handed photographs of Indence and Coco to Dexter.

"He's due back at five?"

"Yes."

"What about her? Where is she?"

"She's on the night shift this week. She's due in at five."

Dexter picked up the photos and stood. "That's convenient." he told her as he turned and left her office.

At 4:45, slightly ahead of Noreen's estimated time of arrival, Sal Indence pulled up in front of the entrance building. Noreen welcomed his passenger and escorted her inside while Sal drove the Lincoln to the parking lot behind the vine covered fence well past the eastern end of the building. He was half way out of the car when the leaded black-jack slammed into his head, just behind his left ear.

Moments later, Coco drove her old brown Ford into the employee parking lot at the opposite end of the building. Windows wide open she was enjoying the beautiful afternoon, the desert at its best. Because she had the radio turned on, she did not hear them approach. It wasn't until a split second before the black-jack hit just above her left eye that she had any inkling of trouble.

One of the men pushed her unconscious body into the passenger seat, then drove to where the car Sal Indence had been driving was parked. Indence's unconscious body was quickly dumped in on top of Coco's then the man who was driving headed down the gravel road, back towards the gate and the two lane highway beyond.

The gate guards did their best to ignore the Brown Ford as it sped past. It had been made clear to them that only Coco and Sal Indence were in that car.

Holly telephoned Peter at nine-thirty. "He hasn't called," she told him.

"Ahh, Holly..." Peter's voice was strangely tight, she thought. "Holly, I was just about to call you. There's been an auto accident. As far as they can tell me now, both the man who was your driver and the nurses who tended you have been killed in an automobile accident.. I'll let you know more as soon as I get further information." Peter hung up before she could ask any questions.

She took a deep breath, and held it as long as she could. Two people were dead. No, three people were dead. A man, a woman and an unborn child. All because of her stupidity. Her carelessness. They should not have tried to blackmail her, but was this the only answer? One answer was obvious. Less drinking and probably fewer pills. When she drank a bit too much she had been careless. And that was not good.

As that thought passed from her mind, another took its place. Peter Best was perhaps more than just Hollywood's best agent.

Holly did not meet Donald Lowman until she and David reached London two weeks before production of, "A Girl Named Anne," was scheduled to start.

Printer had booked an apartment for them at the Dorchester Hotel, just across the street from Hyde Park. Printer maintained an apartment there and was on hand to greet them when they stepped out of the warm hotel limousine, into the damp chill of a February morning.

"Well you two, have a good trip?" He put his arms around Holly and gave her the customary kiss on the cheek, "Come on, let's get inside before we freeze." Turning to David, he clapped an arm around his shoulder, "Good to see you old boy. How long can you stay?"

David told him he had to be in Madrid in ten days to begin pre-production on his next picture and hoped he wouldn't be in the way if he hung about 'till then.

"In the way? Nonsense." Printer slid between them in order to put his free arm around David. "It will be wonderful having you here and you'll have a chance to see your wife as a blond."

Holly stopped, blinked and turned to him. "What did you say? A blond?"

"Oh, quite." Printer bubbled with his usual British enthusiasm. "Ann Bolin was a blond, you know. Real knockout. We'll talk about it all later. Now Donald's dying to meet you both. Can we do tea this afternoon?"

"I don't know," David looked questioningly at his wife. "It's been a long flight, Holly's probably tired. She might..."

"Not at all," Holly butted in. "My berth was very comfortable and I slept fine." They had flown from New York in a TWA Constellation which boasted four full berths in its first class cabin. "By all means, let's do tea," she continued. "I want to find out about this blond business."

"All right," Printer rubbed his hands together, "Four o'clock, then. In the lobby?"

"I guess that works for us... Holly?"

"Sure. You bet."

At age 39, Donald Lowman was the picture of rugged good health. Although he was taller and heavier, his unruly blond hair and well muscled body somehow reminded Holly of Todd Wilson. People who knew him well insisted he looked no different today than eleven years ago when he was discharged from the Navy's CeeBees after serving almost four years in the South Pacific. When Holly had learned Lowman was the Executive Producer and financial backer for Printer's picture, she had made a point of learning more about him.

Donald's father, John Lowman, had once owned the only lumber yard in Colfax, Iowa, a town of some two thousand residents located just twenty miles north and east of Des Moines. As a boy, Donald worked in the yard after school.

Later, at Iowa State, he had studied architecture and worked summers as a carpenter. Like many Mid Westerners, the day after Pearl harbor, he had enlisted. He was assigned to a Construction Battalion where he quickly earned his commission.

Donald had crammed a lot of living into the eleven years since his discharge and had amassed a considerable fortune with the construction company he created for the purpose of building much needed, inexpensive houses for returning GIs.

Nine years ago he had married the daughter of an old money, Wall Street family and together they had two children before she decided she could no longer live with him. Their divorce had occupied considerable newspaper space a year or so ago. Although there was no way Holly could know for certain, she did not believe Lowman was currently "involved" with anyone. If he were, the gossip columns carried no mention of it, and Lowman was enough of a celebrity to warrant reasonably close attention by the columnists.

"I can't tell you what a thrill it is for me to meet you, Holly." He had taken both her hands in his as Printer introduced them, and his broad smile and the excitement in his voice gave proof to his words.

"Mr. Lowman, that's very kind of you, but I must tell you the thrill is all mine. You helped defend our country and you've made home ownership possible for thousands of our boys. You are a true American hero and I am very proud to meet you."

"Oh, wow!" He was overwhelmed by her words and for a moment could only blink his eyes. Nice eyes, Holly thought. Steel blue, but warm and friendly, with slight smile wrinkles at each side.

"Thank you," he said at last. "But one thing we have to get straight right now. You call me Donald, or Don, but no more Mr. Lowman. Understood?"

Being in London was wonderful! And the Knightsbridge Studio, Holly thought, was so... so... British. The high red brick wall that surrounded it, and the ancient looking gate, complete with spikes at the top of each of its iron bars, made the studio look more like an old prison than the entrance to one of England's, if not the world's finest movie studios. It wasn't until you passed through that well guarded portico and reached the inner court yard that you began to feel the warmth and excitement of the film world.

On her first visit to the studio, for makeup tests, Holly met Bryce, a hair stylist who was somehow a friend of Leonard's, the medic who helped her get to sleep after her first day of shooting on "Out West."

As Bryce carefully transformed her into the "ravishing blond bomb shell," Printer had promised. he told her Leonard sent his love and if there was anything he could do for her, she had only to ask.

Surprised, she asked him how he happened know Leonard.

"The film world is very small," he answered. "I've known Leonard for years."

'Since the abortion, she often found herself wanting something to take her mind off things... the sounds of children at play... a baby crying. Especially at night... at night, alone in bed. She didn't like to be alone in bed because that was when she thought about it the most...

But her resolve was strong. That crying baby could have been her's. She was determined to keep the promise she made to herself. "No more pills. And much less booze."

"Bryce," She spoke slowly. "Thank you, but no thanks. Some things happened to me that wouldn't have if I hadn't been 'using.' I don't want things to happen again."

"'Nuff said." Bryce nodded his head. "But just know I'm here for you."

Two days after David left for Madrid, Don Lowman stopped in at the wardrobe department where newly blond Holly Sinclair was being fitted. She walked out of the dressing room and provocatively modeled the dress she would wear in the scene when King Henry sees her for the first time. "Do you think a king would be intrigued?"

"I don't know about a king," Donald grinned, "But I certainly am."

She tried on two more dress for his approval, then, as she thanked the designer and her assistants, Don took a deep breath and asked, "I know David is out of town, and this is probably very improper, but would you consider having tea, or a sherry with me?"

"Oh I'd love to Don. And David wouldn't mind a bit."

Each morning a studio limo stood waiting for Holly just outside the hotel entrance and each evening, when she finished her day's work, it waited next to her dressing room to return her to the Dorchester, or take her where ever she wished to go. Frequently, when her call was not too early in the morning, Don Lowman joined her for the ride to the studio. It was obvious to her that Don was becoming "interested," and she was anxious to let him know his interest was returned, but how to do this without telling him of her situation with David was a problem. She hoped David's failure to return from his "pre-production" trip to Madrid, might give him some idea all was not well with their marriage, but if it had, he gave no indication of it.

One of the marks of a great director is being sensitive to an actor's needs, both on camera and off, and being a great director, Printer was quick to appreciate the situation. He was aware of Donald's interest in Holly, as well as hers in him. He realized she was anxious for Donald to know her marriage to David was not a permanent arrangement, but did not know how to do so without revealing David's secret. Not surprisingly, therefore, Printer took it upon himself to solve her problem.

Malcolm Printer had never been one to approach things head on. To him, the only approach to a problem was obliquely. For example, he would never tell an actor his performance was not good. Instead he would say something about what an interesting interpretation the actor had just given, praise his versatility and tell him he was so entranced by that performance he would just love for him to try some others. In the end, Printer usually got exactly what he wanted from the actor, and the actor was convinced one of the world's great directors thought he was wonderful.

A reporter once asked Printer what his favorite word might be. "Manipulation," he answered with no hesitation, "Not only is it a most pleasing word to speak... the way the tongue and the lips form around the syllables... its meaning is so interesting: 'to deal skillfully with; to manage,' that's what I try to do every day."

He intended to use a similarly oblique, manipulative approach with Lowman as soon as he found an opportunity to do so.

"Golly, that stuff looks good," Donald told Printer as they started out of the screening room one evening. "And Holly looks like a million."

"We don't call it 'stuff', old boy." Printer chuckled as he put his arm around Donald's shoulders. "You have been watching 'dailies.'"

Lowering his voice slightly, Printer continued, "You're quite right, you know; Holly does look marvelous, but we have a little problem there, we need to discuss. Do you suppose we could wander off by ourselves somewhere and have a bite to eat?

Printer tasted the sommelier's recommended burgundy, found it a "bit too young, and rather 'woody'," and asked for a bottle of Romanee Grand Cru '53 instead, then leaned closer to Donald.

"Now about our Holly..."

"Yes?" Donald was all ears.

"The problem is that husband of hers..."

"Oh...?"

"Yes. He's a bit of a rounder, you know. He's taken up with some opera singer off there in Spain." Printer was speaking the truth, however he neglected to mention the opera singer was a baritone. "Our problem," he continued, "Is trying to keep Holly from learning about the situation for at least a few more days."

"I don't understand..."

"Well, you know I'm shooting this picture more or less in sequence. For a few more days I require a happy, youthful Anne Boleyn. By the end of next week we will have her awaiting execution, and whatever unhappy emotions she has then will only enhance her performance. As a matter of fact, if she hasn't found out by that time, I will probably tell her."

Both men fell silent as the sommelier returned with the Grand Cru. Printer examined the color, sniffed the bouquet, then indulged in a carefully measured sip. "Yes... this is far better."

He waited as Donald's glass was filled then proposed a toast, "To Anne Boleyn."

"Printer... Listen, damn the wine, this business with Holly's husband and keeping secrets to get a performances; I can't go along with all that. She's to fine a woman to have people playing games with her life."

"Yes, well I'm not actually going to tell her straight out. She's much to good an actress to need that kind of stimulation anyhow. She'll do those scenes perfectly well without outside help. But really, I am concerned about the news getting to her while we're still shooting."

"I can understand that. I don't suppose news like that gets any worse if you don't hear it right away. But I feel terrible for Holly. How did you find out?"

Printer lifted his glass and looked into the deep red color of his wine. "It's a small world, this world of film making. I've made films all over Europe and I have friends everywhere."

Printer's answer was far from specific, but it seemed to be all Donald needed. In truth, the news was not nearly as upsetting as he pretended it was. If anything, the news sparked his fantasies about her. Which was exactly what Printer had intended.

Holly carefully lifted her skirt and leaned back against the reclining board as Printer joined her for his usual pre-shoot talk.

"Screw the shit about motivation and approach, I know all that," Holly told him. "What's going on with Donald? Does he know about David and me?"

Over the past several days Donald had become increasingly attentive, giving her reason to suspect he had some knowledge of her situation with respect to David. The only person she could think of who might be able to confirm her suspicions was her director.

"Ummm. We are a bit testy this morning, aren't we?"

"Come on, Printer. You are the all wise one. You know everything. What gives?"

"What gives?" His voice was almost that of a purring cat. "How quaint. I do so love those American expressions..."

"Printer!" Her voice raised a notch or two. "You want to shoot something today, or shall I just have a tantrum and walk off the set?"

"All right my dear. Calm down. Yes, Donald is aware things are not good between you two. He knows David is having an affair in Madrid..."

Holly's eyes widened, not in surprise, but excitement. "An affair? I didn't know about that. Do you think that's enough grounds for me to ask David for a divorce now? I promised him I'd wait a year."

"Given the present situation...Yes, I think perhaps you could. I'll have a word with him... Lay some ground- work so to speak,"

"You are a dear man." She blew him a kiss. "Now, if my motivation is believing I'm in love with the king, I'll just pretend he is my wonderful director."

"Ahhh." Printer allowed a smile to cross his face. "You Americans have another rather quaint phrase that comes to mind..."

"Oh...?"

"Ummm. 'Fuck-off!' Is that about right?"

"Seems singularly appropriate."

"Jolly good. Now, do you suppose we can shoot something before elevens?"

"Elevens" and "Fours" are traditional with British film companies. At eleven each morning and again at four each afternoon all work stops for a tea break.

"Rather," she answered in her best British accent. Then, again carefully lifting her voluminous skirt, she leaned forward, stepped away from the recliner board and headed for the set.

"Mister Printer called," David Dill's secretary told him as he returned to his office from a visit to the set. "He wants you to please telephone him at his home this evening."

Life in Spain, David knew, was very different from life in England. When the Brits are breaking for their morning tea, a Spanish company is just starting to work. Dinner in Spain is usually about eleven at night, when people in England are going to bed. For Printer, David decided, "this evening" would probably be just about when his Spanish company closed down for the day.

"Malcolm, how are you?"

"Fine, dear boy, but it's not me we're going to talk about, it's Holly..."

"Oh? What's up?"

"Well, she seems to be getting a good deal of attention from our Mr. Lowman these days, and she's rather anxious to let him know she is not, shall we say, fully committed. But she's an honest young woman and very aware of her deal with you, and me. What I'm wondering is, could you possibly see your way clear to letting her off the hook, as you Americans say."

After a moment of thoughtful silence, David answered, "Maybe I can do that. Let me give it some thought. Tell her I'll telephone her Sunday."

Holly knew David liked to wake-up early on Sunday, have a large breakfast and read the papers. So, in spite of having had too much to drink last night, she awakened to the eight o'clock call she had requested and took two "uppers" in order to be ready to deal with whatever he might have to say.

Knowing Holly liked to sleep late on Sundays, David did not telephone her until a few minutes after eleven. By the time his call did come, she had taken two more pills and her nervous pacing back and forth across the sitting room had almost worn a path in the carpet.

"Have you got today's Daily Mail?" His question confused her.

"Daily what...?" She stammered. "Mail?... David what are you talking about?"

"Calm down, Holly. Printer told me about Lowman, and how you want to break things off a little sooner than we talked about."

She took a breath and started to reply, but he continued, "If that's what you want, it's okay with me. I want to do what I can to help, so I've started a little something that will give you a reason for dumping me."

"David, you are not making sense..."

"Yes I am. You'll understand when you look at the second page of the paper. The London Daily Mail. Call me after you look at it."

She hung up, then quickly flashed the hotel operator. She knew she sounded bitchy and demanding as she told her to have a copy of the paper rushed up to her. She needed to calm down.

She went into the bedroom and realized she was still wearing her nightgown and what could only be described as a very sexy negligee. Well screw it! she told herself. So the bellman gets a little thrill. She didn't need to change her clothes, she needed a pill to help her calm down. She scarcely had time to swallow it before the doorbell sounded.

She gave the bellman a pound, an outrageously large tip, and managed to close the door, without slamming it in his face, while he was still ogling her and trying to tell her "thanks".

On the second page, under the headline: "*When the Cat's Away, Mice Will Play,*" there were two photographs; one, a picture of her at work on the set of "A Girl Named Anne", the other, a picture of David having a drink with a beautiful woman she didn't recognize. Below the pictures, the paper informed its readers that while Lovely Holly was hard at work in London, her husband was in Madrid doing the town with Italian Model Carmella Mondavie.

She joyfully crushed the paper to her bosom, exclaimed out loud, "Oh David, you're wonderful!" then went to the bar, opened a bottle champagne and poured herself a celebratory drink before telephoning David to tell him, “Thank you, you really are a wonderful person.”

Monday was perfect in Beverly Hills. The sun was shining and Peter was looking forward to the drive over to the valley. He had the top down on his convertible, all was right with the world. But.....

From Canon Drive, up Coldwater to Mulholland usually took no more than fifteen minutes but the change from city to country was remarkable. Running along the top ridge of the Hollywood Hills, Mulholland Drive offered an amazing view of the San Fernando Valley, far below on one side, and the rugged wilderness of small canyons covered in a variety of pine, sage, and God knows what on the other.

Mulholland Drive was famous for two things: With all its twisting turns and sharp curves, it was the ultimate speedway for sports car enthusiasts; while for lovers each night, it was also the ultimate park your car, "make-out" road in Los Angeles County.

For Peter it was neither a race track nor a "passion pit." The few miles he traveled along Mulholland, from Coldwater to Laurel Canyon, usually provided him with a brief opportunity to turn his mind away from the office, to things of natural beauty. But.. today was not a usual day. Today Peter found himself not admiring nature, but thinking about last night's telephone conversation with Donald Lowman:

"Can we buy a nomination for Holly?" Lowman had asked.

For an outsider, Lowman certainly had been quick to pick up the jargon, Peter thought. "Nomination," was industry short hand for Academy Award Nomination.

"Last time I looked, nominations weren't for sale," he had answered.

"Yes, well I know you can't just go to the store and buy one, but I've been told, if you're willing to spend a little money, you can sometimes generate one. From what Printer has been telling me, and what I've seen for myself, she's giving a performance that will certainly be worthy, and I'll be very happy to pay whatever it might cost to see if we can get one for her.

"Okay, Donald," he had told him. "I'll see if I can get something started."

Upon reaching the intersection with Laurel Canyon, Peter made the sharp, somewhat dangerous left turn off Mulholland, into Laurel, and headed down the steep, twisting road leading to the Valley and Paris Brest on Ventura Boulevard where he pulled into what had to be the world's smallest parking lot. As an attendant handed him a claim check he quickly turned and headed into the restaurant. He couldn't stand to watch these guys park his car. Somehow they managed to get thirty or more cars into a lot no one would believe could hold more than ten or twelve. But they did, and somehow every time he got his car back it was miraculously free from scratches or damage of any kind.

Virtually unknown to people outside the industry, the Paris Brest was a wonderful restaurant that featured good food and intimate seating arrangements conducive to confidential discussions. Like the parking lot, the restaurant appeared to be much smaller than it really was. The secret, Peter realized one day, was in the fact that although the room was very narrow, it was actually quite long but a series of well placed decorative baffles divided the room into small, intimate sections, and kept the place from looking like a bowling alley.

Nick Benton, "Nicholas Benton" to his readers, was sitting at the tiny bar just inside the front entrance when he arrived. "Hi Nick."

"Hello, Peter. They're just clearing a booth for us."

He lifted the glass he was holding, “Wanna drink while we wait?”

“No, I have a busy afternoon ahead of me. A drink and I might fall asleep.” Peter looked at the bartender, “How ‘bout a coffee.”

“Yes, sir, Mr. Best.” The bartender nodded. “Comin’ up.”

Nicholas Benton was an actor turned columnist. He had played a small roll in Cathy Connors’ first film but somehow had come to her attention and she had asked Peter to represent him. It wasn’t long before Peter realized Nick’s real talent lay not in acting, but in his ability to befriend people and learn all sorts of things about what was going on and what wasn’t. Peter helped him find a job with the LA Herald where an ability to write nice things about Hollywood Celebrities soon earned him a regular column and a loyal following. Thoughts and rumors revealed in Nick’s column often had a way of becoming reality.

“Nick, I wanna talk about Holly Sinclair,” Peter said after they had been seated in a booth and ordered lunch. “From what I’ve been hearing, she’s doing a fantastic job in ‘A Girl Named Anne’, and Printer thinks she’s worthy of nomination.”

“And you want to start the ball rolling?” Nick asked quickly.

“Yes. I think it might be time. And maybe a mention of StayCon thinking the success of their association with Don Lowman may lead to more feature production. What-a you think?"

"Ummm, no, not the business part. Let me deal with her talent and how everybody is getting excited by what she's doing. The business end ought to turn up in something like the Wall Street Journal. That can influence votes because agents and producers will pay attention to what they read there. More production means more jobs."

"Sounds good to me, Nick. I leave it to you."

"Okay, I'll start the ball rolling tonight, and when it opens I'll tell Orin to give her a great review. Then it'll be time for you to start running some adds in the dailies."

"Thanks Nick, I appreciate it, I really do... and tell Orin 'hello' for me."

"Orin" – Orin Quigley – was what Peter thought of as an added bonus. He was one of the top film critics in the country. He was also Nick's "friend."

"As long as you buy the lunch it's okay," Nick laughed, then, turning serious, added, "You know I can never pay you back for all you've done for me, Peter."

Happily, his car once again emerged from the tiny parking lot in perfect condition. He gave the attendant a dollar tip, climbed in and headed for the studio, confident that a nomination for Holly was underway. Now, he thought, if “Homeroom” is everything I expect, this will be a great day.

But the viewing of "Homeroom" turned into a disappointment.

The script was good, he had no doubt about that. Don Stern's camera work is beautiful, no problem there. Crystal is perfect, no doubt about that either, so why isn't it working, he asked himself. The warm and wonderful scenes certainly would bring tears to the eye, but the comedy just didn't seem that funny. He couldn't believe no one laughed when the mud splashed all over Miss Ridley's new dress, but aside from a couple of chuckles, neither he, nor the Lustigs, nor any of the half dozen other people seated in the room had exactly fallen out of their seats with laughter at that scene or any of the others he had expected would get laughs. And that was a surprise. When he read the script he had expected laughs by the dozen.

It was probably his own fault, he realized. He should have insisted Todd ask Aaron Marks to direct the pilot, but Todd had been so adamant about following Megan Schmidt's recommendation, and now the result was not what he had expected it to be.

"...Yes, Meg thinks two hundred should be enough ..."

Peter turned in his chair to look back at the control desk behind him where Todd and his editor were seated. Meg was shaking her head in agreement as Todd spoke into the telephone. "Yeah, Charlie. If we can do it Thursday that will give us plenty of time..."

"You know what's the matter with this picture?" Todd announced as he put the phone back on it's receiver. "Laughter's contagious. Nobody laughs alone. Aaron told me that two years ago. What we're going to do is run this for a couple of hundred people in a small theater. We'll record them laughing and Meg will put that right on the sound track." He turned to his editor, "Just in case, I'll ask Doris to find us a few good laughers to get things started."

Would recorded laughter be the answer, Peter wondered as he headed back to Beverly Hills. He guessed they would soon find out.

The following morning Nicholas Benton's column carried the news that: "Movie Makers in Jolly Old London are all a twitter over the performance being turned in by Holly Sinclair in the role of Anne Boleyn. Bookmaker odds over there are five to one it will bring her an Academy Award nomination!"

Three days after that a column in the business section told readers, "In anticipation of strong box office from what they believe to be an award winning performance by Holly Sinclair in the title roll of their upcoming film, 'A Girl Named Anne', Donald Lowman and StayCon Pictures are making plans for an expanded production schedule next year. More production will mean more work, and that is good news for people in an industry that has been suffering from TV's inroads on its audience"

Next day, with prerecorded laughter added, Todd's pilot was delivered to OGB. A week later the agency began an add campaign announcing "Homeroom," would be Palmer Foods' new entry in the Fall Program Schedule.

Most of the time Sheila Goodman took the stairs from her forth floor office up to the fifth floor, the executive floor, of OGB's west coast headquarters where her boss, J.P. Margolis' office was located. She felt the exercise was good for her and God knew, she got little enough exercise these days. Her job entailed a lot of sitting in meetings, sitting at her desk and sitting in her automobile while she drove from one studio to another. Sometimes she wished JP would call her to his office more frequently just so she could get to climb the stairs. But today she took the elevator, it was more business like and today it was important to be business like. Today, she had a feeling, was the beginning of her climb up the ladder of success at Oren, Gunther and Boyle.

Being young, only a year out of Sarah Lawrence, and attractive, she did everything she could to make herself look older and more business like. She pulled her dark hair into a sever bun at the back of her neck. She wore almost no makeup, dressed in gray business suits with skirts that were too long to show off her excellent legs, and jackets a bit too full to reveal her lovely bust line. And, although her eye sight was twenty-twenty perfect, as a final bit of camouflage she wore heavy, dark rimed glasses which more or less distracted from any indication of her facial beauty. She had a man's position in a man's world and she was determined to be as much a man as any of her compatriots.

Sheila knew the assignment New York had insisted she be given was not going to please JP. Evan if "Homeroom" was "only a family show," aimed more towards a women's audience, her assignment to watch over it was a feather in her cap and was sure to upset JP. JP did not believe women belonged in the programming department. For that matter, she was pretty certain, JP didn't think women belonged anywhere but in the kitchen, or, in the case of attractive bimbos, in his bed. She owed this assignment, and her job at OGB, to an enlightened Vice President in New York who believed it was time the company had a few women in responsible positions. Now all she had to do was work twice as hard as any of her male counterparts to prove that enlightened executive was right.

One day, before too long, Sheila knew, there would be an opening for a junior vice president in programming, and she was determined to be OGB's first woman VP. In her heart and in her mind, she believed "Homeroom" was going to be the stairway to that objective but she was well aware it was an objective not easily reached. TV viewing is dominated by Westerns, Cops and Robbers and Sports. Pretty much a Man's world. "Homeroom" is intended to be family entertainment with a woman star.

Wonderful as Crystal Manning is, "Miss Ridley" alone might not be enough to make "Homeroom" the success Sheila wanted it to be, prayed it would be. She knew its success would also depend on the producer and the scripts he and his writers deliver. That was the area in which she was going to have influence, she told herself as she headed for JP's office and her first meeting with the man who created, and would produce the series.

"Sheila Goodman, this is Todd Wilson." JP said as she entered his office.

She was surprised by his youthful good looks. He was not at all what she had expected. He was young. Maybe younger than herself.

"Mister Wilson," she extended her hand to shake his. "t's great to meet you. I'm really excited about 'Homeroom'."

Following the introductory meeting in JP's office, Sheila and Todd adjoined to her 4th floor office where, all through a take out lunch brought in by her secretary, they talked about

"Homeroom" and Miss Ridley. As they talked, she became more and more delighted by Todd's enthusiasm and sensitivity to her concern about the development of Miss Ridley's character.

Two hours after Todd left her office that afternoon her intercom buzzed. "Mr. Wilson on line two," her secretary announced.

"Todd?" Her voice was a bit more feminine than normal when she answered.

"Hi Sheila. Listen, I have a couple more thoughts about the Ridley character I want to go over with you. Can we have diner tonight?"

"Oh, gee." Her surprise was genuine. "Gosh... Yes, I guess so. Where and when?"

"How about we meet at the Bantam Cock down on LaBrea? Say, seven o'clock?"

"Seven will be fine." She managed to return her voice to its normal, business like register. "I'll see you there."

"Great, I'll make a reservation."

Just down the street from its sister establishment, "The Tale of the Cock," the quaint, brick and wood English cottage exterior of "The Bantam Cock" served as a preview for the warm interior of a restaurant that, during the day, might well have been the scene of more business deals than any place other than the Hollywood Derby. But at night, with soft lighting, flowers and candles on each table, a small dance floor and music from an always excellent soft jazz group, it became far less business like.

In addition to atmosphere, The Bantam Cock featured an excellent menu accompanied by a wine list that defied diners to request a vintage not in stock, as well as a bar that boasted the ability to create any drink imaginable.

Todd was waiting at their table when she arrived. He jumped to his feet and stepped in front of the waiter to hold her chair.

"I took the liberty of ordering a couple of Manhattans," he told her. "I hope that's okay. You look like a Manhattan kind of girl and after a busy day I can't think of any better way to relax."

She settled into the chair and told him a Manhattan sounded good. At least he hadn't ordered Martinis. Although Martinis were Hollywood's drink of choice, she found them to be awfully strong and she did not like their taste. Truth be known, she did not really like to drink at all, but drinking was a very real part of the business world she intended to excel in. Manhattans, at least, were a bit sweet, and by putting an ice cube in hers, something that simply was not done to a Martini, she could dilute it a bit.

As Todd took his seat opposite to her, a second waiter arrived with their cocktails.

"Here's to 'Homeroom'," Todd raised his glass and held it out to her.

"Yes indeed." She picked up her glass and touched his with it. "To 'Homeroom'."

"Do you really need to wear those glasses?" he asked after she had taken a sip of her drink.

"Well, no. Not if they bother you." She was surprised by her own coyness but determined not to completely let down her guard.

An hour later, as a busboy cleared away the dinner dishes and their waiter took orders for desert she unpinned the bun at the back of her neck and shook out her hair. It was something she had seen done in countless movies but never before thought of doing herself.

"My God!" Todd sat back in his chair and looked at her. "Miss Goodman, you look almost human."

She blinked as he continued, "Would you like to dance?"

"All right..." He paused just long enough to get everyone's undivided attention. ...That's a Printer!"

Realizing this was Holly's final shot, applause broke out all over the set as Printer stepped up on the scaffold to help her down from the executioner's block. "My dear, that was absolutely beautiful. Thank you for making our film a true masterpiece."

"Thank you, Printer." She stood on her toes to give him a kiss on the cheek and whisper, "A lot's happened since we first met, not all good, but working with you has been an absolutely wonderful experience."

"For me as well.," he gave her a hug. "Well do it again soon, very soon I hope."

Before either one could say more, Don Lowman arrived at the bottom of the scaffold steps they were descending to embrace them both in a bear hug. "...What can I say? Wonderful. Wonderful..."

"Yes, exactly Donald." Printer changed his tone of voice to something slightly petulant. "Now if you two will kindly clear my set, I still have an execution to film."

"Uhhh, yes," Holly shuddered. "I don't want to see that. Come on Don, let's get out of here."

Before taking his arm to leave, she climbed back up the first two steps of the scaffold and looked out at the cast and crew members who had been applauding her. "Thank you. Thank you each and every one of you. This has been an absolutely wonderful experience for me. I love you all!" She blew kisses to them before adding, "And I'll see ya Saturday Night!"

An hour later, makeup removed and dressed for traveling, Holly slid into the limousine seat next to Donald.

"Are you sure you don't want me to come with you?"

She twisted in her seat to look directly at him, then took his hand in both of hers. "Don..." she began slowly. "It wouldn't be a good idea. I've asked David for a divorce and he's agreed. I'm going to Madrid to meet with him and a lawyer he's flown in from California. There's bound to be a couple of reporters around and God knows what kind of stories they might come up with if I arrive on the arm of a handsome man.

"I'm not sure about the handsome part," he chuckled. "But sweetheart I don't like the idea of you making that long trip all alone."

"Don't be modest," she grinned and gave his hand a squeeze, "You are very attractive. And don't worry, I'm not going all by myself. Merri Farley, from security, is going with me. I'm picking her up just as soon as you climb out of my car."

"Okay, you win." He knew she was right, it would not look good were he to accompany her. "When will you be back?"

"Don, you know I'm going to be back for the party Saturday night."

"Yes, okay. Then what?"

"Then I'm going home and wait for the divorce." She gave his hand another squeeze, "And what about you?"

"I'm going to stay here for a while. Once the bills are paid and Printer's settled into his editing, I'll fly back to New York. Then I'll call you to see where we go from there."

She leaned towards him, gave him a quick kiss, and whispered, "I'd like that."

Much to Holly's delight, Peter Best had invited himself to lunch.

"They tell me you've been back for ten days," he said, "So I decided if I was ever going to see you, I'd better hike out here."

"Oh Peter, it's so good to see you."

She took his arm and led him through the house to the sliding glass doors leading out to the deck. What little morning fog there had been was gone before noon and by one o'clock when he arrived it was a perfect California day.

"Good to see you too," he told her. "Besides, I hear the food's good, and," he handed her a script. "I wanted to give this to you."

"When Robins Fly?" She read the title out loud, making it a question rather than a statement.

"Yeah. It's a mystery your old friend Aaron Marks wrote and is going to direct. He wants you for the lead."

"Oh? That sounds like fun, Peter, but I'm in kind of a time bind. Printer is working like a mad man to get Donald's picture ready for the London opening in September. As soon as my divorce is final I'm going to join Don in New York so we can go over there together."

"Holly, September is a few weeks away. Aaron's ready to go immediately. He has you on a three week schedule. Would Don be upset if you help the guy who got you started?"

"No, I don't think he would."

Further discussion was briefly interrupted by Olympia's arrival with the Manhattans Holly had ordered. Holly lifted her glass and tipped it towards her guest, "Peter you are not only a wonderful agent, you're a very thoughtful person but just in case you have some other things in mind that you're not telling me about, maybe I should tell you that after the London opening, Don Lowman and I are going to be married."

With a broad smile on his face, Peter asked, "Why am I not more surprised?"

The opening scene of "When Robins Fly" is the exterior of a pleasant country house with trees in the front yard and a number of Robins perched on their limbs.

Suddenly two loud guns shots! The birds almost darken the sun as they fly away.

Police cars arrive. Police Lieutenant Betty Hampton is in charge. Betty Hampton is a new roll for Holly Sinclair and she loves it. And working with Aaron again is wonderful

Aaron's schedule is a busy one. And Holly loves that too.

And then it is time to fly to London and her husband to be, Don Lowman.

"Good morning Mrs. Lowman."

Cheerful as ever, Amanda arrives right on time to give Holly her regular morning massage. Together they walk into the exercise room, just behind the billiard room, where Holly stretches out on the massage table, closes her eyes and Amanda sets to work.

Life as Mrs. Donald Lowman was turning out to be quite different from life as David Dill's wife. As David' wife she had been better known as Holly Sinclair. As Donald's wife she was Mrs. Lowman... the actress Donald married.

Their home, their main home, was in New York City. A seventeen room duplex apartment in a building Arnold owned on 5th Avenue between 66th and 67th Streets.

Following the London opening of "Anne Boleyn" she and Donald were married then, following their month long honeymoon in the South Pacific, they had come to New York. .

Shortly after she settled in there, Donald invited two other couples who lived in his building to a "Meet my New Wife" dinner:

The Lunstroms, Abby and Vic – he, a stock broker, she very active in the City Women's Club, and the Van Pelts, Tiffany and Norton. Tiffy, was president of the DAR, Norton – no nick name for Norton – was president of a bank. She could never remember which one.

Even though life in the fast lane of the movie world had been pretty exotic, the dinner party was several layers above anything Holly had previously experienced: Their normal household staff of three was augmented for the evening by a bartender and two waiters.

The bartender prepared excellent martinis.

Their cordon-bleu chef prepared a gourmet menu.

The waiters served with discrete efficiency.

Just as Donald had promised, the Lunstroms and the Van Pelts were charming people who were fascinated at meeting a real live Academy Award nominated movie star.

Tiffy wanted to immediately check out her mother's ancestry to see if she were eligible to join the DAR.

Abby insisted she accompany her to the next City Women meeting where her celebrity would be an enormous help at fund raising.

After two luncheons with Abby and Tiffy and some of their friends, followed by a Women's Club tea, Holly had not been at all sure she was going to last out their fourth month of marriage.

"Turn over please, Mrs. Lowman."

She did and took a deep breath as Amanda's fingers began to work softly, soothingly over her shoulders and down her spine. Completely relaxed now, she closed her eyes and let her mind wander again. At the moment she was living her mother's dream. Donald was wealthy. Really, really wealthy! But she was bored.

Only four months, but already she was beginning to think it may have been a mistake and perhaps she may have carried her mother's advice too far. David had been rich enough. At least his parents were... not like Donald, but rich enough. What her mother had cautioned her not to give away without getting something in return for, David didn't even want. On the other hand, what she had gotten from him had been far more than she needed. Far more then her mother could have ever dreamed of. Maybe she should have quit when she was ahead.

As David's wife she had been free to do pretty much whatever she wanted to do. It was quite different with Donald. She was his wife! Perhaps something of a trophy wife, but his alone. So why did she let him chase her until she caught him?

To have a real husband to live with, to make love with, to settle down with. Those were the reasons she had given herself. "What every girl wants," kind of reasons. It wasn't until after she had it, that she began to realize it might not be what she really wanted. Maybe it had something to do with their age difference. Donald was almost fifteen years older. Maybe not, she didn't know. But quite simply, she was bored with having just one man.

Thinking of a "one man" scenario, brought Todd Wilson to mind. She remembered the apartment on Windsor Avenue. If they had married then would she have become a different woman? Maybe. Maybe not. How could she tell? They were from such different backgrounds: He was from a small Canadian village where he grew up with a mother and father who loved him and cared for him. She was from a suburb of New York City. She had no father and practically no mother. The only thing they had in common was a burning desire to succeed... to make it in the movies. Was that enough?

"Are you asleep, Mrs. Lowman."

"Ummm..." She stretched... "No, not quite. I just feel completely relaxed." And bored out of my mind, she said to herself. "Thanks Amanda. See you tomorrow."

For Don Lowman the marriage was not working out exactly as he had expected either.

Holly was a lovely woman and she grew more beautiful every day but somehow she didn't quite replace Martha and their children.

Part of the problem, he realized, was his own, and his efforts to make Holly into the woman Martha was: A club woman, a New York socialite; a Tiffy or an Abby. Maybe, instead, he should try to fit himself into Holly's world.

He had made one movie and it was turning out to be a great success. In spite of his earlier, "movies are shit!" conviction, once Peter Best put together the deal with StayCon and satisfied Printer's insistence on using Holly, things had not been all that bad. And now, with Peter's success at getting her the nomination he so much wanted her to have, he was beginning to think seriously about their future.

There was no reason why he couldn't, or shouldn't, try to move into Holly's world... at least part of the time. Yes, he decided, he would try.

That evening, when he arrived home, he gave her a kiss, told Joseph to bring the martinis, took her hand and led her into the library.

"Honey, I know life here in New York is different from your world," he began as Joseph murmured, "Mrs. Lowman," and careful placed a well shaken, well chilled Beefeater martini on the table in front of her. "Abby and Tiffy are good people," he continued, "But you don't have to go overboard with them. I want us to make new friends. Your kind of people. You know there's some pretty good theater here in New York. And they make movies here too. When we get back, I think we should look into producing a play or another picture..."

"Get back?"

"Oh, didn't I tell you?" He smiled as he reached into his inside jacket pocket. "I've got some business out on the coast." He drew a slender, pale blue box from the pocket and held it out to her as he continued, "I thought maybe you'd like to go with me. We can spend a few days at your place in Malibu, maybe meet with your agent, see if he has any thoughts about production."

"Oh, Don. That would be wonderful!" Her excitement at the prospect of "going home" almost made her forget his gift. Then, suddenly she blinked. "What's this?"

"I suppose the best way to find out is to open it..."

The color of the Tiffany box was familiar. The diamond encrusted Rolex inside definitely was not. "Oh Don..."

"Happy one hundred thirty-nine days anniversary." He whispered as he bent down to give her a kiss, "I had it set on California time."

Much of a surprise as the trip to California was for Holly, Donald had an even bigger one in store for her. As soon as they settled back in their seats after takeoff, and the first round of cocktails had been served, he casually asked her, "What would you think of spending a few weeks in California?"

His question caused a small flip-flop of excitement in her stomach. She looked away from the cloud formations she had been watching out the window and focused a wide eyed stare at him. "Are you setting up an office out there?"

"No, but I've got two major projects starting up. One in St. Louis and one in Dallas, Texas. Over the next two or three months I'm going to be bouncing back and forth between those two towns. I'll be lucky to get home at all, and I think you'd have a lot more fun out there rather than sitting around New York, or traveling back and forth between construction sites with me."

He could see the sparkle in her eyes as he added, "We want to be out there for the Awards dinner in April anyway... so what-a-ya say? Maybe your agent can even find you a picture to do."

She didn't know quite what to say. The thought of spending some time in Malibu was more exciting than she dared tell him. And the idea of doing a picture... well, she realized, that wasn't too likely. But, there was lots to do in Hollywood without making a picture. Just getting ready for the Awards dinner... and Todd was in Hollywood.

"Don, you know I'd love to spend some time in Malibu," she said after a moment. "But I don't want to be away from you all that time."

"Sweetheart, I'm going to be traveling constantly and if I get to New York at all, it's likely to be only for a few hours. For that matter, I could just as easily come out there and I think you might be a lot happier in Malibu than bouncing back and forth between Dallas and St. Louis or being alone in New York. Give it some thought."

He took a sip of his own martini before adding, "And when we get in we'll call Peter and ask him if there is anything around that might interest you."

"Oh, Don, it's so sweet of you to think of that." She leaned toward him and pushed her lips out in the form of a kiss. "I love acting, and I would like to do another picture."

"Okay." Donald lifted his glass in salute. "We'll call Peter in the morning."

Thoughts of seeing Peter and maybe even doing a picture filled her head so fully she was not even aware of the second martini their stewardess brought to her.

Nearly a quarter of a mile out into the Pacific Ocean, at the very end of the Santa Monica Pier, Jack's At The Beach was considered the best sea food restaurant on the west coast by people who felt they knew about such things. Marvelous as the food was, the spectacular view of the curving coast line from Palos Verdes far to the south all the way north to Malibu, backed by the Santa Monica Mountains and an endless view of the ocean to the west made it sometimes difficult to appreciate the wonders of Pacific Crab, Sword Fish, and the house specialty, Abalone Steak.

"Holly, Don. I can't tell you what a delightful surprise this is," Peter told them as they sat down at their table overlooking the ocean.

"Thank you Peter." Holly reached over and put her hand on his. "It's good to see you again too." She gave his hand a squeeze.

By way of acknowledging her gesture, Peter put his hand on top of her's. "So what brings you out here all of a sudden?"

Before Holly could answer, Donald did. "Several things, Pete. I have some business out here, then I'm off to St. Louis and Dallas for God knows how long and we both thought she would be happier out here... and a hell of a lot warmer..." he laughed and waved his hand at the sunshine and the surfers working the waves just below the pier. "I think it was about twenty degrees when we left New York," he looked to his wife, "Wasn't it sweetheart."

"If that," she agreed.

Perhaps the thing about Donald that annoyed her most was his habit... really his need – his need to always speak for her. If she wanted to, she thought, she could spend her entire life without ever saying a word, just nodding "yes" or "no" to whatever he said.

"Right," Donald agreed. "Anyway, being alone and freezing in New York didn't sound half so good as being out here looking around for a project."

Peter's attention quickly zeroed in on what Donald was saying. "A project?"

"Yes. Holly's getting bored being a New York club woman. She wants to make movies. And, you know, 'Anne' has turned out so well I think it's time we find another picture for her. I thought perhaps the two of you could do a little looking around."

"We can certainly do that," Peter agreed. "You thinking of something to produce yourself?"

"Yes, that would be okay unless StayCon's interested in doing something together again."

Peter nodded his head, "I would be very surprised if they didn't want to."

As Peter and her husband were talking, Holly's mind turned to thoughts of life with Donald. It was all about money, she knew, but was it really worth it? What would mother have thought? The way David Dill had set her up, she would be very well off without Donald's money. And, for that matter, she could damn well take care of herself. She was pretty sure Peter could find parts for her and she liked making movies a lot more than being Mrs. Lowman...

Six "Homeroom" episodes were already "in the can," movie slang for completed and ready for airing, and sponsor enthusiasm was running high when Todd, his star Crystal Manning, and OGB rep Sheila Goodman joined more than three dozen other Hollywood luminaries boarding an American Airlines charter flight to New York, and General Broadcasting Company's drunken bash known as the Annual Affiliates Meeting.

Networks such as NBC, GBC, CBS and ABC, were allowed by law to own only eight television stations. In order to build a network that would attract sponsors, these companies spent considerable sums of money trying to cajole, induce or seduce station owners and programming managers, from cities and towns all over the country, to agree to carry their programming.

As in previous years, GBC's affair, titled "Coast to Coast with the General," was held in late August, just before the new TV season was to get underway. Its avowed purpose was to give folks from the all important present or potential "affiliates," an opportunity to view episodes of new programs they could soon be carrying, and have a chance to communicate their reactions and interests to the producers and stars. In actual fact, it was mostly an opportunity for folks from the hinterlands to become a part of the glamorous world of entertainment. A chance to have a drink with the beautiful star of one show, throw an arm over the shoulder of a handsome actor from another, and, for the surprisingly large number of considerate husbands who left their wives at home rather than "drag them to a boring sales meeting," it was an opportunity to have a date with a gorgeous "starlit."

Call Girls from as far away as Philadelphia and Boston were imported to augment the roster of exceptional looking women from New York in order that no man would be left alone if he didn't wish to be.

These annual affairs, jointly financed by the networks and the advertising agencies representing sponsors who bought time on them, were one of the most envied and enjoyed rewards given to the key people who actually were "the network."

As the agency exec for "Homeroom," it was Shelia's job to introduce her program's star and producer to the VIP's attending the extravagant "get aquatinted" party at the Waldorf Astoria's famed Starlight Roof. And at that party, each of the three hundred guests was a VIP.

Fortunately, everyone wore an identifying name badge, so it wasn't a case of knowing who everyone was, so much as a case of having sufficient social skills to make everyone feel important and admired. Skills a Sarah Lawrence girl was well trained in. But skilled though she was, she was no match for Crystal Manning who became the unquestioned star of the evening.

Crystal was not only a good actress, with a winning personality, she was a very bright woman with an uncanny memory.

As a teenager, she had traveled back and forth across the country with "bus and truck companies" playing in a great many "hinterland," cities and she could remember incredible details about those cities in which she had played "split weeks." Details which paid big dividends at the Affiliate's Party.

Introduced to Walker Pearson, who owned the biggest station in Nashville, she asked, "Walker, is the Rib Joint still across the street from the dock at the end of River Street?"

Blinking in surprise, Walker told her it sure enough was, and how the devil did she know about The Rib Joint. Nobody except natives knew about The Rib Joint."

“Well I was taken there by a man named Joe Henry who managed the theater we played.” Somehow, just a little trace of Tennessee slipped into Crystal’s voice as she spoke. “I’ll never forget the place. Best darn food I ever ate.”

“Crystal, you’re not gonna believe this, Joe Henry now works at our station. He was going to be here tonight but somebody had to stay home and mind the store...”

“Well it’s a small world. You give Joe my love, hear?”

“Yes ma’am, I surely will.”

If it had happened only once, Sheila and Todd would have chalked it up to a happy coincidence. If it had happened three our four times, they would have thought it amazing. But ii happened a dozen or more times. And when Crystal had no personal memory of a city, she seemed to always find another subject for a delightful conversation.

As the evening’s event began to wind down, Crystal whispered to Todd that she was ready to leave “anytime.”

In order to be away from “all that”, as she put it, she had elected to stay right there in the Waldorf rather then the Sherry Netherlands, where most of the guests were housed, She would do her best to be witty, charming and friendly at the parties, but in between, she needed a little peace and quiet.

Todd and Sheila escorted her to the elevator, saw her to the door of her suite where she asked them to forgive her for not inviting them in, but she was going to bed.

"Me too, eh?" Todd laughed and took her hands in his. "It's time for all of us to call it a day. You were great tonight Crystal. Just watching you exhausted me."

"Me too," Sheila agreed. "Thank you so much. You had those people eating out of your hand."

They told her "good night," and headed back towards the elevator.

"Would you like to go back to the party?"

"Not unless you think we have to," Todd replied.

"I think we've done our duty. Let's head for the barn."

There were limousines available for party guests but, as the party was breaking up, it was likely they would have to share a ride with someone and neither of them wanted to continue the somewhat forced camaraderie of the evening.

Avoiding the congestion in front of the hotel, they started walking north on Park Avenue.

Late at night, Park Avenue is not particularly spectacular. The lighting is subdued, there are no "exciting" looking buildings. For many blocks north from 49th

Street, Park Avenue is best described as "reserved."

The evening was warm with humidity in the 90% range, pretty much normal for an August night in New York, and since neither had been drinking at the party, Todd asked if she would like a nightcap. She told him no, she would much rather get back to their air conditioned hotel, and a moment later an empty cab came along.

In the taxi they chatted about how delightful Crystal was with the affiliate people, and how they were certain her personality was going to make the show a big hit. It was, in part, because of their conversation about Crystal's importance that Sheila realized the man she was with was just as wonderful with affiliate people. Perhaps he couldn't match Crystal's ability to connect with people's lives, but his warm, Canadian personality, was a sure road to immediate friendship, and just as important to the success of the show. She probably should not have turned down his offer of a nightcap quite so quickly.

"I changed my mind," she told him as they arrived at their hotel, "I think a nightcap might be a good idea, eh?"

"Great!" Todd laughed at her slightly teasing use of his Canadian expression.

The Sherry Netherlands bar was packed, mainly, it seemed, with people from the affiliate party still wearing their name tags.

"Oh, Jesus, Todd." Sheila backed out of the entrance. "I've had enough of them. Come up to my room. I have a bar set up and we can drink in peace."

Sheila's "room" was a very comfortable "Junior Suite," with a small, well supplied bar set up in front of the large picture window overlooking Park Avenue. She poured a glass of light, white wine for herself, and fixed a scotch and soda for Todd. Tired from the strain of the evening's activity, they sat down, relaxed and sipped their drinks.

"You sort-a went overboard in the glamour department tonight, didn't you?"

"What do you mean by that?" Sheila wanted to know.

"Well that evening gown isn't exactly out of the Sears and Roebuck catalogue like most things you wear."

"Oh, thanks a lot."

"No, no. Don't take offense." Todd held his right hand up like a traffic cop ordering cars to stop. "I understand in the office you think you have to look business like, but you are a very attractive woman and it's just nice to see you looking glamorous for a change."

She pouted and looked at him for a moment. "You know that's the second time you've made a crack about my looks."

"It is?"

"Yes. When we had dinner at The Bantam Cock. Before you asked me to dance, you told me I looked almost human."

"That was after you took off your glasses and let your hair down."

She looked at him. He is really a very attractive man, she thought. She took another sip of wine before answering. Then she told him, "Yes, that's right."

He looked at her thinking she's really very pretty... All right, why not?

"Well God knows what else I might say if you were to come over and sit next to me on this lonely sofa."

"Might be fun to find out," she answered as she put her drink down, stood up, and walked slowly toward him.

Not surprisingly they did have fun, and, as it turned out, that night began a relationship that would last almost two years.

Five "Homeroom" episodes had been aired when Sheila Goodman called. Todd was on the set when he took the call. "Hi Sheila, What's up?".

"Todd, I just got out of a meeting. We're going to exercise our option for the full thirty-nine."

"Wholly shit!" Todd's surprise was genuine. "Are you kidding me?"

"No, I'm not. But I don't blame you for being surprised. This is the first time I have ever seen a pickup this early."

"Hang on a second."

She could hear Todd calling Crystal to join him. A moment later her voice came over the phone. "Hi Sheila, what's up?

"You just got picked up for the full thirty-nine. That's what."

Sheila could hear a gasp then almost a screech, "Oh, Todd. How wonderful..." followed by sounds of what Sheila took to be a hug and a kiss.

Peter Best was almost as excited by the news as Todd, Sheila and Crystal Manning had been.

"They picked up your option, so you're hot and now's the time to strike."

"Please, Peter." Todd chuckled. "Strike, is a very bad word. Actors are threatening to do that. Writers are threatening to do that. Directors are threatening to do that. Producers never even think about doing that. How 'bout now's the time to act?"

"Okay. Act. Make you happy?"

"Yeah. So what-a-ya want me to act?"

"I want you to come up with an idea for a new show. OGB is making noises like they want another "Homeroom" for next season and you have the inside track there."

"I know that."

"I'm sure you do."

The inflection in Peter's voice told Todd he was aware of his affair with OGB's Sheila Goodman.

"And just what does that mean?" A hint of testiness in Todd's voice indicated to Peter he would do well to back off on comments regarding his personal life.

"Nothing. Forget it. Just tell me if you can come up with another show for them?"

"Okay. Just so happens Sheila Goodman and I have been talking about that and I've got an idea. Gimme a few weeks and I may have something for you to take to them."

An idea had been germinating in Todd's mind ever since Shelia first suggested he ought to begin thinking about a second show and Aaron Marks could bring it to life.. Writer, director, Aaron could be a TV wiz, But how to broach the idea to him?

The answer, as it turned out, was almost too easy. As if on cue, Aaron telephoned Todd to tell him Peter Best had just told him of the "Homeroom" pick-up. "How-bout I take you and Sheila out for a celebration dinner."

"Oh wow!" Todd's enthusiasm was obvious. "That would be great! We would love it."

Over cocktails before dinner Todd and Sheila quickly worked the conversation around to TV.

"I'll tell you something, Aaron," Sheila took a sip before continuing. "The way TV is going all you movie guys will soon be looking for work."

Nodding his head slowly Aaron agreed. "Yeah, you may be right,"

"So, why haven't you stuck your toe in?" Todd asked.

"Me? TV?" Aaron's surprise was genuine. "I never thought about it."

"Maybe you should," Todd said gently. "TV is here to stay, so are movies. The thing is, should you put all your eggs in one basket?"

Aaron looked from Todd to Sheila then back to Todd.

"All right. Just what are you two leading up to?"

Looking to see who might be standing nearby, Sheila gently took Aaron's arm and pulled him a bit closer before answering. "OGB is looking for another program in the same family show vein as 'Homeroom'," she almost whispered.

"So...?"

"So," Todd jumped in. "What about your Professor? That character's a natural for a series, Aaron. Keith Phillips hasn't done didle-squat since 'Desperate Men.' I'm sure he'd jump at the chance to do TV, just like Crystal did. With your name on it, and Keith for a star, we can sell it in a minute. My company will produce and you'll make a fortune on royalties."

"Jesus, you are fast talkers," Aaron grinned, then turned to Todd, "Is this how you talked me into Holly Sinclair?"

"You're complaining about that?"

"Hell no." Aaron laughed. "I'm hoping she'll agree to do at least one of my next movies."

"Do an outline for a TV show, Aaron," Todd grinned, "And I'll put in a good word for you with Holly, eh?"

"Fuck-off Wilson." Aaron downed the last of his scotch.

It was almost seven o'clock Friday evening when Holly's TWA flight arrived at New York's Idlewild Airport. The flight had been pleasant. She had been wined and dined like the movie star she was, and the bottle of champagne Donald welcomed her with was quite unnecessary. Unnecessary perhaps, but she loved champagne "almost as much as I love you," she told him as their chauffeur helped them into the waiting car. It wasn't until they reached their apartment a few minutes after eight, that he asked her if she felt up to a serious discussion.

She laughed, "Serious discussion, eh? As Todd used to say. Sure," she held up the Rolex he had given her, "It's only five o'clock by my time." .

"I'm being very selfish," he began slowly. "You've had a long flight and you really don't need this now, but I just can't live with myself any longer..." He leaned forward to rest his elbows on his knees and fold his hands between his legs.

"I've been spending some time up in New Canan... with Martha and the kids," he added before Holly had time to make the connection.

"Oh...?"

"Holly, you are wonderful woman and I can't believe I'm lucky enough to have married you, but... the fact is, I miss Martha and my children."

"Oh..." Holly repeated herself.

"We talked a lot and both of us have realized we were hot headed and unreasonable and should not have gotten a divorce..."

Holly thought for a moment before commenting. She had learned long ago the value of not saying the wrong thing at the wrong time. It was clear he was not aware of her increasing boredom with their marriage. It sounded like he was totally involved with his own feelings of need for his kids and his first wife, and guilt over wanting to dump her. An actress with even a little talent should be able to handle this, she decided.

"Are you saying you want to go back to her Don?"

"Yes. I am," he said slowly.

Once he and Martha had come to understand the mistake they had made, the decision to ask Holly for a divorce had not been hard to make. What was difficult, was telling her. He had thought of a dozen different ways to do it, but finally decided the best way was to be straight forward about it.

"I wish I knew how to tell you more gracefully; with more sensitivity. I just don't. You're a wonderful person. I admire you, I respect you, and I care for you more than I can tell you Holly, but I don't love you. Not the way I love Martha and our kids."

Perhaps if she would say something it would be easier, he thought, but she didn't. She just sat there looking at him as tears slowly filled her eyes.

Holly had always been proud of her ability to cry on cue. It was something she learned early on from her mother and she could tell from the look on Donald's face that the ability was proving very useful now.

"...Holly, I..."

She put one finger to her lips, "Shhhh. You don't need to say anymore." She blinked the tears from her eyes then tried to smile. "You know, if you had told me this before I left LA, you could have saved the price of my plane ticket."

"Don't go back there right away." He reached over and put his hand on her arm. "This place is yours for as long as you like. Stay here for a few days anyhow. There are things I need to arrange for you. I want you to know, you will never have to worry... about anything."

"Anything? Except not having a husband, you mean."

"Yes, I guess I do."

She sat quietly for a moment thinking she had just given one of her best performances and there wasn't a camera in sight. Then, with something of a forced smile she said, "Would you ask what's-his-name to bring me a martini. It's not exactly a substitute for a husband, but it may help."

Following her divorce from Donald, Holly did not return from New York until the middle of TV "hiatus" time. That time in summer when "replacement shows" take over while the regular season programs have a thirteen week rest. Not being much involved with TV, this was not something she had thought about. What she thought about was a movie for herself. "Shit!" She said out loud.

"Chu call Miss Holly?" Olympia asked from the other room.

"No," Holly called back. "But while I'm thinking about it, make me a martini and bring it out on the deck. ...Please," she added.

She had taught Olympia to make the best martinis anywhere in the world. And the funny thing about it was she didn't use expensive gin. Plain old Gordon's London Dry with a little more vermouth than most people used. The secret was in the ice. Shake well with plenty of ice. Make them really cold, then serve with a thin slice of lemon peal. Now that was a martini.

“Here you are, Miss Holly. Nice and cold. Chuss de way chu like.” Olympia handed a chilled glass to Holly, then carefully poured from the frosted shaker. “I put de-ress back in de ice-box ‘till chu ready.”

Holly smiled. No matter that her kitchen boasted the finest, newest appliances, the word “refrigerator” had no meaning to Olympia. To her it was simply an “ice-box.” Never mind that... she took a sip. “Oh God, that’s good, Thank you Olympia.”

She took a second sip, then picked up the telephone and called Peter Best.

“What kind of an agent let’s his best actress sit twiddling her thumbs when she wants to work?”

“All my clients are “Best Actresses, or Actors as the case may be,” Peter answered with over stressed pride. “And none of them twiddle their thumbs.”

“Well this one is twiddling.”

“Oh?”

She waited for him to say more. When he didn’t, she asked. “What the hell does that mean?”

“Does what mean?” Peter asked.

“Oh! What the hell does ‘Oh’ mean?”

“Ummm... I guess it means I didn’t know you were really looking for work.”

“Bull-shit, Peter.”

“Okay, I’ll see what’s out there.“ Then his voice changed from a slightly teasing banter to a more serious tone.

“So, how are you making out? Everything going okay? You really ready to go back to work?”

“Peter, I’ve told you before, the divorce from Don Lowman did not make me unhappy. It made me rich... rich-er!. Now stop worrying about my state of mind and find me a picture.”

“I’ll get right on it.”

Holly took another sip of her martini, then purred,

“Thank you, Peter. I love you madly!”

He chuckled, told her “You’re a nut,” and hung up.

“Olympia, see if you can find my blue pill box and bring me another martini please.”

“Right-away Miss Holly.”

.“No. Wait Olympia. Never mind. Save it for later.”

It’s time, she told herself. It really is time. Enough should be enough. She was smart enough to know that too much booze and too many pills were not good for her. She had told herself before it was time to quit. Well maybe this time she could do it. At least she could try. Really, really try.

And deep, deep down in the back corner of her mind a tiny voice whispered, “Todd Wilson would approve.”

"Get right on it," did not mean Peter would start making inquiries. One thing he had learned early in his career as an agent: a successful agent does not look for work for his clients, a successful agent receives requests for his clients. If you weren't getting calls for a client, you had a problem. You needed to get other, more successful, more in demand, clients! Hollywood's Best Agency seldom had such problems.

In Holly's case, however, Peter decided to plant a few seeds. First, he telephoned Nick Benton who next day mentioned her return to Hollywood in his column. Next, he confirmed to several friends at an industry party that indeed Holly was back, feeling great, and reading a script which she, "found very interesting." Other than that, he waited patiently for the calls he knew would soon be forth coming. To his surprise, the first call did not come to him but went directly to Holly.

"Good morning, Holly. This is David."

It had not been necessary for him to introduce himself, she recognized his voice immediately. "Hello, David." Her voice was emotionless.

"You know I'm not very good at all those 'how are you?' and 'what are you up to?' kinds of chatter. I'm calling to ask if you would like to do a play with Printer and me?"

"Oh, my goodness..." her surprise was obvious. She had just walked into the kitchen to talk with Olympia about dinner when David's call came. Olympia was busy with flour and dough so she had grabbed the wall phone herself.

"Wait a second..." Covering the phone mouthpiece, she pointed to a chair and asked Olympia to push it over to her. She sat down, then turned her attention back to the telephone. "David, would you like to start all over again."

"Printer and I have bought a play," he said slowly. "We want to do it on Broadway and we think you'd be perfect for the lead. He wanted to call your agent, but I thought I ought to call you first. See how you might feel about seeing me again... working with me that is," he added quickly.

How would she feel about it? she asked herself. "David, The whole idea is such a surprise, I don't know how I feel."

"Any animosity towards me?" he asked.

"No, David. I don't think so, not a bit. We parted friends and I will always think of you as a friend."

"Do you think you'd like to do a play in New York?"

"Maybe. I never told you this but ever since I was a little girl in the 'Y' play troupe I've dreamt about doing a play on Broadway."

"Okay, we'll call Peter Best."

"Malcolm Printer on the line Peter."

"Who, Caroline?"

"Printer." Caroline's voice conveyed her slight annoyance at having to repeat the name she knew full well he had understood.

"Jesus, what do you suppose he wants?"

"Gee, Peter, he didn't tell me. Shall I be really efficient and ask him?"

"There are days, Caroline, when I wonder if I really need a brilliant, beautiful, smart-ass assistant."

"Me too, and I have a great offer for a position over at MCA. ...Now, do you want to speak to Mr. Printer, or shall I tell him you're busy with a client?"

"Put him on, Caroline. Put him on."

There was a click in his ear as he looked at his watch before he spoke. "Printer, My God, it must be almost midnight over there..."

"Yes, well I suppose it is, over there. Only thing is, I'm over here, old boy."

"In LA?"

"No, I'm in New York, actually."

"Well that's closer than London. How the hell are you?"

"Peter, I'm well and very excited about a project David Dill and I are working on."

"You and David Dill? Really."

"Yes, Peter. David and I. Now, mind you, I'm only the director. David's the producer, so he must talk to you, but I did want to have the fun of talking first."

Peter could not help but smile at Printer's droll chuckle. "I'm honored that you wanted to talk with me, Printer."

"Yes, of course you are, dear boy. Now here's David."

A moment later David Dill's somewhat pretentious voice sounded in Peter's ear. "Printer and I want Holly to star in a play we are going to do here in New York, and if it goes as well as we think it will, we'll make it into a movie. I've talked with Holly, she sounds amenable."

"Umm-hum," Peter grunted in surprise. If there were going to be surprises in life, he would just as soon they all be pleasant surprises like this one seemed to be.

"That sounds promising David," he continued. "Is this for TDL?"

"No. No, this is something Malcolm and I are doing on our own."

"I see." Peter wasn't sure he did "see." He stood, picked up the phone and carried it to the windows overlooking Canon Drive. Why David would be doing something outside of his father's company, he could not imagine.

"...You're financing this yourselves then?"

As he waited for David's reply, he became aware of a young woman wearing a very short skirt stepping out from between parked cars and nearly being hit by a silver haired man driving a Mercedes.

"Not entirely..." David said after a moment. The tone of his voice was definitely evasive Peter thought. "We have some additional backing."

"Where is that coming from?"

"I'd rather not discus that, Peter."

The woman and the driver on street below were exchanging words and traffic in each direction had come to a halt.

"That's up to you David. But you have to understand that with the success of Printer's picture and her nomination, Holly's in the big leagues now. I can't recommend anything to her that I'm not sure will be able to pay her what she's worth."

"This is getting us nowhere," Printer cut in. "Donald Lowman is backing our play, Peter. He does not want Holly to know that."

The argument down on the street seemed to have ended. The woman in the short skirt went on across the street, the man in the Mercedes drove off, and traffic began to flow again.

“Well the money’s good then,” Peter said with a chuckle. “Tell me about the play.”

Printer took over again. “it is something Philip McIntosh has written. He calls it, ‘The Invisible Wall.’ Has to do with a woman who is very good at her junior executive job but is constantly being passed over for promotions. In total frustration she finally persuades a group of other women to finance her and she starts her own company. She becomes enormously successful. All highly unlikely of course, but very ‘IN’, as you Americans say.”

“McIntosh is a hell of a playwright, Printer. But why’d you think of Holly for something like that?”

“Because, dear boy, a play about a strong business woman is not going to appeal to the male audience. But, and I stress ‘but’, put the girl every man dreams of in the lead, and they’ll buy tickets just to see her, never mind the message.”

“And,” David jumped in. “Lowman won’t finance it if she isn’t in it.”

“Oh.” Peter blinked... “I understand... Why don’t you send me the script, I’ll get it to her and we’ll see where we go from there.”

"I'll let him in Olympia," Holly called as she hurried towards the front door. She had been on pins and needles ever since Peter's phone call an hour ago inviting himself to lunch so they could talk about the project.

"Peter..." She wrapped herself in his arms and gave him a kiss on both cheeks. "It's really good to see you."

"I might say the same." He gave her an extra squeeze before taking a step back to look at her. "I can't believe it, but you get more beautiful every time I see you."

"You just say that because you're my agent." Holly took his arm and led him in. "Which you aren't going to be much longer if I don't get something to do."

She guided him through the house to the back patio. "Now, you've talked with Printer and David, tell me about this play they want to do, and is that what's in your brief case?"

"Maybe," he answered.

It was a perfect beach day with very little wind and a warm sun which made the blues and greens in the ocean look almost as if lit from below. He took a deep breath of the ocean air as he sat in a deck chair and unzipped his brief case.

"So, here." He pulled a script from the case and held it out to her.

"The Invisible Wall," she read out loud. "A play by Philip McIntosh, Wow!" Her excitement was obvious. "Oh Peter, this sounds wonderful..."

"I think it's pretty good. We can talk about it after you have a chance to read it."

"Peter." She gave him a look that expressed more annoyance than her voice did. "You didn't come all the way out here just to play delivery boy and get a free lunch. Obviously you think this is something I ought to do, so let's talk about it now."

Before he could respond, Olympia stepped out onto the deck. "Hello Mr. Best. Can I get chu something to drink?"

"Hi Olympia, yes, maybe a glass of red wine." He turned to his hostess, "What are you going to have?"

"Olympia knows," Holly purred. "Now Peter, you get no wine and no lunch if you don't start right now telling me what's on your mind."

"Okay. If you look at that script, you'll see McIntosh's play is a 'PD Production'."

She looked at the cover, "Yes...?"

"PD, is Printer, Dill."

She blinked in surprise. "You mean Printer and David?"

"Yes. They seem to have gone out on their own. They plan to produce the play on Broadway, then make it into a movie."

"And they want me!"

"For the lead. Yes." He did not tell her their financing was contingent on her willingness. "I think it's a good part. Kind of a trail blazer, the sort of thing people talk about." Peter continued before she could say more. "Thing is, about working with David again. He told me he had talked with you and you seemed agreeable, but how do you really feel about it?"

"Oh my," she shook her head from side to side slowly as she got out of her chair, walked to the edge of the patio deck and looked out at the ocean. "I've been thinking about that ever since he called."

The sound of an approaching beach patrol helicopter caught her attention. She watched it as it flew just beyond the surf line, only a few hundred feet above the ocean. She waved at the pilot and received a quick wing waggle in response. Beach patrol pilots knew who lived in just about every house along their stretch of coast line and a wave from Holly Sinclair was always high on their wish list.

She waved again and blew a kiss even though her mind was not on the chopper nor its pilot. Her mind was on David, and his play.

He was not a bad person. He just was, what he was, and she supposed he couldn't help that anymore than she could help... well, being what she was. They had not seen each other since the divorce, but they had parted more or less as friends. Was there any reason not to work with him again?

My God, she thought, if she did the columnists would have a field day. But doing a play... on Broadway. Wouldn't that be wonderful.

The helicopter slowly disappeared from view, but she continued to look at the sky in the direction it had gone until she finally turned back to Peter.

"I'm not sure... David asked me if I had any animosity towards him and I told him no, but honestly, I'm not sure. I think I need to know a little more about it."

Peter put his fingers to his temple and scratched lightly just where his gray hairs were becoming more and more noticeable. Gray hair that made him look ever so distinguished, ever so handsome. She wondered why she had never tried to flirt with him. Was it because she was fond of Beverly and knew he was happily married? Was it because he was something of a father figure for her? He certainly was that, she realized. He was a man she respected and trusted. Not someone to go to bed with. Still... he was awfully good looking.

"David and Printer are doing this on their own," Peter said after a moment. "No TDL backing. And they think you're essential to making it a success. I believe that can open the door to a real opportunity if, and I stress if, if it's something you want to do and you'll feel comfortable with."

"What kind of an opportunity are you talking about?"

"There is no way a play can pay you the kind of money you command now, so my thinking is you only agree to do it if they take you in as a full partner. It wont be PD Productions, it'll be PDS. Better yet, maybe SPD. You own a third of everything and if the play's a success, and they make the movie, I think it could be very good for you."

And if Lowman wants to keep his involvement secret, he thought to himself, he can keep it a secret.

Before she could reply, Olympia appeared with a glass of wine for Peter and a very cold looking silver cocktail shaker and glass for Holly.

"Let me read the script, Peter. I'll think some more and I'll call you tomorrow."

"Ask The Professor" was the second Todd Wilson production acquired by OGB for its client Palmer Foods and it too had been assigned to Shelia Goodman. In spite of the enormous excitement of the presidential campaign, and the debates between Nixon and Kennedy, or maybe because of it all, more people were watching television than ever before and "Professor" found its audience much more quickly than "Homeroom" had the year before. By the end of October it had already established itself in the top twenty-five, and each week was seeing an increase in its audience share.

And with its growing success, Shelia had rapidly become JP's favorite programming executive. Around the OGB office the rumor was that the Vice Presidency she had so long coveted would not be long in coming. And for once, the scuttlebutt had it right... almost right.

She poured herself a cup of coffee then stepped out onto the narrow, balcony like deck that ran the full length of Todd's house on Overlook Drive. Cantilevered out over the edge of a steep hillside the balcony offered an awesome, 180 degree view of everything from the Hollywood sign on the hillside several miles to the east to Santa Monica and the ocean to the west. She had always been glad Todd rented the place even though she had turned down his offer to stay there full time.

Election night had been exciting. The party at the Ambassador... the thrill of having "their man" win... their love making that followed... He's a wonderful man, she told herself, and if she was interested in marriage, he would certainly be her choice. But if there had ever been any question in her mind about her decision, last week in New York had convinced her how right she was.

Overlook Drive" was appropriately named, she thought. All of Hollywood was spread out right below her. She would miss it. And she would miss him. Now her only problem was how to tell him. Shouldn't be that tough, she told herself. They had always been very straight with each other... just tell him.

The sudden realization that he had joined her on the balcony was a little disconcerting, but her resolve was not diminished. She held her half empty cup up and in her happiest voice said, "Here's to our wonderful, new president!"

"I'll drink to that," Todd responded and held his own cup aloft.

They each took sips... hers almost cold, his too hot.

"Now, another toast," she said coyly, "To our new vice president."

"Come on," Todd's tone of voice expressed his distaste for President Kennedy's running mate. "That was what they call 'political expediency.' He'll never keep Johnson around for his second term."

"Actually, I wasn't talking about Johnson... I was talking about another vice-president. Sheila Goodman."

It took Todd a second or two to realize what she was telling him. "Oh shit!" he almost spilled coffee on his robe. "You mean they've finally recognized your fabulous ability?"

"...Umm, I guess you could say that. Only not at OGB."

"Not OGB? Who then?"

"General Broadcasting. The main reason I went to New York last week was to meet with Terry Deerfield. Todd, the TV world is changing drastically. You know your production costs are accelerating faster than many sponsor budgets so General is turning to the magazine format NBC invented with 'Today' and 'Tonight,' and they need programming people to supervise them."

Todd's grin expressed his delight at what she was telling him. "And how could General find anyone better than you! Congratulations, Madam Vice President!"

"Thank you sir." She did a slight curtsy. "There's just one drawback... the job is in New York."

Todd's grin was quickly replaced by a rather somber, slightly surprised look. "And... ah, just exactly what does that mean as far as we're concerned?"

"I have to be in New York by December 15th," she answered.

"You mean living in New York."

"Yes. My office will be there. In all likelihood I'll make several trips to the coast every year and you're likely to be in New York every so often... but it won't be the same, Todd."

"No," he shook his head sadly from side to side. "No, I guess it won't."

Standing alongside Camera 1, which was focused on TV host Larry Miller, **t**he stage manager held up his hand with all five fingers extended... "In five..." he called out as he closed his thumb. "Four..." He closed his index finger. "Three..." His final counts were silent, indicated by his fingers only... The red light blinked on above the lens of camera Number 1.

"Our 'Breakfast This Morning' guests today are beautiful Holly Sinclair..."

Holly watched the monitor and smiled as the picture changed from host, Larry Miller to one of Duke Mitchell and her.,

"...And all pro quarterback, Duke Mitchell"

Holly had met Mitchell, briefly, in the "green room," where they spent a few minutes together with one of the show's producers who explained how he would escort them to the set, show them where they would sit, and basically what they would be asked.

"Miss Sinclair, Larry will want to talk about your play opening last Thursday, and the critics raving about you being the best thing to happen on Broadway in ten years... And Duke, I know he'll want to talk about that 'Hail Marry' pass yesterday. That was really something.

"You bet it was," Duke answered. "And I'm here to tell you, sure as shit, we're goin' undefeated this season."

"From what I know about football, I think you may be right, but Duke, when we go on the air, please leave out the profanity."

"Okay," Duke laughed. "If you say so."

God, he is a good looking son-of-a-bitch, Holly thought. "Built like a brick shit-house," was the expression that came to her mind. Six three, maybe six four; at least two hundred twenty-five or thirty pounds; jet black hair, and a face that was a cross between Errol Flynn and Tyrone Power. Looking at a hunk like him, she couldn't help wondering what he'd be like in bed.

Trying to dismiss that thought from her mind, she returned her attention to Larry Miller and the monitor:

"Don't go-way," Larry Miller was telling the camera, "We'll be back to talk with our guests right after these messages from our sponsors."

As planned, Holly talked about what a wonderful playwright Philip McIntosh is, what a great director Malcolm Printer is, how none of it would have come together without their producer, David Dill.

Host Miller resisted the temptation to ask how she felt about working with her former husband and, instead, asked about the dress she wore in the first act.

"Everybody seems to think it was designed for me," Holly told him. "But actually, I found it on a rack in Macy's."

Next it was Duke Mitchell's turn. "The Duke" talked about the "Hail Mary" pass that beat the Lyons, "team spirit," his great receivers, his offensive line, their great defense and how all their success was due to a great coaching staff, and the "Breakfast, This Morning," segment came to an end.

"Thank you, Holly. Thank you Duke. You guys were wonderful," the producer told them as he escorted them off the set, to an elevator, and down to the underground parking lot where limos were waiting for them.

"Enough of that shit," Duke exclaimed as the producer left them. "I'm ready for a drink and some decent food."

He turned to Holly, "What-a-ya say. You wanna go to Nate and Al's?"

"Actually, no," Holly cocked an eyebrow at him. "I'm tired of having to sign autographs before every bite, I have a wonderful cook and a very complete bar at my house. Wanna give it a try?"

"Hell yes!" Duke turned to one of the two limos waiting for them and pulled the door open. "Climb in, Miss Sinclair. We can tell the other car to get lost."

Not surprisingly, even though she had not spent that much time there, with Sheila gone the house on Overlook Drive began to feel strangely empty. At night, with no one next to him, Todd sometimes found himself thinking about his former roommate. Not Sheila, Holly Sinclair.

It was a long time ago when they shared the tiny apartment on Windsor Avenue. Today, if someone were to come to him with a script about two youngsters who came to Hollywood with absolutely no idea about the impossibility of finding work here, and then made it big, he would politely throw them out of his office. Such things just don't happen in real life. One of these days he was sure he would find George Fredenhoff shaking him and telling him to wake up, it was Show Time, time to stop dreaming, put on his skates and go to work.

But it had happened. To both of them. In less then ten years he had become one of the top TV producers in Hollywood. And Holly had already been nominated for an Academy Award.

Has success made us happy? He sometimes wondered. It was a question to ponder. Actually, he wondered, what constitutes happiness? Is there a separation between professional happiness and personal happiness? Was he personally happy? Is she?

Since her divorce from Donald Lowman... a divorce that made all the papers and reportedly netted her ten million in cash plus a New York Apartment, and another in London... since that divorce she had been in New York staring on Broadway and reportedly doing the town with Life Magazine's "Professional Athlete of the Year", Quarterback Duke Mitchell.

Christ, Todd thought, she's been in and out of more beds than Heinz has beans and she's worth millions. She's like a world traveling, really high price hooker and I'm just a simple kid from a tiny town in Canada. So, if she's such a tramp, how come I still think about her so often. Especially at night. Late at night, when it's very dark and I'm very lonely...

"Counter Productive!" The voice inside his head seemed unusually vehement. You should be thinking about the future, not lying here feeling sorry for yourself! What was it President Kennedy said about the future? Plan for it. Not just tomorrow and the next day but five years from now...ten years. Things are going well enough now, but where will you be in five years?

"All right," he said out loud as he plumped up his pillow and twisted over on to his side... "I'll think about that."

The next five years... I'd like to develop one new series each year. Aaron can certainly come up with one, maybe two. Ron and Lucenne should be good for at least one more. That means I have to get busy and come up with a minimum of two more new ideas myself. But when do I find time for that? Obviously I need some help keeping an eye on things already in the works. But who?

God damn! The answer is right in front of my eyes. Meg! Megan Schmidt. A wonderful film editor, but she's capable of more. A hell of a lot more. She loves editing, and she'll never give that up entirely, but she can still help run the company and do that too.

Screw lonely, he told himself. I'll talk to Meg tomorrow; tonight I'm going to sleep.

The words "Can't a guy have a little privacy around here" were on the ttp of his tongue when Meg pushed open his office door and rushed across the room to his TV set. He would have said them were it not for the fact that she was in tears, sobbing.

The TV set came to life...

Oh my God...

The "Homeroom" set was always a happy place to work. A set where a cast, and a crew that had been together for what in Hollywood seemed forever worked smoothly and efficiently with very few problems.

Although the Red Light was on, indicating a sound take in progress, and thus entrance to the stage prohibited, much to the annoyance of director Michael Lange, the street door opened.

"Cut! Cut! What the fuck...?"

Michael quickly squelched his annoyance as he discovered the door had been opened to admit his boss, everyone's boss, Todd Wilson.

"Sorry Mike, I need to gather everyone together please."

The look on Todd's face told them he had not come bringing good news.

"...I don't know how to tell you this," He began slowly. "...Our President, President Kennedy has just been shot. They don't think he's going to live."

Part 2
And the World Was Never the Same

"It probably isn't fair to blame it all on Lyndon Johnson," Todd told Peter Best as they sat having lunch at the Paris Brest. Peter had suggested that place because it was close to Todd's office and he had to be in the valley anyway for a meeting at Warner Bros.

"This damn Vietnam business got started long before he had anything to do with it, but it's certainly fucking up the country," Todd continued. "That and the "hippies," and all the rest that's going on. It's hard to believe things can have gotten so out-of-hand."

"You sound pretty depressed," Peter told him when he finally could get a word in edgewise.

"Yeah, I am," Todd agreed. "Not only me, the whole 'Homeroom' gang. 'Homeroom' just isn't a show for the current market."

"So?... What am I hearing?" Peter wanted to know.

"What you're hearing," Todd answered wearily, "Is this is gonna be the last season for the show and I think you should let the network know."

"And your other shows?"

In the years since "Homeroom" ventured onto the TV screens across the country Todd Wilson Productions had developed four more shows that were now on the air. Peter did not want to hear that Todd was thinking of canceling any of them.

"Oh, we're not going to dump any of them." Todd's voice suddenly returned to its normal, upbeat tone. "They came later and they can fit into the new world. 'Homeroom' can't."

"I could argue that point, Todd," Peter told him, "But I won't."

The day after Todd's lunch with Peter, Sheila Goodman telephoned to express her disappointment at his decision to cancel the show, but with four other Todd Wilson Productions helping keep her network on top in the ratings game, she was not all that unhappy.

"Have you got something new in mind for next season?" she wanted to know.

"As a matter of fact," Todd answered. "The Rubins are working on an idea even as we speak, but I think Peter's going to send it over to CBS."

"Over my dead body!" Sheila screeched.

As she had done one hundred ninety–four times in the past, Miss Ridley collected the papers on her student's desks, walked slowly to the classroom doorway where, with a wistful look back over the empty room she whispered, "Good night girls and boys," then switched off the lights, stepped out into the hallway and slowly closed the door behind her.

The 250 people in the audience, some with tears in their eyes, applauded... slowly at first, then with more and more enthusiasm. Unlike the end of previous shows, "Miss Ridley" did not immediately return to the stage for a bow. instead a good looking young man appeared and waited patiently for the applause to die before speaking:

"Hello. I'm Todd Wilson, eh?"

Tears were quickly replaced by laughter and renewed applause. At the end of each of Todd's shows, an announcer's voice told the viewers, "This has been a Todd Wilson Production, eh?"

"As most of you know, this was our final episode," Todd waited for audience reaction. "...And I wanted to take a moment to thank you, and the lady who made it all possible." He paused again as the audience reacted with sighs, smiles and a smattering of applause.

"Five years ago no one had any idea 'Homeroom' would last this long, and I'm sure you'll agree it would not have, were it not for Crystal Manning who has made Miss Ridley a national treasure."

Todd turned toward the classroom door and called out, "Crystal," then led the audience's applause as "Miss Ridley" re-appeared and made her way down stage to join him. The audience could see she was trying to hide something from Todd, something she was carrying in her hand.

"Shortly after election day in 1958," she began slowly, "A driver from Toyo Griffith Park Florist delivered two dozen beautiful roses to my door. With the roses there was a note." She revealed what the audience and Todd could now see was a small picture frame. "This note," she continued as she held up the framed piece of paper. "I've kept it all these years.

"Dear Miss Manning," she read. "I hope you remember me and will permit me to telephone you this afternoon regarding a project I think might interest you. Sincerely, Todd Wilson."

She looked up from the framed note and turned to Todd. "Eh?"

The audience laughed at her "eh?"

"The project was 'Homeroom' and," she slipped her arm around Todd's waist and kissed his cheek, "Thanks to you boss, I have had the five best years of my life."

In spite of his success in television, Peter knew that deep inside, Todd Wilson still had a craving to make movies, real movies made to play in theaters, not on 16 inch TV screens, so he leaned back against the booth's red leather upholstery, which was as much a part of Musso and Frank as the liver steak he had just finished eating, looked at Todd, and told him, "I think it's time you make a movie."

"Jesus, Peter, that's what I came here to do ten years ago," Todd said wistfully, "And you pushed me into TV. What brings it up now?"

"Ten years ago nobody knew you, or had any idea what you might be capable of. Now with 'Homeroom' finished and everything running smoothly, it just seems like the right time for you to give it a shot."

Peter winked, "And I bet Meg will be glad to get you off her back for a while."

"I wouldn't be surprised if she would," Todd laughed. "So Okay, what-chu got in mind?"

"...Well, StayCon is looking around for some new movie projects and I can't think of a better person for them to get into bed with than you."

"Have you got a script in mind?"

"No," Peter reached into his ever present brief case, "But I read this book..." He pulled a paper back from the case and handed it to Todd. "I think it might make a great movie so I had Irving negotiate the film rights for me."

"'Pursuit'," Todd read the title. "What's it about?"

"It's a love story about an Inspector in the Canadian Mounted Police who goes from Vancouver to a small town hospital to question a man he thinks may have been shot by an escaped murderer. He's intrigued by the victim's nurse. Then a few days later, he gets shot in a gun battle with the murderer and finds himself in the care of the same nurse. She helps him recover and they fall in love."

"It's as good a story as any." Todd riffled a few pages with his thumb. "Shall I read it?"

"I want you to," Peter answered.

A week after their lunch Todd telephoned Peter. "Where the hell did you get the idea you know how to pick a story that will make a decent movie, eh?"

"You don't like it?" There was both surprise and disappointment in Peter's voice.

"Like it? Shit!" Suddenly Todd's voice brightened, "I think it's absolutely terrific"

"No kidding?"

"Not in the least." The excitement in Todd's voice was contagious. "I want to shoot it in Canada, next summer. I know just the place. Now, have you got a writer?"

"Yes..." Peter hesitated. "If you aren't in a big hurry, I have someone in mind I'd like to have take a shot at it."

"If we shoot next summer we'll need a script by January, February at the latest."

That's plenty of time Todd. Let me give this writer six weeks to turn in a first draft. If you don't like it we'll have time to find someone else."

"Okay. So who's the writer?"

"Her name is Deandra Washington." Peter paused. Then, with a reassuring nod to himself, he continued, "She's a black woman who lives in Chicago."

"In Chicago? How the hell did you find a script writer in Chicago?"

"That's a good question."

Todd could not see the smile of relief that broke out on Peter's face as he answered. He had been confident Todd would not object to a writer who was a woman, and a black woman at that, but...

"You know Cathy Connors and her husband are clients of mine..."

"Yeah, so?"

"So, there's this guy, Freddie Washington, who played with the Stacey band. He and

Chuck have been pals ever since Chuck first started in the business. In fact, Chuck was sitting in with Freddie's group in Chicago when he first met Cathy. Deandra is Freddie's daughter. He sent some of her work to Chuck, Chuck sent it to me."

"I can almost follow that," Todd laughed.

"Right... But the truth is, the girl has real talent. I think she can give you a script you'll love."

"So what are you waiting for, Pete? Wind her up and get her started."

It was four degrees below zero and that was supposed to be too cold for it to snow, but in Chicago, the weatherman was not aware of this, so it was snowing. Not hard, just enough so it was necessary to de-ice the wings of United Flight 237 twice before it could take off.

Deandra had a window seat in First Class. She had never sat in First Class before, and the truth of it was she felt intimidated and very much out of place. She wished Peter Best would have sent her a Tourist Class ticket. Black girls didn't fly First Class. In fact, black girls didn't fly very much at all. And they certainly didn't go to Hollywood with a script they had sold tucked under their arms.

"Pursuit." She looked at the cover sheet, read the title to her self, then folded her arms around the bound script and held it to her breast as the engines revved up, the breaks released, and she was forced back in her seat as the plane started its takeoff run. She closed her eyes and told herself, if this is a dream, please don't wake me up.

Five hours later they landed in Los Angeles, where the pilot advised them the temperature was 73 degrees, and Deandra walked up the exit ramp to a meet a man she had talked with several times over the telephone, but had never seen.

"Deandra."

She turned towards the young man who had called. "Hi, I'm Todd Wilson."

"Hello." She reached out to shake his hand. "How did you know it was me?"

"I saw you were carrying a script and I recognized the cover, eh?" he answered with a grin.

Now this is a pretty good guy, she told herself. He didn't say because I'm the only black girl on the flight.

Todd took her baggage checks and handed them to a porter, then led her to a convertible parked in a "No Parking" zone just outside the terminal door. A uniformed Airport Police officer was standing next to the car. Oh-oh, trouble, Deandra thought. Then she blinked as Todd slapped the cop on his shoulder and said, "Thanks officer."

"You're very welcome, Mr. Wilson. You gonna be shooting here again soon?"

“As a matter of fact, I think we’re scheduled to be here next week.”

“Great.”

Deandra didn’t know the officer’s happiness was partly due to the fact that a film company working at the airport was a welcome relief from the normal, pretty dull routine, and partly due to the $20 tip he knew he and his partners would each receive when the company shot there. All she could think of was this wasn’t at all the way she would have been treated in Chicago if she had parked in a No Parking Zone.

With the top down and the warm sun shining as they drove out of the airport, Deandra could hardly believe that only a few hours earlier, she had been freezing in sub-zero Chicago.

“I tell you, Mr. Wilson, I could sure get used to this weather.”

“I wouldn’t be at all surprised it you just may have to do that, Miss Washington.” Todd maneuvered around two trucks then turned left onto a freeway. “Now if we can get past the Mister and Miss business, maybe we can talk about your script.”

“Okay, Todd.” She held up the script that had not been out of her hands since she left her apartment that morning.

“I think I made all the changes you wanted.”

“Let’s not think that way,” Todd glanced at her. “I had some questions but it’s still your script and what you decided to do was up to you."

"All right. Let me put it another way... I thought about your suggestions and questions and decided to make some changes. Which I hope you'll like."

"I'll read it as soon as I drop you at the hotel. The Roosevelt is right in the middle of town, so you can have fun looking around. Tomorrow's a holiday for some folks, but a work day for us. We have a one o'clock lunch date with Peter Best at the Hollywood Derby. It's on Vine Street, just a short walk from your hotel. They can tell you how to get there."

"We're meeting him for lunch?"

"Yeah." Todd smiled at her question. "You'll find that here in Hollywood, most business is done at lunch. I sometimes wonder why I even bother to have an office."

They waited patiently while the waiter carefully poured their champagne. "Body language," Todd thought, amazing how clear it can sometimes be. Their waiter was obviously uncomfortable serving a black woman. He knew Deandra was aware of the waiter's attitude too. No matter Kennedy's legacy of civil-rights laws, no matter how many "equal rights" fund raisers Hollywood personalities attended, the film colony was still very segregated. Very Jim Crow.

With the wine finally poured, Todd looked from Deandra to Peter Best, picked up his glass and lifted it in a toast. "Here's to a great script."

As they clinked their glasses together, Dendra said, "Who would ever have though the great, great grand daughter of a slave would one day write a Hollywood movie?"

Peter could see tears in her eyes. It was time to change the subject. "Any thoughts about casting?" he asked.

"Yesss." Todd looked at Deandra. "It's your idea Dee. You tell him."

The tears were gone, replaced by a gleam of excitement.

"A long time ago I saw a movie I've never forgotten. It was a western but sort of a love story too. The boy and the girl who fell in love were wonderful together. They will be perfect for our picture."

"Sounds good to me. Who were they? What movie?"

"Todd thought you would know, Peter. The movie was 'Out West'.".

"Oh my God." Peter couldn't have been more surprised. It took him several seconds to respond.

"Holly Sinclair and Keith Phillips." Almost laughing he added, "Dee, are you out of you mind? She's on Broadway and he's tied up with Aaron's hit TV show."

"Ummhumm," Todd spoke slowly. "I talked with Aaron and he thinks if we shoot this summer we could work things out with Keith.."

"Okay," Peter nodded his head, "Maybe Keith Phillips, but Holly? Dee, Todd, they are sold out every night for weeks in advance."

"Yes." Deandra put her finger over her lips, "But a little bird whispered 'maybe' to Todd."

New York life had become a bore. Doing eight shows a week on Broadway had become a bore. And Todd Wilson's call was intriguing.

So what's a girl supposed to do? Quit? Yes, Quit. So where's the telephone?

"Miss Sinclair's on line two David."

"Thanks Tommy." He picked up the phone. "Good morning Holly. What's up?"

"David, I've had enough Broadway. Let's go make the movie."

"Whoa, whoa, whoa. Say that again."

"I'm serious David. I can't take this eight shows a week business any longer. Being on stage is great but not doing the same damn thing ever time."

Holly took a deep breath then continued in a less strident tone of voice. "Really David, I'm a movie girl. Can't we go make the picture?"

Now it was David's turn to take a deep breath. Be careful, he told himself.

"Holly, this is too much to deal with on the telephone. How 'bout lunch? One o'clock at the Plaza? That's close to you."

The Plaza Hotel was only a few blocks away from her Apartment on 5th Avenue, A walk there would do her good. "Okay David. Plaza. One o'clock."

She was not surprised to find Printer standing half way down the Plaza steps waiting for her, "My dear, even in dark glasses, that hat and that coat, I'm surprised you aren't being followed by a hoard of screaming fans,"

"Fans don't scream on Mondays Printer," Holly told him as he led her up the steps. "Then they start all over again on Tuesday."

Martinis delivered and luncheon ordered, David was ready for serious talk. "You said you want to quit. Why in God's name?"

"As I told you on the phone, David, I'm sick and tired of doing the same thing every night."

"Holly..." Printer spoke very slowly. "You do not do the same thing every night. Each performance you give brings a new light, a new shading to your character."

"Bull shit, Printer. Now why can't we forget Broadway and go make our movie?"

"Holly," David broke in. "We have advance sale tickets sold for three months. We have commitments to the theater, the cast... You're a partner in this Holly, you can not just walk away."

"And Holly, " Printer spoke up again. "We do not have a movie script. It is going to take us a while to write one..."

"As for being a partner," Holly spoke very slowly, "I abdicate. Script or no script, partner or not, I'm out of here in two weeks. My understudy will be thrilled to take over." Holly put her napkin on the table. "Now, if you gentlemen will excuse me, Duke and I are going to Coney Island to ride roller coasters."

As the Canadian Government mini van left Penticton for the fifteen mile drive to Summerland the sun was just climbing over the mountains on the east side of Lake Okanagon. None the less, it was already getting warm. Warm for May in Canada, that is. Over the past few days it had been warm enough to bring out buds on hundreds of peach trees in orchards along the lake shore. The buds, silhouetted against thousands of sparkling points of light bouncing off ripples in the lake, made it a picture postcard morning.

As they drove past the turnoff for Trout Creek and up the long hill from the lake's shore to the little town of Summerland they could see the raising sun beginning to push shadows off the rock formation, known as "The Old Man", on one of the low mountains surrounding Summerland. Mountains which extended north, all the way up to lake Kelowna, and a hundred miles beyond, to Vernon. Fruit trees might be in bud in the Okanagon Valley, but there were still large patches of snow to be seen on those low mountains.

Emily Yalding expertly wheeled into to a parking spot at the far end of Summerland's four block long main street and announced, "Here we are. Everybody out."

"Everybody" being Todd, Deandra, Production Designer Marvin Kline and John Poer.

When Todd had decided he would direct "The Pursuit" himself, he asked Aaron Marks if he could borrow John for the project. He had not done all that much directing and although he was confident he would know what he wanted, he knew there might be times when he would not be certain how to get it. John Poer would.

Aaron had graciously agreed.

Standing on the sidewalk, looking back towards the lake far below, they were all struck by the beauty of the little town. Being used to eight or ten new buildings every time he turned around, along with several thousand new arrivals to California each day, it was hard for Todd to realize there were parts of the world where "progress" is a bit slower.

"I can't believe it," he told Emily. I haven't been up here since mom and dad moved to Penticton and it hasn't changed a bit. It's just like it was. What-a-ya think Marv?"

What Marv may have thought was lost for the moment because of an interruption from a delightful sounding female voice.

"Todd Wilson! Is that you?"

"Nancy?" He was startled, but recognized her voice immediately. Nancy Nelson, his high school crush. Probably the last person in the world he expected to run into. He turned to face her. "Nancy. I'll be damned! How are you? What are you doing here?"

"What am I doing here?" She laughed. "What are you doing here?"

"We're looking at Summerland and thinking about shooting a movie here." Then, turning to the group with him, he continued, "Nancy Nelson, this is Emily Yalding from the BC Film Commission, our writer Deandra Washington, our Production Designer, Marvin Kline, and our Producer, John Poer."

John Poer blinked. He had just been promoted from Assistant Director to Producer.

"Hi Emily, Deandra, Marvin, John." Nancy said as she reached out to shake their hands. "A movie, eh?" She put a little extra emphasis on "eh!"

"Cut it out," Todd smiled. "What's your story? I thought you and Worthless moved to Toronto."

Trent Worthington had been in Nancy's class at Penticton High, one year behind him. When Todd started Junior College, he and

Nancy drifted apart. A few years later his mother told him she and "Worthless" had married and gone to live in Toronto.

The smile she had greeted him with disappeared from Nancy's face. "Worth's dead, Todd. He was killed in Vietnam."

"Oh, my God, Nancy..."

"Over a year ago now," she continued. "My mother and dad live down below in Trout Creek. I moved back here with our son to be near them."

"Nancy, this is too much to assimilate standing here in the middle of the street. Can we have a cup of coffee somewhere?"

"Best coffee in town," she pointed to a small restaurant just across the street.

"Why don't you two beat it over there and assimilate," John Poer suggested Emily can show us around. It'll do Marv good to see a real small town that isn't on a back lot somewhere. We'll meet you back here in half an hour."

"Good idea, John." Todd took Nancy's arm and started across the street. "Come on."

"How are things with you, Todd?" Nancy asked. "I suppose you're married and have lots of kids?"

"No to both of those," Todd answered as they reached the entrance. He opened the door and held it for her. "No wife. No kids."

"Really?" She waited while he pulled out a chair for her, and was hardly aware of the tiny little light that suddenly flashed on in her head.

"I would have thought down there in Hollywood, with all those beautiful women…?"

"Beautiful, yes." Todd sat down opposite her. "But not the kind you want to marry. Besides, I've been too busy to think about things like marriage."

"Really?" Nancy said again, and the tiny little light inside her head got a bit brighter. "Just goes to show you. Back in high school we all thought you would be one of the first to go."

"Two coffees," Todd told the waiter. "You want anything else Nans?"

"No thanks."

"Okay then, just a couple-a cups of coffee, eh?"

Nancy could not help laughing, "You can take the boy out of Canada but you can't take Canada out of the boy. Eh?"

"I guess not," Todd grinned. Then turning serious he asked her. "You said Worth died in Vietnam. What in the world was he doing there?"

"He was a photographer covering the war for the Toronto Telegram."

"Nans, I'm so sorry… I don't know what to say."

"There isn't anything you can say."

Tears were starting to form in her eyes and a change of subject seemed very much in order. "Now what's this about your son?" Todd asked. Tell me about him."

"Trent, junior. He's the joy of my life, Todd. He's four years old and he's just beautiful." Her tears vanished in the smile that lit up her face. "I'd love for you to meet him."

"Gee, I want to. We will be up here for a couple of weeks when we start production, and once or twice before that, I'm sure we can find time. But what about you? What are you doing to keep yourself looking so young and beautiful?"

"Well, I've got a job. Up at the hospital, eh? I'm the Assistant Administrator, no less."

"Wow! Now that's a coincidence. We're going up there next to see if the hospital can work as a location for us."

"Great. I'll show you around."

The waiter brought their coffee and for a moment they were busy with sugar and cream.

As they were working on their third cups of coffee, John, Deandra, Marvin and Emily looked in the doorway.

"What-a-ya say, boss?" Marv called. "At my rate-scale you're spending a lot of money to have me standing around doing nothing."

"You're quite right, Kline. Let's get to work!" Todd put his cup back on the table. "Nans, are you headed for the hospital? Can we give you a lift?"

She told him, "no," her car was parked around the corner. She would meet them up there.

Located on top of a small hill above Summerland's Main Street, the Summerland Hospital looked over the town and Lake Okanagon beyond. "Jesus, this is spectacular!" Marv Kline said to no one in particular. Then, looking at Nancy he added, "How the hell can you get any work done with a view like this?"

"Our offices are on the other side of the building," she answered.

"Oh."

Half an hour later, Todd took Nancy's phone number and promised to call as soon as he got back to Summerland,

"No phone call, no hospital," she laughed. Then she watched Todd, Deandra, John and Marv climb into Emily's mini van and head down the curved driveway leading back to Summerland's Main Street and the world beyond.

The small light that had been flashing in her brain went dark and the smile she had been wearing slowly faded away.

"Todd, this place is perfect. It's just what I had in mind while I was writing."

"It works for you, then?"

"Oh yes!" Deandra clapped her hands together. "Couldn't be better! I want to make a couple of changes in the first hospital scene though."

"Yeah, I agree." Marv Kline's voice was not quite so up beat. "But I hope you aren't thinking about shooting inside those tiny little hospital rooms."

"No," Todd chuckled. "Not hardly. You, Marvin Kline, are going to build the inside of that hospital on Stage 5 back in Studio City."

Turning to their guide and host, Todd continued, "Emily, if we can work things out, we want to shoot here. I'll call you from the coast when John tells me what we need and how long we'll be here."

"That's wonderful, Todd. I can promise Canada will do everything we can to make things good for you."

Emily drove them right to their chartered Aero-King at the Penticton airport and less than an hour after leaving Summerland they were airborne for the flight to Vancouver for customs clearance, then on to Burbank.

At Todd's request, the pilot made two circles over the lake shore from Penticton to Summerland allowing them a good overview of the entire area where they planned to shoot. After the second go round everyone settled back in their seats as Todd told the pilot, "Okay, let's go home."

"No talking, please. I'm going to write," Deandra said to no one in particular as she flipped open her note pad.

"No talking please," Marv Kline mimicked her voice as he spread out his sketch pad on the pull down table. "I'm going to sketch."

John Poer opened his production board and began studying the various colored strips. His only comment was a loud "Hummm...."

"I haven't said a word," Todd told them in a stage whisper, then rested his head back on a pillow, closed his eyes and was alone with his thoughts.

Out of nowhere he began to hear Claude Thornhill's beautiful theme, "Snowfall." "Snowfall," a recording Nancy had given him for Christmas, his senior year in high school. A song he and Nancy used to listen to. Used to dance to, used to think of as "our song."

Nancy Nelson. My gosh, she hasn't changed a lot since high school. Still cute. Still fun...

He tried to turn his mind to the locations they had been looking at and how various scenes would work in them, but it kept coming back to Nancy. They had "gone steady" all during his senior year. They had done a lot of high school style "necking" but never went "all the way."

They had been good friends. They had shared their dreams for the future. She expected to study architecture in college and she used to kid about the houses she would design for Todd and his father to build. The only problem with that, Todd often reminded her, was that he was not going to build houses with his father, he was going to Hollywood.

"Hollywood." He remembered her resting her head on his shoulder as they sat in his father's car looking at the moonlight reflecting off the lake. "Hollywood. Wouldn't that be spectacular."

"Spectacular" had been the "in" word at Penticton High in 1954. She had told him his ice skating was "spectacular," and his English thesis was "spectacular," and he was "spectacular!" And she had told him, more times than he could remember, how she hoped his dream would come true.

While he had been on the road with Capades, he had thought a lot about Nancy. Until he met Holly.

Holly was much different from Nancy. Holly was like himself. Driven with ambition to succeed in the movie world. During those few weeks he and Holly lived together he had dreamed of spending his life with her. He had thought more than once about asking her to marry him. But neither of them had been ready for marriage, and then it was too late.

First she was off with Keith Phillips. Then she was married to David Dill. No sooner than she divorced Dill, she married Donald Lowman. How long did that last? Six months? Seven? Now the NFL quarterback. She had really been around..

It was nearly ten years ago when they briefly shared the tiny apartment on Windsor Street. Was she in any way the same person she was then? He knew he wasn't. He had become more successful and wealthy than he had ever dreamed. During part of that time he'd had what the pop culture referred to as, "a significant other," Sheila Goodman. He smiled at the thought of the woman who had been so much a part of his life for nearly two years. They still saw each other from time to time, and when they did it was not unusual for them to wind up in bed together, but neither of them thought of it as love. Never anything like what he had felt for Holly that summer they were together. But is she capable of real love? Was he? He wondered. Real, spend the rest of my life with you, love. The kind of love his mother and father shared. The kind of love he was sure Nancy was capable of.

...Nancy. Had it been more than just a couple of old friends seeing each other for the first time in many years enthusiasm in the way she reacted to seeing him? Was there more to his inability to get her off his mind than just... just what? Is there still an attraction? Obviously there is, he told himself. In his mind the sound of "Snowfall" grew louder.

When they landed in Vancouver, Todd took a moment to find a pay phone and call the Summerland Hospital. He asked the hospital operator for Nancy Worthington.

"Hello, this is Nancy."

"Hi Nans. We ducked out of there so quickly this morning I didn't really have time to tell you how good it was to see you again."

"Todd... Hello." There was surprise, then genuine warmth in her voice. "It was wonderful to see you again too. I'm hoping you wont forget your promise to call me when you get back here."

"Don't worry, Nans," he assured her. "I'll call you from California just as soon as we get our schedule set."

"I'll be waiting."

"Spectacular!" ...He wondered if she remembered.

Two days after their return from the location survey, wearing his Assistant Director hat, John Poer brought his production board into Todd's office. "I've got it laid out for thirty-five shoot days."

He spread the board out on Todd's desk. "Have a look."

Todd had learned long ago that each thin strip of colored cardboard represented a scene in the script. John used yellow strips to designate "day exterior," blue strips for "night exterior," white for "on stage – day," green for "on stage – night."

Each actor in the cast was assigned a number. If that actor was in the scene represented by a strip, his or her number was listed. Brief phrases indicating the scene's location and action were written at the top of each strip, the scene's page count was indicated. The strips were then assembled by production day in such a way as to make the most efficient use of cast and production requirements. For instance, if there were three scenes to be shot inside a location house, even though those scenes might be far separated in the story, it was likely John would schedule them on the same day in order to avoid a costly, company move in and out of the place more than once.

As Todd examined the board, John explained he had scheduled six day weeks in Canada, because all the crew would be on location pay, so they were being paid for Saturdays anyway. Monday, August 3rd, would be a travel day for the Canadian crew coming from Vancouver. Tuesday the 4th, a prep day, Wednesday the 5th, first day of shooting. He had laid out a total of twenty-one shooting days in Summerland and the surrounding country side. A move back to Vancouver on the fourth Saturday, then five days shooting there, before saying good bye to the Canadian crew and returning to LA for nine days back at the studio.

"Looks pretty good, John." Todd's eyes quickly scanned the daily page count. "A couple of those days in Summerland seem a little heavy though... You really think we can do everything along Trout Creek in two days?"

"I think so. The thing is, I scheduled that for our last two days. If we need more time, or run into problems, we can work that last Saturday there, travel Sunday and still keep our schedule."

"That sounds okay."

"Only thing," John continued, "We need to have Dennis look at the locations before we lock it."

Todd had insisted to Emily Yalding that he be allowed to bring Dennis Stern into Canada along with his camera operator, his chief electrician and his key grip. Without Dennis and his three key crew men, Todd had told Emily, he would scrub the Canadian locations and shoot everything in California. That would mean the loss of several weeks work for seventy or more Canadians as well as lost income for equipment rental houses, hotels and restaurants.

The day after Todd advised Emily of his crew requirements, she telephoned to let him know temporary work permits for his "essential, below-the-line crew personnel" had been approved.

"That's great, Emily. I really appreciate your help in this."

"Believe me, Todd, you don't have to thank me. Your picture is the biggest thing to hit BC since I've been on the Commission. We were not about to let your good American dollars get away from us."

"Fair enough," Todd laughed. "So, you can help me start spending some of these US bucks. I need a Production Manager up there. A really good Production Manager. John and Dennis, Marv Kline and I are coming up for another look-see in about a week. Do you think you can line up a couple of candidates?"

"Todd, you know that as a representative of the Canadian Government I can not show any preference or in any way promote any person or business over any other."

"Yes, I know that. Of course. Sorry I asked." Todd chuckled. "But there's something else you can do... my assistant Susan likes to make new 'pen-pals' whenever our company travels to new places, do you suppose you can think of a couple or three bright people she might get in touch with?"

"Ummm. Okay. I can probably send a few names to her."

"Just a couple, Emily. She won't have time to write to very many."

"Right. I'll get a couple of names to her by tomorrow morning at the latest."

"Thanks, Emily."

Todd put the phone back in it's cradle and looked down at his desk calendar for a moment before picking it up again. The number he wanted was written on the top, right corner. A moment later she answered.

"Nans, I'm going to be up there next week. Can we get together for an early dinner some night soon?"

"When and where?" The delight in her voice was contagious.

"How about Tuesday? At Theo's?"

"That sounds wonderful, Todd. Where will you be staying?"

"The Lake Side, in Penticton," he told her. "Why?"

"Because I'll pick you up, if that's okay."

"Couldn't be better. Is six o'clock too early for you?"

"No," she assured him. "Six is fine. See you Tuesday."

Theo's is one of the few, maybe the only, excellent restaurant in Penticton. Although the menu is in Greek, the restaurant itself is more in the style of a Swiss mountain chalet with several fireplaces, lots of warm wood posts made from full tree trunks supporting a beamed ceiling, country style windows with flower boxes, shutters and curtains.

Todd and Nancy were seated at a comfortable table alongside one of the windows that looked out over Penticton's Main Street.

Intermixed with expressions of delight at the Greek dishes Theo's prided itself on, their diner conversation dealt mostly with lighthearted, where is so-and-so, reminiscences of high school life, and chit chat about Summerland's up coming major event, the making of a real, honest to goodness Hollywood Movie!

In answer to her question about what was involved in making a movie in Summerland, he began to tell her about the "ultimatum" he had delivered in order to get Dennis and his people approved for work in Canada. He explained that Canada had no problem with Above-the-Line people but basically did not want Below-the-Line people brought into the country for fear of depriving Canadian workers of jobs.

"Todd. Just what the hell line are you talking about?"

"Sorry," he couldn't help laughing. "I can see I have to teach you movie talk. 'The line' is actually a real line on a piece of paper that divides the budget into two sections. What we like to think of as 'creative' people and costs are listed above that line, in the top half of the budget. The crew people who do all the work, obviously non creative," he said with heavy sarcasm, "Are listed in the bottom half."

"Am I supposed to understand that?"

"Not really," Todd told her. "But you asked. The thing is," he continued, "Above the line or below, there aren't many more creative people in a movie company than the cameraman. This is the first feature I've directed and I wasn't going to do it without all the help I can get."

"And Dennis is that important to you?"

"Yes, he is."

"Well I'm certainly glad our government agreed."

It wasn't until they had both declined desert but agreed on coffee that Todd introduced a more serious note.

"Nans, I've thought a lot about you since we ran into each other last month."

"I've thought about you too, Todd. I was kind of hoping you would have called sooner."

"I should have," he began. "...But..."

"But?" She smiled, "But what, Todd?"

Holly's name was on the tip of his tongue. "Oh, nothing really. Just busy... business."

"Who is she?"

Shit! Todd said to himself. Why did I get myself into this? "You're too damn perceptive," he said finally. "She's someone I met when I first got to California..."

"Obviously she made quite an impression on you."

"I guess so," he admitted. "But not the impression you do."

She blinked, and it took several seconds before she was able to bring the smile back to her face.

"Todd, until last month we hadn't seen each other in ten years. I admit it was exciting running into you again, but really, I'm not in competition with your Hollywood friend."

Before he could think of a response, she added, "Listen, I should have been home to put Trent in bed an hour ago. Let me drop you at the hotel and get going."

Todd picked up his telephone as Susan's voice came over the intercom telling him, "They're both on."

"Hi Holly, Keith. How are you guys?"

"Rarin' to go!" Keith answered as Holly was saying "Oh Todd. I'm so excited we'll be working together after all these years."

"Me too, Holly, Glad you two are ready because it's time we start to work. I'd like for all of us to meet here at the studio Monday morning. Will that work for you both?"

Following visits to the wardrobe department, Holly and Keith met Todd for lunch in the studio's executive dining room.

Attentive, uniformed waiters and waitresses discretely served the diners who were comfortably seated at well spaced tables, thoughtfully situated for maximum privacy, on each of the room's three, semi circular levels. Each level, six inches higher then the one below, afforded a view of the tiny English

Garden like park just outside the ten foot high arched windows that constituted one entire wall of the room.

"The food here is as good as anyplace," Todd assured them, "Plus, it's convenient."

Vodka was becoming the in drink in Hollywood and both Holly and Keith ordered Vodka martinis on the rocks. "Ask the bartender to put a little extra Vermouth in mine please." Holly told the waiter.

Todd ordered ice tea.

"Todd, I'm not too happy with the nurse uniform Sarah designed for me."

"Oh? What's the problem Holly?

"Well it's very loose. It doesn't do much for my figure." As she spoke the word "figure" she took a deep breath and straightened her shoulders, making her fabulous thirty-sixes a bit more prominent.

"Ummm. That's kind of the idea, Julie is a working nurse taking care of critically ill people. not a Playboy Bunny. The Inspector is intrigued by her brain, not her body. He doesn't really get to appreciate that until they're in the canoe in the rain."

Todd reached across the table and took Holly's hand. "You're a hell of an actress, Holly. I want people to see that side of you first. It's your acting that will finally get you an Academy Award, not your tits."

Holly's eyes widened at Todd's mention of an Academy Award.

“I think the man’s right.” Keith agreed.

“Maybe.” Holly was not in complete agreement. “But I think my ‘tits’ are what keep people buying tickets to see my movies.”

“That may be,” Todd agreed. “I’ll ask Sarah to re-work the uniforms, but I want you to think more about your character. It’s a beautiful part about a young woman who has real depth to her. It’s a part not too many actresses can handle. And it’s perfect for you.”

“Thank you, Todd.” Holly’s eyes became almost misty. “I appreciate that, and together I know we can bring ‘Julie’ to life.” But a little help from my costume will make me so much more confident.”

Morning was never Holly's favorite time of day and having spent last night alone hadn't helped. Memories of the exciting week she spent with Keith in Palm Springs "rehearsing" had filled her mind, but thoughts of more "rehearsing" came crashing down when Keith told her he was anxious to have her meet his wife who was coming to join them for the trip to Canada.

Without her little blue pills she had not slept well, and now, Olympia had awakened her and turned on the shower because the damn studio car was here. All she had to do was get out of bed, stand under the shower, she knew it would be icy cold, get dressed and go. But did she really want to go? Did she ever want to see Keith Phillips again? Did she really want to make this picture? Would Todd Wilson give a damn?

Besides, she had a headache..

"Olympia. Call Mr. Wilson and tell him I don't think I can do his picture. Tell him I'll call him when I'm feeling better. "Maybe tomorrow," she added softly.

"Do you want me to call her, Todd?"

"No Peter. Holly and I go back a long way. Let me handle it for a while. I just wanted you to know what's going on."

Todd returned the telephone to its cradle and looked around the small office the charter company had provided him with. Outside the window he could see their plane. Loaded and ready to leave.

"John, I think you should get everybody on board and head for Penticton. Tell them Holly's had a slight accident. Nothing serious. She and I will probably be along tomorrow. I will be for sure. If this is really anything serious we have the rest of the week to figure out what to do."

"Okay." John folded his ever present production board, got to his feet and left Todd sitting with his legs stretched out on the chair next to the desk, deep in thought, staring out the window at Burbank Airport's busy runways.

Peter had asked if he should suggest some replacements, but replacing Holly was the last thing Todd wanted to do. He knew pairing her with Keith Phillips was exactly the right mixture for a great picture, and Deandra's script was just too damn good to screw up with the wrong casting. But what he did right this minute would either get things back on track or really fuck it up good.

He watched John herd Keith and his wife, Dennis Stern and his crew, Deandra and Marvin Klein onto their plane and watched it taxi down the runway until it was out of sight.

What do I do now? He asked himself.

Then it came to him. He looked at his wrist watch and reached for the telephone.

"Hello?" Olympia's slightly accented voice sounded in Todd's ear.

"This is Todd Wilson," he told the voice. "I wonder if you would give a message to Miss Sinclair for me please."

"Chess. Chess of course Mr. Wilson..."

"Please tell her I'm going to go have lunch today where they make the best Caesar Salads in the world and I would love it if she would join me. About two o'clock...?"

"Chess-sir, Mr. Wilson. I tell her right away."

"Thank you. Ah... if she doesn't seem to remember where they make those salads, tell her Nickodels."

"Nickodel," Olympia repeated, "Okay, Mr. Wilson. I tell her right away."

Movie hangout though it was, Nickodels did not often find major stars among its patrons and the appearance of Holly Sinclair in the entrance vestibule caused a considerable stir. Before the "stir" could turn into more definite action, the hostess appeared.

"Right this way please, Miss Sinclair."

She led Holly to a booth and seated her facing the Melrose Avenue entrance. Seconds later a voice from behind her asked, "Would you like to go?"

Tears almost hid her smile as she turned and looked up at the no longer quite so young man with the good build and the shock of blond hair.

"Hello H.A.P." Her voice was little more than a whisper.

"Hi Holly."

Over the years Todd had learned that one of the most important functions of a producer is the care and feeding of talent. "Feeding" not food, but succor for the emotional instabilities so many were burdened with.

In the case of Holly Sinclair, he began to realize as they talked, emotional instabilities ran deep.

"You know," Holly smiled, "Ever since Windsor Avenue I have thought about you but we went our separate ways. Now here we are, together again."

"Holly, I don't know what to say..."

"There's nothing you can say. If I'd had any brains I would have hung on to you years ago when I had the chance..."

Suddenly it was Todd who was emotionally unstable. Over the years he had thought of her so often. One of the reason he wanted Holly for the picture was to find out if there was anything left of what he liked to think they once had. Then Nancy reappeared in his life. Now here was Holly telling him she had made a mistake by leaving him while Nancy was waiting for him in Summerland. Yes, okay These were things to think about but right now he had a movie to make.

"Holly, this is my first feature and I really want you to be in it, but if you can't, it's okay. I understand. Peter will find someone."

Suddenly the tears were gone as she turned back to him with a determined look on her beautiful face. "Todd Wilson, don't you dare make this picture without me, eh?"

Day six was the first day Todd was nervous about. During the first six days the interaction between Nurse Julie and the inspector had been limited to several brief, out door meetings near the hospital and on Summerland's main street. Day seven was the first big, romantic scene they were to film.

Down by the lake, silhouetted by morning sun bouncing off the waves, Nurse Julie walks with the recuperating inspector. Limping from the bullet wound in his leg, he must use a crutch. She wants to help, but he insists on walking by himself. Suddenly his crutch finds a soft bit of sand. He nearly falls. She catches him almost as he catches himself. She is in his arms. There is a moment... their lips almost meet, but she pulls back and looks up into his eyes. Then, with full commitment, she presses her body against his and hungrily finds his lips.

"Cut." Todd's voice is a whisper.

"Print that," he tells his script clerk, as he walks to his two actors. Still whispering he tells them, "That was the most beautifully sensual, romantic kiss I ever saw. Holly, that hesitation... just as you were about to kiss. That was absolutely breathtaking."

"And guess what, Todd," she said to herself. "I was thinking about Windsor Avenue."

If Todd needed any reassurance that he had been right to insist on bringing Dennis Stern to Canada, he got it during the two days along Trout Creek. The sequences to be filmed there involved the inspector's discovery of the murderer's camp; a chase through the rugged woods and an exchange of deadly gun fire. A daunting five and three-eights pages.

Starting with their first set-up on Thursday morning, Dennis and his crew were "ready-ready," almost before Todd finished rehearsing his actors. With any other cameraman he knew, there would have been the usual, seemingly endless delays while cable was dragged to locations, lights placed, flags set, dolly track laid... on and on.

By Thursday night, he was five-eights of a page ahead of John's most ambitious schedule and he knew they were home free. There would be no question about moving the company back to Vancouver on Saturday. Sunday would be clear. He could catch a plane to Vancouver

Sunday night or Monday morning. He picked up the telephone and called Nancy.

"Nans, I haven't quite finished digesting Theo's lamb chops yet, but we need to see each other again before I leave. I've got Sunday pretty much clear, so tell me when we can get together."

There was a moment of silence before she answered his question. "All right. I promised Trent a beach picnic Sunday. I'll make sandwiches, you bring a bottle of milk and maybe some wine or something. We'll meet you by the lake, in the little park about noon time."

"Spectacular, Nans." He hoped the word would stir some thoughts in her. "I'll see you there."

Trent Worthington, junior, was a bundle of four year old energy. Together with half dozen other youngsters his age, Trent spent every minute, other than when his mother insisted he come eat his lunch, racing up and down the beach, in and out of the water, climbing the jungle gym, swinging on swings and generally expending more energy than it seemed possible any boy could posses.

"My God, Nans. That kid of yours makes me tired just watching him. Where does he get all that energy from?"

"It's called 'being four', Todd. Don't you remember being four?"

“I can hardly remember being thirty,” he laughed. “Which I only just became.”

“Oh...” She pulled herself together in a make believe shudder. “Don’t mention thirty to me. It’s getting much too close.”

“Hell, Nans. You’re twenty-nine for three more months, if I remember right.”

“Please. Don’t remind me.”

A particularly loud shriek from one of the youngsters suddenly caught her attention. “Trent. You boys, be careful now.” She watched them for a moment before turning back to Todd.

“I want to talk about what you said when we had dinner at Theo’s, last month. About somebody else and competition.”

“All right.” Todd took a deep breath. “When I first got to Hollywood, while I was still with Capades, I met a girl who was looking for a way to get into the business too. We became fairly close and played house for a while. Then she got her big break and we drifted apart.”

Paying full attention now, Nancy waited for him to continue.

“And...?”

“...I don’t know, Nans. I’m up to my ears with this picture. In a way that’s good, because it keeps my mind off really important things,” he drew in a deep breath and let it out with a sigh. “Things like being thirty and wondering where I’m going with my life.”

"Yes, I guess that is fairly important." She took a quick look towards her son and the other boys, then back to Todd. "And why are you telling me all this?"

"Because I can't get you out of my mind and I want to know if you have any thoughts about me?"

She considered his question for a few seconds then asked, "This other girl. Are you seeing her now?"

"Practically every day," he answered slowly. "She's Holly Sinclair."

"...Holly... Sinclair?"

Whatever had been going on in her mind a few seconds ago had suddenly run into a brick wall. He isn't the same boy I went steady with in high school, she realized. He seemed the same when we met on Main Street. He seemed the same when we had dinner. And this afternoon, until now. But he isn't the same. He's become a famous producer. He lives in a different world, Holly Sinclair's world. Holly Sinclair! The most sought after, written about, celebrated movie star in the world. I must have been crazy thinking he was still the same Todd Wilson I used to know. Why is he even here with me? She looked at him and asked, "Why are you even here with me?"

"Why?" He turned and looked out at the lake. "Because I keep hearing 'Snowfall' in my head and I keep wondering what we might have had together, and if maybe there is something we can still have." He turned back to her, "That's why, Nans."

Sunday evening seemed to be over almost before it began. He had intended to use the time to get his mind back on the picture and off his personal quandary. Yeah. Sure. Way to go Todd. Shit! Some dinner, a good night's sleep, and all would be well. The scenes scheduled for Monday were no-brainers. Everything was in or around the police office. The inspector in and out, on the telephone, talking to his chief. Julie out of a taxi and into the building. Pieces of cake.

A car picked him up at the airport in Vancouver and drove him to the hotel. He went directly to his suite, ordered dinner from room service and left a message for John Poer letting him know he was back;

Twenty minutes later the room service waiter rang his door bell.

"It's open," he called. "Come on in."

The service cart appeared first, followed by a beaming waiter and, with a champagne bottle in her hand, Holly Sinclair.

"We're all safely back from the hinterlands," She waved the bottle at him. "I thought we should celebrate."

She looked around the room than turned to the waiter, "Michael, set up Mr. Wilson's diner over there near the window where he can see the harbor please, then, if you could open this bottle and pour some champagne for us..."

"Yes, Miss Sinclair."

Todd turned his head away so that Michael could not see the grin on his face. It was painfully obvious the poor guy was completely overcome by the thrill of doing the bidding of the world's most beautiful movie star.

Over looking the harbor, Vancouver's Prince James Hotel stands on a low hill, not a hundred yards from the rocky shore line. For those who can afford rooms with a southern exposure, the view of Vancouver's harbor is nothing short of breathtaking. For Todd, the view was even better because Holly had stationed herself in front of the picture window and lights from the harbor as well as a half moon low enough in the sky to shine in the window, silhouetted her beautifully body beautifully.

"God damn!" Todd said to himself. If her body language is telling me what I think it's telling me, I'm going to break all my rules about screwing around with members of the company and really celebrate our reunion tonight!

As she slipped into his arms Windsor Avenue suddenly seemed not so long ago. They were both much younger then. She was not the first girl he had made love to, but she was the first girl who was still there in bed with him next morning. She was the first girl he had lived with. And that's what it's all about, isn't it, he thought. Being together with someone, not just for a few minutes of passion but waking up each morning next to the girl you went to bed with last night.

His mind turned to the other woman he had been with since Holly, Sheila. He and Sheila were together for almost two years. But it was never like this. Neither of them had ever thought seriously about marrying each other. For Sheila, sex was like exercise and they exercised well together. Then she had moved on... without too much argument from him.

But Holly. She was a very different kettle of fish, as his mother used to say. Is she the "mate that fate has me created for," he asked himself.

As he wondered about that, Nancy returned to his mind. What a time to think of her. What strange twist of fate had brought them together again after all these years. Peter's idea to do a movie?..

Deandra's script?..

Running into Nancy on Main Street?..

Worth's death?

You could never put all those things together in a script and have anyone believe it. Nancy had been his high school steady and she was still lovely and warm and all the things any man could want in a woman. But…

Holly's mind was mulling over very similar thoughts. She tried to snuggle even closer as she too remembered Windsor Avenue. She was in love with him then, she might have married him if he had asked her. But he was poor and she was poor, and they were more interested in success than marriage. Now they had both achieved success, and it was even better with him than before. And now they were both single and… and… Oh God, is he what I've been looking for all my life?

If John Poer's phone call hadn't awakened them, they might have slept 'till noon.

"John, I guess I sort-a slept in. Sorry," Todd told him. "Let me get a shower and I'll meet you at the set."

"I'll be waiting," John assured him. "

After a quick shower Todd returned to the bed room to find Holly, wearing one of his Tee Shirts, seated in a large, overstuffed chair, gazing out the window at a cruise ship headed for the open sea and some no doubt romantic destination. As he entered, her eyes turned away from the ship and followed him. He resisted the impulse to go to her. Instead, he went to the desk and picked up his script and some notes.

"We better break this up for a while," he told her. "I need to get to the set and I can't think about the picture and you at the same time. Let's take a breather until we get back to LA."

"What about tonight...?" Her voice had a

warm, husky quality to it, he thought.

"I can't, Holly. I'm having dinner with my folks. They moved down here a few years ago after my dad had a heart attack. I don't get to see them as much as I should and I'm going to stay there tonight. I'll see you tomorrow on the set."

"All right, Todd. If that's what you want."

"It isn't exactly what I want, but it's what I need to do." He looked at the strange expression on her face. "Are you all right?"

"Yes, why...?"

"Oh, nothing. Your voice just sounds a little strange."

"That's what a Windsor Avenue night with a handsome man can do." She pursed her lips in a kiss. "Are you sure you wan-a dash off to the set?"

"No, Maybe I'm not. Maybe we need to talk."

Picking up the telephone he asked the hotel operator to connect him with the production office. A moment later, John Poer came on the line.

"John, something has come up and I can't get there today. Take over, will you."

"You want me to direct?"

"Yes John."

"Wow. Gosh. Well yeah, sure boss. If that's what you want."

"That's what I want, John.".

Todd put the phone down and turned back

to Holly. "Why don't you go put some clothes on while I order breakfast. Oatmeal with brown slugger, Rye Toast, Jam and coffee. Right?"

There were real tears in Holly's eyes as she answered, "Strawberry jam. Can't you remember anything?"

Twenty minutes later, a knock on the door brought glamorous Holly Sinclair out of the bathroom before Todd could get out of his chair.

"Good morning," she told the two Room Service waiters. "Can you set us up in front of the picture window?"

"Yes mam. We certainly can."

"Pass the butter and can you reach the cream doesn't seem like much from a man who said he wanted to talk," Holly said as she finished her oatmeal.

"You're right," Todd smiled. "I'm just not sure I know how to say what I want to say."

"I remember Printer once got some script pages..." Holly couldn't help laughing at the memory. "There was a scene where the words 'ad-lid greetings' were in place of actual dialogue. Printer sent it back saying 'actors can't ad-lib. They don't know how!' But Todd my darling, you are not an actor. You're a Producer. So produce."

"Yes...well..." a pause, a deep breath, then, "Holly, ten years ago we found each other and had three weeks together. In my memory that could have been a week ago, a year ago… or yesterday,"

"I share that feeling Todd."

"If I'd had any sense I would have told you I love you and asked you to marry me. But common sense told me that was stupid. You can't marry a girl you have known less than a month. That was a decision I have regretted almost every day since then.

Holly sat quietly while Todd swallowed some cold coffee.

"There's been a lot of water under the bridge since Windsor Avenue Holly and I have been wondering how you feel about all this."

Now it was her turn to tell him her feelings. Don't fuck this up, she told herself. It may be the last chance.

"Todd, if you had asked then, I probably would have said no. My mother always told me 'men just want one thing so be sure you get something in return.' Well you were just getting started, Keith was a star."

Now it was her turn to stop for a minute. There was no cold coffee left but there were some real tears in her eyes she could dab at with her napkin.

"I don't really remember when thoughts of Windsor Avenue began to creep back into my mind. Oh screw Windsor Avenue, thoughts of you, Todd. Thoughts that have grown so strong they brought me in here to you last night."

"Where would you like to go from here,"

Todd asked.

"Back to Windsor Avenue."

"Really?" Todd turned back to her.

"Yes," she answered. "Yes, really."

"And would you like to get married?"

"Yes." **Holly Would**.

The End

www.ingramcontent.com/pod-product-compliance
Lightning Source LLC
Chambersburg PA
CBHW060601310726
48982CB00008B/1197/J

* 9 7 8 1 9 5 1 9 8 5 4 9 3 *